Perfect LITTLE PLAN

a pretty little lies novel

JENNIFER MILLER

Cover Design: Wicked By Design
Formatted by: Kassi Cooper of Kassi's Kandids Formatting

dedication

To all my amazing readers that asked for Pyper's story. This book is for you!

Perfect
LITTLE PLAN

chapter 1

UPON OPENING MY EYES, the pain resonating through my head is so fierce, I quickly close them again. Groaning softly, I massage my temples to try to soothe the demanding ache. God, what did I do last night? As if by magic, vivid flashes of images from the night before come to my mind. Engagement party. Surprising feelings of longing. Drinks. Lots of drinks. A sexy man with a slight southern drawl, and sex. Hot, amazing sex. "Oh God."

Last night was Luke and Olivia's engagement party. Honored and excited to be my best friend's maid of honor and have a front seat in helping celebrate her dreams coming true, I sat next to her, smiling like a Cheshire cat at her happiness. Her smiles made me smile, her laugh made my heart feel full of happiness. I love seeing Olivia so happy. Memories of a shared childhood streamed through my mind. I still remember when she would come to my house when we were little, and we dressed up in my step-mom's heels and jewelry. We'd dress in old evening dresses and white scarves, pretending they were veils and conducted our own little pretend weddings. My mom has a picture of us somewhere.

What I didn't expect to feel last night, was the small ache I felt in my chest while watching them interact. Luke and Olivia are so in sync with one another. It's like watching poetry in motion. He completes her sentences, and she his, without even realizing it. No matter where one of them is in the room, the other's body seems to automatically lean toward its soul mate, as if the distance is difficult and the soul keeps seeking to connect with its match. Intense longing for something comparable found its way inside of me, and I remember needing to numb the feeling any way I could.

With a swagger of my hips, and a broad smile on my face, I sauntered up to the bar and started ordering one drink after another. Just thinking about the alcohol now, makes me emit another small groan of pain. In hindsight, perhaps using alcohol to numb my feelings wasn't such a good idea. Hindsight's a bitch.

Laughing a little to myself and letting out a big sigh, I ease onto my other side, eyes still closed, forcing out the light that begs for entry. Feeling restless and uneasy for some unknown reason, I stretch out my legs and toes, trying to counteract the feeling. I smile a little as I recall getting to know one of Luke's friends better last night – Rixton. He's sexy as hell and I flirted with him shamelessly, thinking why the hell not? No harm, no foul. He's been working at the club for the last six months or so. From what I understand, he called Luke about eight months ago and said he was trying to get back to Chicago. He and Luke went to college together, and then I understand, he moved back to Texas at some point. When Luke had an opening for a manager, he called Rixton, hired him, and, as they say, the rest is history.

Rixton and I have treaded lightly around one another since his arrival. I see him at the club whenever I go and we flirt constantly. He's jokingly asked me out a few times, but I always laugh it off. He's hot, smart and extremely full of himself; a dangerous and fun combination. He's easily the kind of man you could lose your head and heart with if you aren't careful.

At one point last night we even did a shot together. I was laughing at something meaningless, finding most everything funny at that point. Rixton didn't seem to mind. While it was certainly fun to just flirt and let myself go, it can't happen again. I know I will see him at the club of course, and since he is Luke's best man in the wedding, some contact will be inevitable, but I need to try to avoid him. He's seriously not my type. At all. I sigh and amend that thought. He's not my type, aside from his killer good looks, built body, amazing laugh, panty-dropping smile, his light southern drawl that's almost undetectable unless he emphasizes it on purpose when he calls me "darlin'." Dammit, focus! Besides all that, he's not my type, but I'm smart. I didn't let that fact keep me from admiring the qualities he otherwise clearly possesses.

Reflecting, I remember being totally over the top, flirtatiously flinging my hair behind my shoulder, and God help me even leaning slightly forward, making sure my cleavage was provocative and that my breasts were thrust out just enough to attract his attention. Clearly no stranger to flirting women, his eyes twinkled at me in amusement and interest. I feel my grin grow as I picture his golden brown eyes, the color of aged whiskey.

"Rixton," I moan to myself in recollection.

"Good morning to you too, darlin'."

My stomach slams up into my throat, as I open my eyes and simultaneously let out a blood-curdling scream, realizing there is a person in bed next to me. And not just any person – Rixton. Oh God. Rixton is in my bed. And grinning. At me. Right now.

I jump out of my bed, arms flailing like a damn muppet as I jump up and down. Looking at Rixton, his grin becomes wider and it takes a complete thirty seconds to realize that I'm completely naked and my jumping is giving him quite a show. I squeak out a noise then find myself gasping for huge amounts of air. Oh hell, I can't breathe. My mouth is opening and closing like a fish.

"You're going to pass out, darlin'. Need a paper bag?"

I ignore the jackass in my bed and feel myself swaying from side to side, trying to decide if I should make a dash to my closet, or what the hell I should do. Grabbing a pillow, I press it tightly to my body, using it to cover up the important parts while yanking at the blanket on my bed with the other hand.

When the blanket is safely around me, I look at my bed and take in the naked, yes *naked*, man lying there. Seeming completely unconcerned about the fact I've taken the only thing covering his nakedness, he casually crosses his legs at the ankle, throws his arms behind his head and smiles, yes *smiles*, at me.

"Who… what… how…" While on one hand I can't wrap my mind around what I'm seeing, at the same time, my traitorous eyes scan his glorious nakedness. My eyes run down his firm chest, over his navel, down to his should-be-illegal abs and lower. I blush and quickly look away.

"Pyper?" My eyes snap to Olivia standing in my doorway in nothing but a skimpy baby doll nightgown. "What the hell is going on?" Her attire makes me raise my eyebrows, even in the middle of this insanity. If I wasn't in the middle of Nightmare in Pyper's Room, I'd probably laugh at the sight. Apparently, I'm not the only one that had a good time last night. *Go us! Wait. Focus Pyper!*

Before I can respond to Olivia's question, my attention is diverted to Luke walking up behind her. Thank goodness he took the time to throw on some pants, even though they're unbuttoned and hanging low on his hips. "What's wrong?" Luke looks from me to the bed, and back to me. Realizing what he just saw, his eyes dart back to the bed again. The look of initial concern on his face, immediately turns to mirth and he laughs. "Rixton? What's up dude?"

"'Sup, Luke?" Rixton nods his head at Luke in greeting, apparently having no concern over the fact he's completely bared to all of us. Hello, full frontal nudity everyone!

All I can do is stare at the bed, my mouth still opening and closing like a damn ventriloquist's dummy – like that isn't creepy. "I don't even…" I trail off, not having a clue where to begin. I'm mortified. I gesture to him at a loss, looking back to Olivia, my eyes begging her to help me.

"Cat got your tongue, Red?" his southern drawl is thick with his words, "I don't think you've finished a sentence yet."

I glare at him, still at a loss for words. "Pyper, you screamed. Are you okay?"

Olivia's concern makes me turn to her once again. "Yes, I'm sorry if I scared you. I received a shock when I woke up and found…" I nod his way again. "I didn't remember…."

"Need a little help rememberin', darlin'?" I don't know how it's possible but Rixton's smile broadens even more. making me want to abandon my modesty, drop my sheet, tackle him like a bear and strangle the life out of him. "I'm happy to help you out with that, maybe you'd like a reenactment? Just say the word."

"Oh my God," I whisper as feelings of humiliation wash over me like rain.

"Aw, looky there! A complete sentence this time."

Luke snorts, which makes me toss him an angry glare. For the first time I understand the saying 'If looks could kill.' I'd be happy if mine could just wound him a little. Okay, a lot. The look on Luke's face makes it obvious he finds this whole scene extremely funny.

Forcing myself to push past the embarrassment, I apologize to Luke and Olivia again for scaring them. "I'm sorry, I was just confused when I woke up. As you've likely figured out, I didn't remember falling asleep…" I gesture at Rixton again… "with that. Right now, I don't remember much of anything." My cheeks flood with color, especially when Luke throws his head back and laughs.

"That's not a good thing there bro," Luke teases, "Sounds like you need to brush up on your skills or something."

Ignoring Luke, Rixton looks at me, "Come on over here, Red, I'll help jog your memory. We can clear up that alcohol fuzzed brain of yours, no problem."

Oh my God, I am such a freaking idiot. Not only do I take a guy to bed and not remember it, but in true Pyper fashion, I let everyone else pay witness to my shame. Who needs a walk of shame when you can just invite everyone to your bedroom to witness it in person? Awesome. This is the stuff reality show TV producers live for.

I rub my temples, feeling the pain from my hangover magnify and look at Olivia, embarrassment clearly written all over my face. "Okay, well… we are going to leave you two… you know… to…" Olivia now gestures to the both of us clearly now at a loss for words herself. It's like a twisted game of charades.

"Aw, you don't have to leave, sweetheart," Rixton says looking at Olivia while she studiously looks at me instead of glancing his way. "I mean if you want to join us, I certainly don't mind one bit." He laughs at his own joke and Olivia looks choked as her eyes widen. "That reminds me, Luke, remember that one time in college when…"

"OKAY!" Luke quickly cuts Rixton off and places his hands on Olivia's shoulders turning her around to face him. "I'm really glad everything is alright. I figured I was going to have to kill one hell of a big spider after that scream."

"I wish," I mutter. A spider would be so much better than reality. I would take a room filled with spiders over this right now. I doubt a can of Raid would get rid of Rixton.

"Wait… what about that one time in college?" Olivia asks, making Luke's cheeks redden.

"Angel, let's go before I'm forced to kick Rixton's ass now, instead of later." He starts ushering Olivia down the hall but I hear her response, "Oh no, don't think for one minute you're getting off that easily. It sounds like you have a story to tell me."

I hear Rixton chuckle, which prompts me to look over at him. He's still lying completely comfortable in my bed, like this happens to him all the time. Maybe it does, I don't know. Memories have started to come back to me now that the shock is wearing off. I remember again how I was drinking with Rixton at the bar. Our flirting leading to touching. My flirtatious toast, which was clearly an invitation. He taking me up on it, and bringing me home, and coming inside.

6

I remember our clothes falling to the floor in our haste to get each other to bed. We didn't waste any time with formalities when we walked in the door. I just led him straight to my room, not even pretending I wanted him here for anything other than sex.

I remember our bodies touching, exploring, tasting. Tongues sliding, gasps taken, fingers pressing, and moans surrendered as our bodies came together and we chased our needs, our wants. I remember the feel of his lips, the sounds he makes at the end when he loses himself, and even the sweet way he wrapped me in his arms afterwards.

"I see the memories have returned."

I realize that once again I was looking between his legs while remembering our interaction. What the hell am I doing? "You need to leave."

"What? No round two? No breakfast in bed? No sweet kiss goodbye? What the hell?"

"Ha. Very funny. You and I both know what this was. Why the hell did you even stay over anyway? I can't believe you did, and oh my God, how embarrassing all of this is. For Luke and Olivia to have seen this!"

I see a flash of something in his eyes, but before I can wonder about it further, he grins again. "Cool your jets, woman. I fell asleep, no big deal. Luke and Olivia are your friends, it could be much worse."

"If you say so," I mutter, having trouble picturing anything worse. Pulling the blanket tighter around me, I walk to where I see his clothes lying on the floor and pick them up and throw them at him. "Here you go. You can go to the bathroom to put them on."

He looks at me for a moment then slowly makes his way out of my bed. He stands up with a groan, reaches his arms up to the sky stretching as if he has all the time in the freaking world. He's facing the wall, so I let my eyes run over his fine ass. I'm embarrassed – not dead.

Without a care in the world he reaches down and slowly starts putting his clothes on, no bathroom needed apparently. I admit, it's erotic watching them slide over his skin. *Wait, what am I thinking? Dammit! Focus!*

"You sure you don't want to go grab a coffee or something, Red?"

My traitorous heart shouts "yes," but after peeking a glance at the clock, I curse, making him smirk like he's never heard a woman cuss before. "Thanks, but no thanks. I need to get my butt to work."

"Okay. Maybe some other time then?" He looks at me with his eyebrows raised, one hip cocked, waiting for my reply.

"Yeah sure," I tell him absently even though I hope I never see him again after this. I'm humiliated enough, thank you very much.

He walks over to me, and I find myself backing up as he approaches. He smiles and I can see amusement flickering in his eyes. Once I'm to the wall and can't back up any further, he places a hand beside my head against the wall. "Thanks for a memorable night darlin'. Hope I can see you again real soon." He leans toward me like he's about to kiss me and I feel my heart race in my chest in excitement. I close my eyes, lift my face and open my mouth in anticipation only to feel a soft brush of his lips against my cheek.

I suck in a breath, feeling disappointed. I take an extra moment to open my eyes, feeling like a fool for appearing eager or desperate for him to kiss me. I'm not stupid and my memory is now fully intact. I remember his lips on mine last night and I want them on mine again. When I finally have the courage to open my eyes and look at him, it's to see his back as he exits my room, closing the door behind him.

I sink down to the floor and place my head on my knees trying to calm my racing heart and cool the fire in my blood.

chapter 2

I DIDN'T LIE TO RIXTON – not exactly. I don't *have* to go into work today, but I should at least make an appearance. I'm the boss, I make my own schedule, but burying myself in work is just what I need after the morning I've had. Sighing to myself, I mentally acknowledge the fact that I'm a complete coward. It was easier to make an excuse, than to stay and deal with the stupid mistake I made.

Thoughts of last night invade my mind and I return to the scene of the crime. First, I'm sitting at a table at Zero Gravity, covetously watching Luke and Olivia. Wrapped up in each other's arms, like they cannot get close enough, dancing slowly on the floor; the center of attention. They were the envy of everyone in the room, their love for one another palpable. Everyone knows what they've been through and all they've overcome. To see them in that moment was an honor – a privilege. A lie that tore them apart, an abusive ex-husband of Olivia's that refused to let her go, and a kidnapping that rocked their world. Yes, they more than deserve to have found happiness, and every moment, every touch, every look that brings them happiness for the rest of their lives together. They are the real life example that love truly does conquer all.

The surprising thing, the thing I didn't expect to experience last night, was longing. The undeniable ache in my chest caught me off guard, threw me off balance, and led to my attempts to drown the feeling in alcohol. And as quick as a blink, it's back.

Shaking my head free of the emotions suffocating me, I switch my thoughts to the work that awaits me as I walk into the spa. Greeting my staff at the front desk, I head to my office, then immediately flip on my computer. As soon as it comes to life, I begin placing an order with our skin care vendor. A couple of hours later, I'm feeling very accomplished. I finalized the order for our new tanning beds that will go in the rooms we are converting for tanning treatments. I've ordered the spray tan machines for the adjoining rooms for those people who want to avoid the UV rays. I've also gone through several samples from local businesses and carefully selected the items I'd like to carry in our gift shop.

I'm so involved in my work that I jump a little when there is a knock at my door. "Yes?"

"Excuse me, Miss Lexington?"

I look up to see my new hire, Lily, hesitating at my office door. Instinctively, I scrutinize her attire. All staff members are required to wear black and white. As long as they don't look like strippers, I generally don't care what it is. We aren't *that* kind of massage place. Moreover, I enjoy learning of their individual personalities through their chosen attire.

"Yes?" I repeat, trying to keep a look of annoyance off of my face.

"I'm sorry to interrupt, but there's a Miss Brooks here to see you. I told her you were in your office with your door closed and I didn't think you wanted to be interrupted, but she said you would want to see her?" She shuffles her feet nervously and for the life of me, I can't understand why she's acting afraid of me. I'm never unkind to my employees. Not ever.

"It's fine, Lily. She's right. Remember when I told you once before that Miss Brooks is my best friend? She's to get any treatment booked she wants without charge, and can interrupt me any time. She's the only person ever allowed to do that."

"I'm sorry, Miss Lexington. I promise to remember that the next time."

"No problem. I know when you're new it's hard to remember everyone and everything. Please just tell her to come on back." I smile reassuringly at her because it dawns on me that when I arrived, I was so consumed in my thoughts about Rixton, I must have stormed in here like a crazy woman. Something they only see rarely – and admittedly, usually because I am troubled or upset about something – feelings that seep through in my heavy footsteps and excessively quick gait, despite my best attempts to conceal it all and maintain a professional décor. Likely, the gossip is buzzing out there. Joy.

"Okay, I will." She gives me a smile and walks out, looking relieved.

My gaze falls to the picture on my desk as I wait for Olivia's entrance. It's my favorite picture of my father and me. It's the day he surprised me with Shimmer & Soothe. I smile fondly, remembering the thrill of that day – how excited, how shocked, I was. We're standing in front of the entrance and there is a huge bow on the glass doors. He's handing me the key, and my step-mom happened to capture the perfect look of elation and happiness on my face while my dad looked at me with a prideful look.

My father may have bought this spa for me as a graduation gift, but I've been determined since the doors opened to do well enough that he would never need to put any of his own money into my business to assure its success. In the beginning, I came awfully close a few times to giving in to his assistance when getting our client base established proved to take a little longer than I planned. Somehow though, we made it through the slow months, and have continued to grow steadily ever since. It isn't that I think my father wouldn't help, or that he would have been disappointed in my request, it's just I'm determined to make him proud. I didn't expect such an elaborate gift from him. I had already drafted plans, in fact, to do it all on my own, so I guess part of me wants to make him believe that I'm worthy of such a gift.

Distracting me from my thoughts, Olivia walks into my office. Adorned in a hot pink skirt, black blouse, and heels for miles, she looks fabulous. Being in love certainly agrees with her, and I find myself automatically returning her smile. "Hey gorgeous," she greets me with a smile, her eyes twinkling.

"Hey yourself, beautiful. This is a surprise!" I'm totally lying. I knew she was coming.

"Oh please," and I smile larger because she knows. "After this morning, you really thought I wouldn't be showing this fine ass of mine in your office today? Pah-lease. We've been friends for how long again?"

"Well, right now I'm starting to think too long," I inform her with a lift of my eyebrow.

"Oh ha, ha. Look who's a comedian. I guess that's a good thing though because I figured you'd be a total bitch right now, stewing in embarrassment and horror." I stare at her without responding, which makes her laugh. "You know what I want… give it to me."

"Yes, I know what you want, because you're a gossip whore," I tease.

"You know, I would be offended by that except for the fact that the only person I ever gossip with, is *you*. That means we are both gossip whores."

"Alright fine, you've got a point. Bitch."

"Floozy."

"Bridezilla."

"Harlot."

"Hey!"

"Stop stalling and spill. What the hell happened last night? How did you end up with Rixton?"

"Well, this woman I know is getting married to this man that adores her more than anything, and last night was their engagement party. I went, drank, hung out. You know that, so whatever do you mean 'what happened last night'?"

"Wow. You are totally on a roll today. You know damn well I'm talking about the very fine, sexy, and let's be honest here, well-hung naked man that was lying in your bed this morning." At this, she lifts an eyebrow and I can feel myself blush as red as my hair. Damn her. "And as far as that naked man goes... first of all I must say... *damn* fine job, Pyper. Good hell that man is....well..." a huge grin spreads across her face, "good job! I mean, you certainly could have done worse. So yeah... I want details and I want them now, you red-headed devil."

I can't help but laugh at her enthusiasm and teasing. "Well, as you saw in vivid high-definition color this morning, I had a one-night-stand with your fiancé's college buddy and employee, Rixton."

Both of her eyebrows raise this time, "Well, that much I figured out for myself, but I must say, I'm SHOCKED."

I snort. "Oh please. It's not like I'm some virgin and you know it. That ship, as they say, sailed a long time ago."

She snorts in return, geesh we sound like hogs trying to have a conversation. "I know that, obviously, but come on. Do you think I forgot the dating profiles we filled out together like a year ago? You convinced me to start dating again. But while I went on date after date, you only dated a few guys and then quit."

"Well, that's because I was being way too entertained by all of your exploits."

"Yeah right... more like you were too busy putting yourself in the middle of my business."

"Well, if I do recall, that seemed to turn out pretty great for you." I pointedly look at the dazzling engagement ring adorning her finger and watch as a smile forms, lighting up her already pretty face.

Sighing, she smiles dreamily and looks lovingly at her ring. Then, as if she was pinched, the smile falls from her face and she winces, "Nice try. You aren't going to distract me from having this conversation."

"Damn," I mutter.

"Yeah, so what gives? Because even those few guys you dated, you never brought them home."

"Well that's not my fault. All those guys were duds. In fact, I'm seriously thinking about suing all dating sites. I mean come on, there is no way those quote unquote realistic commercials stating all those moony eyed couples met and fell in love through their site is legit. In fact, I think I should challenge these companies to produce proof of this shit so there aren't other victims like me that fall for their empty promises." I'm liking my idea more and more and my enthusiasm grows with my idea. "Yeah. That's what I should do. I should call my father and ask to talk to his company attorney."

When Olivia finishes laughing she responds, "I'm sure that would go over well. 'Hi dad, I want to sue all the dating sites because the only guys they say I'm compatible with are men that just want to hook up or cop a feel'."

"Yeah okay, I see what you're saying. That would be awkward."

"My question is, again – what happened? What makes Rixton different? Do you really like him? Luke says he's a great guy, you know."

"He does, huh? Well he seems pretty nice, but I don't remember being too worried about his personality."

Olivia laughs, "Yeah I can see that being the case."

"Ha. Ha. We started hanging out at the bar…" I hold up my hand when I see Olivia open her mouth to comment. "Please hold your comments until the end, thank you." She promptly closes her mouth, making me smile. "You want the truth, Livvie?"

She gives me a look that screams that I should know better, "Do you even have to ask?"

I let out a sigh and look at her for a long minute while my thoughts run through my mind like a movie. I look away and swallow hard, looking at the wall while I gain the courage to tell her my feelings. It isn't that I think she will laugh at me or call me crazy; it's more that this is out of character for me. I'm a self-described optimist; I'm happy and always encourage others to go for it and take risks. I don't sweat the small stuff generally, and do my best to keep the heavy stuff buried, so I'm having a hard enough time wrapping my mind around these new feelings – let alone sharing them with someone else.

"The truth is, I couldn't take my eyes off of you and Luke. You are both so very happy." I look back at her and smile, "The two of you just radiate love for each other. Every inch of each of you is connected to the other and it's apparent to everyone around you. It's like… like you're two magnets, and even from across the room your bodies lean towards one another. It's the most beautiful thing I've ever seen." Livvie's eyes well up at my words and I continue to boldly look her in the eyes, "and the truth is, I want that. For the first time, I felt myself looking at you and feeling jealous and desirous of a love like the two of you share."

"Pyper—"

I hold up a hand again, stopping her, "No, don't get me wrong. No one deserves it more than you, and it makes me *so* happy that you're happy. I mean that, and I think you know that, or at least, I hope you do." She nods absently. "Plus, I like to consider myself partly responsible for helping the two of you find your way back to each other," I laugh, knowing exactly how I interfered as far as that goes. "But the fact is, I want that. I want to have a love like that. To be the fire to someone's ice. To see my soul reflected in them and know they see the same in me." I grasp my chest, "I know it sounds crazy, but I swear I feel my heart ache with longing when I think about it too much. "

"It will happen for you too. I know it. These things always happen when we least expect them to."

"I know. My sexy business man is out there."

"Business man?" Olivia looks confused at my words.

"Yeah. You know that's the kind of man I picture myself with. An intelligent, independent, confident, sexy, well-dressed of course, business man."

Olivia's mouth opens, and then closes. "I do seem to remember you saying something like that before. Well...it sounds like you have this all planned out."

"Of course I do. It's partly why none of those other dates worked out. I have a picture in my mind of exactly how this should go."

"Well, honey," Olivia says gently, "I've told you before, and I know you know, that life doesn't always work like that."

"What do you mean?"

"You know very well what I mean. These expectations you have... your plans... are you sure you're being fair to yourself? Realistic, I mean?"

"Realistic? What isn't realistic exactly? It isn't realistic that I would end up with a successful business man?"

"No, that's not what I mean. What I mean is that sometimes we set ourselves up with expectations. Instead, we should just let destiny and life happen."

"Well, I guess I haven't really given that much thought. I just know what I want, and what my family expects, so why settle?"

"I'm not suggesting you should settle, but the fact is that these things... well they can't be planned out every step of the way. For goodness sake, if anyone knows that, it's me. And as far as what your family expects, I think what makes you happy is far more important. Besides," she smirks at me, "I know for a fact you didn't plan Rixton."

Truer words have never been spoken.

chapter
3

"I ALMOST DON'T WANT TO TELL you about how Rixton and I ended up hooking up because it's so embarrassing. I can't believe how I behaved."

Olivia's eyes widen and she wiggles in her seat in excitement, knowing the details she's dying for are coming. "Well, now you have to tell me because I'm even more intrigued than I was before. Plus, I'm your best friend so that automatically gives me rights to know everything."

Giving Olivia a look that portrays my annoyance, I try not to laugh because truth be told, I would say the same thing if our roles were reversed. Closing my eyes, I take a big breath and instantly, as if he was just waiting for me, an image of Rixton appears in my mind. I open my eyes, smile with just a curve of my lips because I can't seem to help myself, and tell Olivia how I made a fool of myself.

"I was sitting at the table during your engagement party watching you and Luke," I begin. "It was after we had eaten, and you and Luke were surrounded by family and friends at the table, but you were in your own world. You were so absorbed in one another, Livvie. At one point, I laughed at something and turned to you, calling your name, and you didn't even hear me. Luke was whispering something in your ear and you had a smile on your face that lit up the room. I had a couple of drinks with dinner, and then when people started leaving the tables and socializing and getting drinks and all that, I made my way to the bar."

"Well, I did figure it had to be a drunken moment that made you drop your inhibitions and bring him home."

I laugh sardonically, "You got that right. I think I thought… no who am I kidding?" I pause briefly and restart. "I knew that alcohol would help numb the loneliness I was feeling. I wanted to drown out the unfamiliar and uncomfortable feeling and not feel anything at all. I went to the bar, sat down, and ordered another drink."

It doesn't take long for me to request my second drink … that made it three… no four… no definitely three. Who the hell cares? I didn't drive here, and wouldn't be driving home. I turn, scan the room and watch from afar. Luke and Olivia nearly float around the room, chatting easily and thanking their friends for attending, frequently catching brief glimpses of each other. Olivia looks radiant in a black dress with a tulle skirt and lace top. Luke looks equally as sharp in a gray suit obviously tailored to fit his nice physique. They are such a striking couple.

Luke can't take his eyes or hands off of her. He's always holding her hand or has his hand at the small of her back. When they are separated, her by a group of women and he by some guys doing that back slapping hug thing guys do, they make their way back to one another quickly, as if the separation is painful.

I sip my drink slowly and glance around the room. A lot of people turned out for the party; colleagues, old friends and even some new friends. As I'm flirting with a man next to me, Rixton catches my eye at the other end of the bar. Whoa – holy hot boy! He looks amazing tonight. Usually dressed in his typical jeans, t-shirt and boots, his attire —or how he looks in it – makes my breath catch. I almost don't recognize him in a sleek black pinstriped suit. We make eye contact and I quickly look away when a smile appears on his lips.

Focusing once again on my friends, I smile as they make their way to the dance floor. The live band, aware that they've walked onto the dance floor, starts playing a little louder. Luke and Olivia wrap themselves around each other, holding on tight, bodies moving slowly, completely unaware of anyone else. They are clearly in their own world. It's difficult to tell where one begins and the other ends.

I sigh again in longing and take a big gulp of my drink, then tilt it back, realizing I've nearly emptied it. Didn't I just get a new one? If I can't remember, perhaps that's a sign I should be done for the evening. Just as I set my glass down and pick up my purse from the bar, intending to call a cab with my cell phone, I'm startled when in my left ear I hear a voice purr, "Well, hello there."

Turning my head, the first thing that captures my attention are Rixton's eyes. I remember I've noticed them since Luke first introduced us. Not quite dark brown, but not quite gold either, framed with dark brows and lashes. They're simply striking. His hair is dark and slicked back, the ends brushing the collar of his shirt. He's sporting a sexy five o'clock shadow and his lips that look like they are made for kissing and whispering dirty thoughts, are curved in amusement. My eyes meet his again and see they're twinkling, like he knows all my secrets.

I raise my glass in a mock toast, "Hello yourself."

He smirks and it's damn sexy, "Can I buy you another drink?"

I look down at my glass and immediately develop amnesia, forgetting that just moments ago I was thinking that it was time to quit drinking for the night and head home. "Sure, why the hell not? I guess I don't plan on quitting any time soon after all." Especially not with your gorgeous self right here in front of me.

His eyebrows rise at my response, but his only question is, "What are you drinking?"

"A vodka martini straight up, please." He raises his finger signaling to the bartender and orders my drink with a whiskey neat for himself.

His gaze falls back on me while we wait for our drinks, "Having a bad night?"

Groaning softly, I run my hand through my hair. "No, not exactly."

Seeing that I'm not going to say any more than that at the moment, he switches gears. "So, you see that guy over there?"

I follow the direction he's pointing and see a man seated at a table, drink in hand with his eyes on Luke and Olivia. "Yes, I see him."

"Someone was saying he's totally crashing the party."

"Crashing?"

He runs his hand over his mouth as if he's trying to cover a smile. He then places an elbow on the bar and leans back looking as if he hasn't a care in the world. "Yes. You don't know him?"

"I've never seen him before. Hmm, maybe he just really likes parties? Oh! Or maybe he's from one of those TV shows that broadcasts people's weddings and he's here to watch Luke and Livvie to see if they would make good material."

Rixton chuckles, obviously not buying my idea, "Okay, I want to play this game too. Maybe he's been best friends with the beautiful bride-to-be for years, but what she doesn't know is that he's been secretly in love with her forever. He's here to finally tell her the truth about his feelings before he loses his chance forever."

I can't help it, I reach out and touch his arm while I laugh, "Isn't that a movie?" His arm is firm under my touch.

"I have no idea what you're talking about," he says dryly. The amusement in his eyes clearly displays the opposite of his words.

"Wow! I wouldn't take you for a chick flick watching kind of guy."

"Oh really? What kind of guy do you take me as?"

"Not going to answer that one." I smile.

"Oh come on!" He leans close to me, "I dare you."

I lean forward as well, and we are so close, our lips will touch if either one of us moves an inch. I whisper, "You look like a man that has a lot of stamina and can show a girl a really good time."

His eyes widen, but then a slow and sexy smile curves his lips up making my breath catch in my throat. "Wow, so I hit that jackpot. You're beautiful and smart."

I grin, the alcohol making me feel like I'm freaking brilliant. "Damn skippy."

He laughs full out, and I like the sound. A lot. It makes the hair at my neck and on my arms stiffen, and butterflies flutter in my belly.

"I have to admit I'm surprised that you were sitting at the bar all alone."

"Ah, well, I was contemplating calling a cab and slipping out, but Luke mentioned he really wants me to meet some friend of his tonight. He asked me to stick around until he could introduce us. Olivia started going on and on about how great Luke says he is, and that she's seen a picture of him and he's hot. She said I definitely want to get in on that action." He laughs at that, making me chuckle too. *"I probably shouldn't tell him that part when I meet him,"* I confess. *"Anyway, I don't think he's shown up."*

"Ah, so his loss is my gain."

"I think that remains to be seen doesn't it?"

"Ah, fair enough."

"So, I understand you're from Texas?"

"You have something against Texas? You say that with irritation."

"Did I? No, not at all. I've never been there."

"Well, maybe we should change that some time. Texas is great."

I turn and look at Luke and Olivia again and find them still wrapped up in each other's arms. Out of the corner of my eye I see that Rixton is gazing at them too. He turns to me, but I keep looking at my friends. *"Have you ever been in love like that?"*

His question startles me. I look away from Luke and Olivia and try to meet his eyes, but find myself staring at the expanse of skin exposed at his open shirt collar. *"No,"* I respond simply, *"it hasn't been part of my plans."*

"Plans? That's an interesting comment. You can't plan something like love."

"You can plan anything." He just stares at me, prompting me to ask, *"Have you? Ever been in love like that, I mean?"*

"No," he states simply, then turns to the bartender as he places our drinks before us.

"Here are your drinks, sorry it took so long." He's staring at me. *"Can I get you anything else, beautiful?"*

Before I can respond, a cold voice answers, *"She's fine, thanks. I'll let you know if she needs anything else."*

The bartender looks surprised, but shrugs his shoulders and holds up his hands as if in surrender. *"Message received."*

21

Whoa. That seemed like jealousy, unless I'm just too drunk to have a clue, because holy hell, I'm drunk. I think my lips are numb. And my toes.

I look at my sexy company and he picks up my drink and hands it to me, then holds his up. "A toast." I hold up my glass too. "To love."

"To love," I repeat and clink my glass with his. He smiles and we watch each other as we sip.

"Mmm," he says softly.

"Good?" I ask gesturing towards his drink, but he doesn't look at his drink. He looks at me.

"Delicious."

I feel myself flush, "I have a question."

His eyebrows lift, "Hit me."

"Is it true what they say about Texas?"

He looks at me in confusion. "What they say? What do you mean?"

"Well… is everything really bigger in Texas?" I blatantly look at his crotch and back up again. Rixton throws his head back and laughs. I lift my glass, "My turn then. To Texas."

He's still chuckling, "To everything definitely being bigger in Texas." We clink our glasses, smile and sip.

"How come you don't have much of an accent?"

"I do a bit, you just haven't noticed, darlin'," he drawls on purpose making me laugh.

He raises his glass to toast again, "How about this time to sexy redheads that have a great laugh."

We drink again, holding eye contact the whole time. I don't know if it's the alcohol thinking for me, or what, but I want him. Under my top, I can feel my breasts swell and ache in that oh so good way that's all about longing, and a shiver runs through me from head to toe. My breathing starts to get a little choppy and suddenly getting him naked seems like a really good idea.

He notices the change in me, and his eyes drop to my thin top, meet mine again, and I almost gasp – they're liquid fire.

What I do next, I barely think about because if I do, I won't act. I take my glass, and deliberately run my tongue along the rim of the glass closest to my lips nice and slow. His eyes follow the movement, when they meet mine again, I say, "Save a horse?" And let the second half of that saying, 'ride a cowboy' go without saying.

He doesn't even take time to think about his answer. He slams down his glass and grabs my hand, "Let's get out of here."

chapter
4

OLIVIA'S MOUTH IS WIDE OPEN when I finish my story, prompting me to sarcastically say, "Wow, no wonder Luke loves you so much."

Her mouth pops closed, then opens, then closes again before she blinks and eloquently states, "Huh?"

"I said, no wonder-"

She shakes her head, "No, I heard what you said. What do you mean?"

"Well with your mouth open that wide-"

She gasps, "What?! Shut up!"

"Just sayin'," I laugh at her.

"Stop trying to distract me. You actually said, 'Save a horse, ride a cowboy'?"

"I didn't say 'ride a cowboy,' but it was implied."

"And you actually asked him if it was true that things are bigger in Texas?"

I looked down before meeting her eyes, "Um, yeah. And stared at his crotch like I said." Olivia throws her head back and laughs. And laughs. I cross my arms, getting annoyed and can feel the flush build from my neck rising up to cover my face. "Stop laughing!"

"Why, oh why, couldn't I have been there to hear you say that? Oh my God, I would have DIED! Like seriously, best pick-up lines ever!"

"Whatever. I thank God for small favors. Telling you about it is bad enough."

"So, when you woke up, you had forgotten about the night before? I'm assuming that's why you screamed bloody murder this morning. Well, and because that's what I could comprehend from your babbling and crazy hand motions."

I put my head in my hands, "I bet I looked like a demented crossing guard."

Olivia laughs, "Maybe a little."

"You are totally loving this, aren't you?"

"It's just kind of nice to see you all riled up over a guy for once."

I shake my head at her, "I am not riled."

"Sure you're not."

Dismissing her, I change the subject, "How are the wedding plans coming? Anything I can help you with or should be doing?"

Olivia smiles at me her face instantly brightening and I feel a little relieved that we've moved on from me. "Well, I think I already told you we have the venue booked for the wedding, and Luke really wants to have the reception at Zero Gravity. It makes sense – it's free and the bar is stocked," she smiles and I nod in agreement. "I hired the florist and Luke is in charge of getting a band for the reception. I'd really like to go dress shopping with you some time soon."

"Of course. Just say when and I will be there. I can't wait to see you in your gown too. Oh, and I told Bridget how you'd like her to do our makeup for the wedding and she's booked that morning for us."

"Oh, perfect. I had forgotten about that, thank you."

"Hey, just doing my job as maid of honor."

She reaches across the desk and grabs my hand. "You're perfect. I wouldn't want my maid of honor to be anyone else." I squeeze her hand in return. "I need to call the wedding boutique downtown and schedule an appointment for us to look at dresses and for you. I can't wait for you to try some on. I will let you know when they can get us in."

"That's fine, I'm flexible, but you have to schedule an appointment?"

"Oh yes, it's all very posh. They'll bring us dress after dress for you to look at and try on. We merely get to lounge on their comfortable couch or chairs, drinking the best wine. They spoiled me when I went in for my gown too."

"Oh fun! I still can't believe I wasn't with you for that."

"Oh it wasn't a big deal. I saw it in a magazine, found out who carried it locally, and when I called they said I could go over right away. I was so excited I just went. I'm excited for you to see it too. In fact, I'll schedule the dress shopping and my next fitting for the same time."

"Perfect! We will have a blast! Anything else?"

"Did I tell you that I went ahead and bought the shoes I told you about? They were to die for online, but holy shit you should see them in person!"

"I want to see them!"

"I had them sent to the club and they're in Luke's office. Come with me to see them and we can grab some lunch after if you want to."

"They're at the club?"

I tried to be super sneaky Mission Impossible with my question, but she sees right through me, "Yes, at the club."

"Well maybe I will just see them tonight. Bring them home and I can take a look at them then." I look down and shuffle some papers on my desk. Then reshuffle them again. She doesn't speak, but I hear her start tapping her foot. I don't want to, but I look up and meet her eyes.

Her eyebrows rise, "Cut the crap."

I drop the papers, "Excuse me?"

"You and I both know you want to see him. Whether it's morbid curiosity or you want to get another glimpse at his sweet ass, you want to see him. So how about we just skip this whole, 'no I don't', 'yes you do' back and forth part and go?"

It's my turn to catch flies apparently. "Damn."

"Just keeping it real, bestie."

We both laugh and with a sigh I stand up and grab my purse and keys so I can follow her to the club.

I hesitate outside the doors of Zero Gravity, grab Olivia's shoulder, stopping her. Olivia looks at me questioningly, "Okay, I hate that I'm even going to ask this because really I don't care."

Her eyebrows rise and her mouth tilts up on one side, "Sure you don't, but proceed."

"Do I look alright?" I fiddle with my hair and look down at my black capris and sea green off the shoulder top.

Olivia chuckles softly but breaks off into a small squeak when I teasingly yank a piece of her hair. "You look fabulous. Like always."

I roll my eyes, feeling pleased with her assessment and follow her into the club. When we're inside it takes a moment for our eyes to adjust to the darkness, but when they do, like a beacon, my eyes narrow in on the bar. Not even realizing it, I come to a stop and stare. Rixton is bent over next to the bar opening a box of what looks to be alcohol bottles. It's clear he must be replenishing stock. What made me stop is not only the amazing view his position presents, but because of all the women that are currently standing around, staring as well.

Olivia, who stopped when I did, turns to me, a questioning look on her face. Before she can say anything I ask, "What is with everyone being here right now? The club doesn't open for a bit yet."

"Luke said there was a staff meeting today."

"I see." I follow Olivia and we make our way past the bar. Rixton, hearing our approach, looks behind his shoulder and first takes in all the ladies behind him with a smile, then catches sight of me. I look away, wishing Olivia would walk faster so we can get up the stairs to Luke's office. What was I thinking? Curiosity is totally going to kill the redhead.

Out of the corner of my eye I see him stand to his full height, but I keep walking until I hear, "Hey, Red."

I pause, "Are you speaking to me?"

He blatantly looks around the room, taking in the other girls, "I don't see another red haired beauty here," then he smiles a kick-ass grin that simultaneously makes me want to smack him and jump him at the same time. "No offense of course to the dark and light haired beauties that are currently gracing my presence," he says, being sure to emphasize his accent. They all giggle in response, causing me to roll my eyes and start up the stairs after Olivia.

Before I get more than a few steps, I'm startled by a hand gripping my arm, silently asking me to turn around. Obeying, I turn to find Rixton in front of me, eye level. Damn he's tall. "Where are you going?"

I stare at him dumbly, man his eyes are pretty. No! Do not fall into his mesmerizing sexiness, dammit. "Up the stairs," I point as if he needs the gesture to understand. Man, he makes me stupid.

"Be sure to see me when you come back down, darlin'."

"Why should I?" I hear a few gasps from women behind Rixton that apparently can't believe I would speak to him in such a manner. Gag me. It takes everything I have within me not to roll my eyes at the bimbos. Harsh, probably, but I'm beyond caring.

A lazy smile covers his mouth and he gives me a look that says he knows I'm acting like I don't care when I really do. Damn him, ugh. "I just want to ask you a question."

I sigh, "Fine. I'll be back."

"What was that about?" Olivia inquires when I reach the door to Luke's office.

I shrug my shoulders, "He says he wants to ask me a question."

Olivia's eyes light up with amusement, "Oh yeah? What do you think it is?"

I look down and see Rixton still staring up at me. I turn back to Olivia, "No doubt something obnoxious."

I follow her into the office and wave at Luke, who's sitting behind his desk talking on the phone. He waves back politely, but he only has eyes for Olivia, and they are following her across the room as she grabs the box of shoes. When she turns, she catches his eye and blows him a kiss on the way over to where I'm standing.

"Wait until you see these."

She takes the lid off a white box with a very pricey designer name, and starts separating the pale blue tissue paper inside. When she pulls out her shoe and I get a good look, I understand. It's the kind of shoe you bow down before to worship. It's perfection. White, at least four inches high, ruched at the toe with a crystal applique at the peep toe that's just wide enough to show off a gorgeous pedicure my spa will treat her to, of course. "Oh, Olivia. You weren't kidding," I whisper as if the shoe is a holy artifact that should be looked at and not touched.

She giggles, takes the other shoe out and turns them both over, "I know it's kind of cheesy, but I love this part."

I take in the crystal word "I" on one shoe, and the word, "Do" on the other. "I think it's adorable."

"Yeah?"

"Yes, seriously Livvie. They're perfect. Perfect shoes for what will be a perfect day." We both sigh when the shoes disappear from view as she places them back into the box and tucks them back into the tissue. "They were definitely worth the trip here to see," I smile.

She laughs, "We are such girls."

"Girls who love shoes, there's no shame in that."

"Definitely not."

Luke hangs up the phone and beckons to Olivia. Smiling, she makes her way over to him and he pulls her into his lap and whispers something into her ear, making her giggle. I quietly leave the room, and start making my way down the stairs, not wanting to feel like a voyeur.

As I reach the bottom, Rixton suddenly appears in front of me, "What put that pretty smile on your face?"

Startled to see him, I reach my hand out and touch his shoulder to steady myself, then quickly pull it away when a grin flashes on his face. "Luke and Olivia are all cutesy and lovey dovey."

"Ahh, yes. I've been witness to that myself around here plenty of times. It took me ten minutes to get Luke's attention once because he was too busy staring at Olivia across the room."

I smile and do my best to refrain from sighing with envy or making some immature girlish comment. I start to move past him to leave, but stop when I feel a hand on my arm again. Raising my eyebrows, I silently give him an inquisitive look.

"Relax darlin', I just have a question." I hate what the sound of his voice does to my body. My nipples harden, my tummy flutters and my mouth salivates. It's ridiculous.

"Make it quick. I need to go."

"Oh yeah?" He crosses his arms over his chest, "You have plans or something?"

"Yes, actually, I do."

I can hear steps behind me, "Hey," Olivia admonishes, "you left without me."

Turning toward her, I shrug my shoulders, "I thought maybe the two of you could use some time alone."

"Are we still going to go to lunch?"

"No, you stay with Luke. Let's catch lunch later."

"You sure?"

I smile, reassuring her. "Of course."

"Well, I still would have wanted to say good-bye."

"No big deal if you hadn't. You know I will talk to you later."

"I know, but still."

We are interrupted by Rixton, "What plans do you have?"

Turning back to him I put my hands on my hips, "Excuse me?"

"Well, I wanted to see if you want to go out with me tonight? I was thinking maybe for dinner, or we could grab a coffee, or something? You can choose the place."

I stare at him for a minute, for the life of me forgetting what it is I have to do and why I can't go with him. I blink. Dinner. With my parents.

"Sorry," I say with a flip of my hair over my shoulder, "I can't come."

A smile that can only be called wicked crosses his face, "Oh darlin', we both know that's not true."

Warmth spreads over my face and I have no doubt my face is as red as my hair yet again. How does he keep doing this to me? "Wh… um… we…" I am completely at a loss for words. I look at Olivia, and she is staring at Rixton with her mouth on the freaking floor.

Completely flustered, I make my way to the door and walk out with Rixton's laugh following me.

chapter
5

RACING THROUGH THE DOOR of my condo, I quickly run to my room after turning off the security alarm, and start to remove my clothes. Dinner tonight at my parent's house requires me to dress the part. My eyes quickly dart to the disheveled sheets that are still on my bed. I try to ignore them, but hear them calling out to me, so hurriedly strip them from the bed and dash down the hall to throw them into the washing machine. Pulling fresh sheets out of the linen closet, I make my bed, knowing I don't really have time, but do so anyway. I don't want my stupid impulsive decision to be staring me in the face upon my return, yet again.

Stripping and trying to freshen up my makeup at the same time is a challenge, but one I've accomplished before – thank you so very much – so I finish quickly and run a brush through my hair. It's grown out a lot and quickly catching my reflection in the mirror, realize I like it longer again. I pull on a classic black dress and pumps for dinner, add pearls and switch out bags before heading out the door.

On the drive over to their house, my Mercedes affords me the quiet time to relax my brain and reflect again on last night. Why I can't just let this go like I have with similar prior situations causes me an extra pause, but I quickly dismiss it. Rather, images of last night start flashing through my mind against my will and better judgment. I can almost hear his whispered moans again in my ear, and feel the brushes of his skin upon my neck. He repeatedly kissed the spot between my collarbones and then would continue nibbling the right or left side up to my neck. Each time my body would react to his touch with wanting, longing, and I even begged him for more as I met each of his thrusts with my own.

Suddenly, it feels so hot in my car, I can barely breathe. Turning the air conditioning to a lower temperature, I try to find a song on the radio that will distract me. The first station is playing S&M by Rhianna, and I quickly turn it, the next station is playing Come & Get it by Selena Gomez, prompting me to turn it again. When I hear Justin Timberlake singing Rock Your Body, I let out a slight scream, "Really?"

Okay so apparently the radio is a bad idea, and I need to find music other than pop to listen to. I distract myself with playing the alphabet license plate game until I finally arrive at my parents' home. Living in Highland Park, a suburb of Chicago, their home is only a twenty minute drive from my own. After I moved into my condo, my father purchased the entire high rise it's located in, likely to make sure my home wasn't too far from their own. He also knew that he would be in a position to be sure everything was taken care of and there would always be abundant, excellent building security. My father goes over the top and over indulges me in everything. I've learned not to fight it, and just give in because it seems to make him happy, although sometimes I feel suffocated by his involvement in everything I do. I know it's all out of love, though. He just wants the best for me.

I pull up next to a car I don't recognize in the driveway. Out of the car, bending to grab my purse, I feel perplexed. It's unusual that I can even make it this far out of my car before my mom or dad are coming to greet me or at least standing in the entryway welcoming me. But there is no sign of either. Hmmm.

When I approach the front door and reach to turn the knob, it opens and I see Mrs. B, the amazing woman that runs my parents' home. She has been part of our family since I can remember, yet she never manages to age at all. I don't know how she does it, but if she can figure out how to bottle it, she'd be a billionaire. "Hi, sweet pea," she greets me.

I give her a hug in return, "Hi, Mrs. B. You look pretty." She has one of her favorite dresses on – blue with white flowers all over it. An apron around her hips and her hair pulled into a low bun completes her familiar appearance. She is also wearing lip gloss – a sure sign – if I hadn't already noticed the car in the driveway – that my parents have company. "Where are they?"

"They are already in the dining room, sugar."

Giving her one last squeeze, I walk toward the dining room, able to hear voices as I approach. Walking through the room's threshold, my eyes instantly fall on my father. Seated at his usual spot at the head of the table, my mother is at his right side, and the left is vacant, a clear indication of where I am expected to sit. My eyes flick to the two men I don't recognize. One is my father's age and clearly a business associate. The snippets of conversation I'm catching from them clearly indicate as much. The other man looks close to my age and he's looking at me with a small smile. I return it hesitantly and look at my father once more.

"Pyper!" My father stands and holds his arms out to me when he finally becomes aware of my presence. I smile and easily walk into them, exchanging a strong embrace.

"Hi, daddy." He squeezes me once more (for good measure, as he has always said) and lets go so I can greet my mother. I lean over the back of her chair and am able only to give her a somewhat awkward hug since she's still seated. "Hi, mom."

May is my step-mom but I still call her mom. My mother died when I was only five-years-old from cancer. My father married my step-mom only a couple of years after that, so my memories – perhaps other than a rare few and those I've contrived from pictures – are mostly of the two of them. "Hello darling, you look lovely."

"Thank you," I take in my mom's smiling face, and the love in her eyes, "so do you."

"Pyper," my father puts his hand on my back to get my attention, "let me introduce you to my work associates."

I turn expectantly and plant a smile I really don't feel on my face. I wish my parents had told me we were going to have company. It doesn't make much of a difference I suppose, but still, a heads up would have been nice.

"This is my work associate, Richard, and his son, R.J." They each stand and offer me a hand. Ten bucks says R.J. stands for Richard Jr.

"Hi, nice to meet you Richard," I shake his hand firmly and turn to his son. "And R.J. Is that for Richard Jr.?"

R.J. smirks, "You are correct."

"Ah, I thought so." I knew it. Seriously, sometimes these guys are so predictable. He holds my hand a little too long and even runs his thumb across the back. Ew. I want to yank it out of his grasp, but I politely wait for him to let go before sitting down in the chair my father is holding out for me.

"I'll let Mrs. B know we are ready for the first course," my mother says. But before she can do so, Mrs. B comes around the corner with a tray in her arms ready to serve the salad. She places a lovely plate in front of each person before disappearing and like synchronized swimmers, we all pick up our flatware and begin eating.

I really hate this kind of thing, but I've done it since I can remember and know what is required of me. I've been to more stuffy parties than I care to remember. My parents drilled me in appropriate manners and etiquette when I was younger so I was sure not to embarrass them. I know that they love me, I don't doubt it for a second, but I also know what it means to be the daughter of Ted Lexington, entrepreneur, capital investor and owner of one of the top grossing mobile phone companies in the country.

Through the salad, soup, and then finally the main course of steak, asparagus and rice pilaf, I listen to my father and Richard talk business. It's boring as hell and I try to stay tuned in, but often wonder how my dad finds it all so fascinating while wishing this were just a one-on-one dinner with my parents. I would be happy with that. Instead, I'm counting down the minutes until I can bail.

My thoughts turn to Rixton and the way he embarrassed me at the club today. I can't believe he actually made that suggestion about our night together. I'm somewhat shocked my phone didn't ring immediately after I left the club with Olivia on the other end dying laughing, the bitch. Man, I love her.

"Pyper?"

Jumping a little at my father's voice, I turn to him. "I'm sorry, what?"

He smiles at me, "I was just telling Richard that I'm sure you would be happy to take R.J. to our country club Saturday evening while Richard and I have a business dinner that same night." It's useless to ask why he's having a business meeting on a Saturday night. I know better. "R.J. doesn't know anyone here and no doubt he would prefer an evening with you showing him the club as opposed to just being alone in a hotel room."

I look over at R.J. and find him looking at me expectantly, interest shining in his eyes. "Um, okay. Sure. I can do that." Not like I can say no anyway, after being put on the spot like that. Of course, my father knows that. I look at him, my eyes clearly stating that he owes me for this. He nods his head, acknowledging my unsaid feelings so discreetly I wonder if I imagined it.

"Sounds like fun," R.J. says.

Trying to look like I agree, I smile at him, "There's a great restaurant at the club and it's open to the public on the weekend, so it will be packed. I will make reservations for us. I hope you like

Italian food? We can go there and then I can show you the club's other amenities."

"Sounds perfect. Why don't we meet there at 7:00 PM. You can drop me off, right, father?"

"That's fine, son. I can drop you off on my way to meet Ted."

The conversation returns to business once more and I'm left dreading a date with daddy's boy. My mother catches my eye and smiles, her eyes giving me an apology. She knows how much I hate these expectant gestures. I'll just suck it up, though. These are the duties and life of a daughter that has a successful businessman for a father. After everything he's done for me, there is very little my father could ask of me that I would not do. He knows it though, and that's the problem.

Considering a man just like him is likely in my future, I suppose this is good practice. I just wish I could get my heart to be more into it though. I know it's my destiny in my mind, but sometimes my heart has other ideas. Out of nowhere, Rixton's face pops into my mind, and I make a face. Why does that keep happening?

"You don't like the asparagus, dear?" my mother asks.

"Oh, no, mother, it's wonderful. I think I just got a part that had a little too much seasoning." *Great Pyper, make stupid faces at dinner, what are you, twelve?*

I'm thankful when dessert is finished and I can excuse myself from the table. My father and Richard are pouring themselves after dinner drinks and my mother is joining them. I think it's the perfect moment to make my escape.

"Thank you for a wonderful dinner, mom and dad, but I need to get back home. I have an early morning at the spa."

"Oh, I wish you didn't have to leave so soon," my mother tells me as she takes me into her arms for a hug.

"Me too, but we will do it again soon, okay?" Then I whisper into her ear, "Just you, me, and daddy please?" She nods her head and gives me a squeeze.

My father hugs me too and I turn to Richard, "It was very nice to meet you, sir."

"You as well, dear. Take good care of my son Saturday night."

I smile at him and turn to R.J., "I will. I will see you then, R.J."

"Great," he smiles. "See you then."

I walk out of the house as fast as I can and breathe a big sigh of relief as I get into my car. I pull my hair out of the restrictive bun I had it bound in and drive away quickly, eager to get home and out of these clothes.

On the drive, my phone chimes a few times. I ignore it in an effort to stick to my no cell phone in the car rule since I don't have my Bluetooth setting turned on. Upon arriving to the condo building, I pull into the underground garage and whip out my phone before I head to the elevator. I have a text from a number I don't recognize.

Unknown: Hey, Red. Give me a call.

I immediately know who the text is from. I get out of my car, stride to the elevator, and wait to arrive at my floor, all the while contemplating my response. I let myself into the condo when I reach my floor. The alarm starts beeping as I walk in, loudly telling anyone that would be home that someone has walked in the door. I'm still getting used to the thing. I've not had it installed all that long, just since Olivia was kidnapped and I was held at gunpoint. Funny how something as simple as a security system can bring much needed comfort and peace. I close the door, punch in the code, then lock the door. It's quiet, and no one came running at the alarm going off, so I don't think Luke and Olivia are here.

Opening the refrigerator in the kitchen, I grab a bottle of water and make my way to my room. Throwing the bottle of water and my purse on the bed, I type out a reply to Rixton, then add his name and number to my contacts.

How did you get my number? I ask, then head to my closet, unzipping my dress as I go. While changing into some yoga pants and a tank top I hear my phone chime again.

Rixton: I told you to call me. Why are you texting?

I roll my eyes and then type: so what? You tell me to do something and I should do it? I don't think so.

Rixton: Feisty. I like it.

Me: You didn't answer my question.

Rixton: I have my ways.

I growl in my throat because I know what that means.

Me: I will kill her.

Rixton: It's not her fault.

Me: Explain

Rixton: Well, I may have held her wedding shoes hostage until she caved.

I can't help it. I laugh. Then I type again.

Me: You savage! No wonder she gave it to you – a girl would do anything for those kinds of shoes.

Rixton: Storing that information away for the future.

Me: Whatever. What do you want?

He doesn't text me back right away and before I can wonder where the hell he went my phone rings. I politely answer, "What?"
"Wow, is that how you always greet callers? Rude."
"No, you're just special." He makes an indistinguishable noise, "So what do you want? Why are you calling and texting me?"
"Well, because darlin,' you are the kind of girl that a man can't get out of his head."
I scoff, "Stop doing that."

"Doing what?"

"You purposefully make your accent harder when you try to be all sexy."

He pauses. "You think I'm sexy?"

"That is not what I said."

"Oh, yes you did, I heard it."

"I said when you *try* to be sexy. I didn't say you *are* sexy."

He laughs at me, "Okay, Red, you keep telling yourself that."

I sigh into the phone, "If you don't tell me the reason for this call, I'm hanging up."

"Maybe I just want to hear your voice," he purrs and instantly my body reacts to the sound. Ugh, traitorous skank. Out of irritation more at myself than him, I hang up the phone. He immediately calls back. "What?"

"Okay, fine. I was calling because I need you to do something for me."

I lay back against the pillows on my bed. "What could you possibly need me to do for you?"

"Oh Red, that list is endless. Do you really want to know all the things I have on it?"

"Rixton!"

"Alright, alright. I need you to check your dresser drawer. The first one."

I sit up again, "What? Why?"

"In the top right hand corner, underneath these amazingly skimpy red lacey thong and matching bra," my mouth hangs open at the description of a lingerie set I own, "I need you to see if I left something there."

Is he serious? "Left something there? How could you possibly have left something in my drawer? And what could you have left there."

"Just go look."

I walk to my dresser and slide the drawer open. In the top right hand corner, sits the lingerie set he just described. I move the set to the side and see a black ball underneath. Picking it up, I shake it out and almost choke when I realize what I'm holding between my fingertips.

"YOUR UNDERWEAR? WHY IN THE HELL AM I HOLDING YOUR UNDERWEAR?"

"See? I knew I left them there!"

"Oh my God, why in the world would you have done that? That means you went through my lingerie drawer!"

"Oh yes, that is not something I'm soon to forget, you sexy little vixen. There are some amazing pieces in there. Will you model them for me some time?"

I'm speechless. He went through my drawers. I don't know if he's crazy, or a stalker or what. "Why in the hell were you rummaging through my drawers?"

"I don't know why it seems to bother you, I mean hell, it's just some underwear. I'm way more familiar with you than a pair of underwear. Don't you remember when I-"

"RIXTON!"

I hear him sigh through the phone line, "Isn't it obvious? I left them there so I could have an excuse to call you. Or randomly show up at your place and retrieve them. Either one would have worked fine."

I throw his undies on the floor and walk back to my bed, "You are insane."

"Some would say charming." I can hear the smile in his voice over the phone.

"Maybe so, but not me!"

"Go out with me."

"What?"

"Go out on a date with me. I want to take you out. People call that a date. Maybe you've heard of it?"

"Take me out?"

"Yeah. I want to take you out. For dinner."

"For dinner?"

"Are you going to repeat everything I say? Okay awesome. Rixton, you are so sexy, yes, yes, I want to go out with you! And I'll model all my lingerie for you too."

That snaps me out of it, "Ha. Nice try. Why should I go out on a date with you?"

"Because it will be fun. And don't deny it, you are attracted to me, can't get me out of your mind, and are dying to get to know me better."

"That is not true," I insist, but dammit how does he know that? "I haven't thought about you at all."

"Wow, you are great for a guy's ego."

"Um, sorry?"

"Come out with me on Friday night. We will have a good time. We can talk, and laugh and get to know each other better. You know… other than the biblical sense."

"I don't know if that's a good idea."

"Look, I really need you to bring me my briefs back. They're my favorite pair. I'll pick you up for dinner Friday night, and take you out as a way to thank you for keeping my briefs safe for me. I'm off that night. Does that work for you?"

I find myself laughing at his ridiculousness. "Okay fine. I will let you take me to dinner. One dinner. Only because I don't trust you and fear you'll tell everyone I have your briefs if I don't get them back to you."

"Oh, that's an excellent idea. Why didn't I think of that?"

"Because apparently, I'm more of an evil genius than you are."

"I'll have to remember that."

"Okay, well I have to go. It's been a long day. I was getting ready for bed when you called." I pull the covers over my legs and settle down into the bed.

"Oh yeah? Are you in bed now? On the same sheets we slept in together? Do they still smell like me? What are you wearing?" He shoots off his questions like rapid gunfire.

"Bye, Rixton!" I hang up the phone and laugh despite myself.

I'm staring at the wall, wondering what the hell I agreed to when my phone chimes in my hand. Looking at it I see he's texted me.

Rixton: I'll pick you up at 7:00PM. Good night, Pyper.

I stare at my phone a few minutes thinking I will just ignore it and not respond. I reach over, turn out the lamp at my bedside. Then, before I can think twice, I'm typing out a reply before placing my phone on the bedside table.

Good night, Rixton.

chapter
6

THE FEW DAYS LEADING UP to my date with Rixton move very slowly. It's given me plenty of time to doubt my decision. Why did I ever tell him I would go out with him? I don't know what I'm thinking. *Yes you do. You were thinking with your hormones.*

Spending time with him isn't going to lead anywhere. It can't. All it will do is screw up my carefully, well-thought out plan for meeting the man of my dreams. I try to picture him in my mind. Navy blue pinstriped suit, shiny black shoes, pants that hug his legs, a shirt tucked in with a shiny belt catching the light at his waist. His jacket and dress shirt will hide a solid and sculpted body underneath and the light blue tie at his neck will match his eyes. When I try to see into my dream guy's face, it's blurry, but then suddenly Rixton is staring back at me. I shake my head, trying to rid myself of the image. *Yep, this just interferes and interrupts my plans – plans that I need to get busy putting in place.*

A one-night-stand, Rixton, dates with Rixton – none of this is part of that plan. So, what the hell am I doing? Why am I wasting my time this way? I should be going out on dates that have potential to actually lead somewhere. Time seems to pass quicker and quicker all the time. If I really want what Livvie has, I need to get busy. I shouldn't be screwing around anymore. It's time to be serious, grow up and look towards the future. It's time I find Mr. Right. And Rixton? Well he's not my type at all – certainly not the type you bring home to your parents. Especially my parents.

But how long might this plan thing take? Is it really wrong to just have fun in the mean time? Hanging out and hooking up with Rixton doesn't have to *mean* anything. We are both consenting adults that are attracted to one another. It isn't crazy that we would consider having a no strings attached relationship, right? I mean Rixton probably has those kinds of relationships with chicks all the time. And why does that revelation make me feel queasy? No worries; I will choose to push that particular thought away.

Remembering how funny Rixton was on the phone, makes me smile despite myself. Pushing away the unwelcome thoughts, I choose yet another outfit option from my closet and look it over. Dissatisfied, I toss it onto the ever-growing pile that keeps mounting on my floor. I make a noise of exasperation, put my hands on my hips and glare at my clothes. I have no clue what to wear. Why the hell didn't I go to the store and buy something? No wait, it's good that I didn't go and buy anything. This is just a one-time thing, not anything to go crazy over. It's not buy-a-new-outfit worthy. Oh God, who am I kidding? Everything is new clothing worthy – I'm just being stubborn.

With a feeling of determination, I grab my favorite Kelly green sheath dress out of the closet, unzip the back, and slide it up my body, and over the matching lace bra and panty set I'm wearing. Pulling up the zipper, I look at myself in the full-length mirror on the back of my closet door. I smooth the dress out around my hips, then with a contented nod, grab my nude stiletto heels and put them on.

Standing tall, I glance down at my shoes, "Perfect." In the bathroom, I put the finishing touches on my lip gloss and rub my lips together while I turn my head side to side looking at my face.

My makeup is soft — not too over the top, emphasizing my blue eyes. I've left my hair down and loose around my shoulders. When I find myself twirling and fidgeting with it, I force myself to stop and walk out of the room.

Picking up my bag off my bed, I walk out into the living room and open a closet to grab a sweater in case I get chilly just as I hear a knock on the door. I'm grateful that Olivia and Luke aren't here. I really don't want to deal with Olivia's inquiring looks and Luke's sarcastic comments. I have loved living with Olivia, but sometimes, three is definitely a crowd. Besides, I only agreed to go on a date with Rixton so that he would stop bugging me about it. That's all.

Opening the door, the first thing I see are Rixton's warm golden eyes shining at me. A combination of amusement and heat, they make goose bumps flutter over my skin as a smile curves his lips. "Hello, Red." His gaze rakes me from my feet to the top of my head, causing me to shiver involuntarily. "You look amazing." He lifts a sunflower up, handing it to me, "this is for you."

I'm surprised not only by his thoughtfulness, but that he would give me a flower other than the typical roses I've gotten from other dates. It's refreshing. I realize he must be able to read the thought on my face when he says, "We have a field of them back home and I've always loved them. It seemed like the perfect flower to bring to you."

"I love it. Thank you so much." I smile at him and he returns my smile with one of his own. I quickly get a vase for the flower, turn back to Rixton, only to find that he followed me into the room. He walks toward me, and with each step he takes, I walk backward in kind. I gasp when my back hits the counter. He stands right before me, and picks up a piece of my hair and twirls it around his fingers. "You look gorgeous, Red," he purrs. I can't take my eyes off of his mouth. He leans toward me and I'm so captivated by his eyes that I barely turn my head in time to avoid his kiss. His mouth lands on my cheek, and lingers, until I feel him smile against my skin. Taking a few steps back, he looks at me, giving me a chance to appraise him from head to toe. He's wearing blue jeans and a dark blue shirt that's rolled up to his elbows, exposing strong tan forearms. Sure, I've seen him many times at the club, but there's something about having him here, in my place, up close and personal, right now, that makes him seem even more remarkable. His shirt is open at the collar, the flash of skin there holding my attention for a moment. And just as the heat starts to form, I look a little lower and see... he's wearing cowboy boots.

I smirk and look up into his face, "Nice boots, cowboy."

"You like them?" He grabs his jeans at his knee and pulls them up, exposing his entire boots to my gaze. Turning one of his feet side to side, he is clearly admiring his boots while making sure I get a clear view as well. "I wore these just for you. I wanted to look my best."

I roll my eyes – he makes me do that a lot – trying to cover up the fact that I'm feeling a little uncertain. He's dressed much more casual than I am, but he didn't say anything so I'm not going to worry about it. Plus, he's a cowboy; this probably is dressing up for him, and I admit, he looks hot as hell. The last thing I want is to embarrass him by asking if I'm dressed okay thereby suggesting he's not dressed up enough. Besides, he could pull off a towel. Oh God, now I'm thinking about him in a towel. Wet. With water trickling down his chest, and abs, and... I swallow hard... lower. I try to distract myself with something horrendous. *Dead puppies... dead puppies... dead puppies....*

"You ready to go, or would you like to have a drink here before we leave?" I squeak out as I grab a bottle of water from the fridge myself and quickly take a drink to try to calm my nerves. And cool my hormones.

"Thank you, but let's go ahead and head out if that's okay with you."

"Okay, sure." I set the bottle on the counter and follow him to the door. After I set the alarm and lock the door, he escorts me to the elevator with a hand on the small of my back. I can feel the heat of his hand through my dress. It's... nice. Once inside the elevator, the confined space increases the scent of his cologne. The aroma reaches and penetrates my pores. He smells divine, like first dates and sexual tension. It feels as if my blood starts rushing through my veins. Is it loaded with sex pheromones or something? I move subtly to the other side of the elevator, hoping the space makes the tingles I'm feeling subside. I not only feel hyper aware of him, but of myself. Rixton looks at me with a raise of his eyebrows, "You okay? I'm not going to bite you know."

I giggle nervously, "I know. I'm fine." Giving him what I hope is a casual shrug, I stare at the elevator doors, anxious for us to reach the garage level and have the doors finally open. Leading me out, with a hand once again on the small of my back, I'm not at all surprised to see he takes me to a huge black truck. "Good hell, I'm going to need a step ladder to get into that thing!"

He smirks, "No you won't." With a beep the truck is unlocked and he opens my door. As I step onto the running board and grab hold of the handle at the top of the door, I feel a hand push against my ass helping me into my seat. I sit with a plop and turn to look at him, "Really?"

He wipes his hand over his mouth as if he's trying to cover a devilish smile, "Just trying to be gentlemanly."

I lift an eyebrow at him, "Well that's a good thing, considering that once people get a look at your mode of transportation, they are likely thankful at least for your manners."

His brows lower in confusion and he leans on the door, "What do you mean?"

"Well you know what they say about big trucks, right? It usually means the guy is trying to make up for something they may be," I look at his crotch suggestively, "lacking."

He laughs, the sound low and husky. "It's a good thing you know better. Isn't it, darlin'?"

I flush, which makes him laugh harder, but makes me feel irritated. So I lie. "I wouldn't know. I hardly remember it at all."

"Well now, Red, that sounds like a challenge to me."

"It isn't."

Jennifer Miller

He ignores me, "I accept." He closes the door and walks around the truck. Truth is, I do remember. My memory may be a bit fuzzy about the evening, but I remember our interaction and I recall the morning quite clearly. Fact is, Rixton is definitely not trying to overcompensate for anything. Damn him, and his big dick.

I wait until he starts the truck to ask, "So, where are we going? Need any suggestions, or do you have a place in mind?"

Buckling his seatbelt he turns to me, a smirk on his face. "I'm insulted."

I look up from buckling my own belt, "Why?"

"Do you actually think I would work so hard to get you to go out with me and then not have a plan?"

I shrug. "I wasn't sure. Besides, I don't mind."

"Well I do. And I've got a place in mind. Just sit back and enjoy the ride." He winks at me and then puts his keys in the ignition, starting the car.

"Okay," I smile and lean back, making myself comfortable, but when he eases into traffic, I can't help but turn my head to watch him. His thigh muscles tighten when he pushes the break, the muscles in his forearms and biceps flex as he turns the wheel. He has one hand resting casually on the wheel, and the other is on the console between us. What is it about men driving that's sexy? The way they handle a vehicle – it's a casual sexiness that makes me salivate.

He turns his head, his eyes catching mine and he smirks, "You think I'm sexy don't you?"

How does he do that? Read my mind like that? "Um, what?"

"You know… where I'm from… in Texas? We have two tractors on the farm. I would drive them a lot."

"Okay," I reply, drawing out the word, "What does that have to do with anything?" My mind flashes to Rixton shirtless and operating a tractor. The powerful machinery between his legs, sweat glistening on his skin, muscles bunching in his arms as he turns the tractor. I shift my legs yet again.

49

He pushes the power button on the stereo and after a minute, Kenny Chesney's voice comes blaring through his expensive sound system singing, what else? 'She Thinks My Tractor's Sexy'. I outright laugh when he sings, "It really turns her on."

Rixton winks at me, "Don't worry, darlin', I'm happy to give you a ride on my tractor."

Is it wrong that I now picture myself straddling his lap on that tractor? Oh hell. I'm doomed.

chapter
7

AS WE PULL INTO A DIRT PARKING LOT, I realize we've arrived at our destination. The truck bounces as we go over the uneven dirt and I white knuckle the passenger door, trying to maintain my balance. Trying to identify our location, I quickly scan the surroundings as a large building with a neon sign hanging in front comes into focus that says, PRIME STEAKHOUSE.

Rixton is out of the truck and holding my door open before I process what I am seeing or have the chance to unlatch my seatbelt. "Let me help you down," he holds his hand out for me to grasp. I do and gingerly step down out of the truck. He holds onto my hand a few beats longer than necessary.

Walking toward the front of what I'm guessing is a restaurant, my stilettos sink into a soft dirt patch, making me lose my balance. I quickly try to adjust to keep my ankle from turning and avoid falling. "Whoa, are you okay?"

"Yes, I'm fine." I push away the hair that has fallen into my face, and flash him a quick, but somewhat insincere smile. He grasps my elbow and holds it tightly the rest of the way to the entrance. We walk up wooden steps to the door and I try to maneuver over the natural cracks in the wood, distracted by the concern that my heels might get stuck. A picture of myself falling flat on my face flashes through my mind. That's all I need.

As soon as we walk into the restaurant and my eyes adjust to the lighting, I quickly skim the interior, immediately feeling both surprise and embarrassment. Rixton should have told me we were going somewhere very casual. To say I'm overdressed is an understatement. The place is really busy. There are people everywhere and practically everyone is dressed comfortably in jeans. I see a few cut off jean shorts and even girls in comfy looking flowered dresses, all accessorized with cowboy boots. The ladies all look great – I look ridiculous. I am immediately aware that this place is very much Rixton and not at all me. I should have expected something like this. But no, I'm all stupid, fancy, five-star venues with their over-the-top five-course meals, while he does off the beaten path steakhouses decorated with peanut shells on the floor.

Trying to distract myself, I absorb the environment and its, uh, ambiance. The room is large, filled with high bench seats and tables. The walls are decorated with what appears to be old country album covers and pics of country and western performers in haphazardly positioned black frames. There is a prominently displayed guitar on the wall as well. Wood beams ascend to a high ceiling, carving out various seating areas. Otherwise, it is one large open area. There's even a huge tractor in the corner of the room, affixed with a prominent John Deere sign. Rixton catches me staring at it and winks, "I can pose on it for you later if you'd like."

Ignoring his comment, I see a large red lettered sign over a side door stating "BULL OUT BACK." Somehow, I'm easily convinced it's a statement of fact, when I swear I hear an audible snort coming from that direction. Oh lord.

Coming back to the moment and not wanting him to think my pause meant that his arrogant comment got to me, I hastily answer, "Maybe *I* will pose for *you*."

His response communicates that it was the wrong thing to say. His lips curve into a smile and his eyes fill with heat. "Promises, promises. I would really like to see that, Red. Tell me what it would take."

I laugh, "A few drinks, for sure."

He smiles and turns to the hostess when she comes back from seating another couple. They exchange a few words, and then Rixton grabs my hand and begins leading me through the room. The peanut shells crunch under our feet as we walk. When we reach the back of the restaurant, large open doors leading outside welcome us. Passing through, I see many tables await guests in an open air environment. The hostess seats us and hands us menus.

"Your waitress will be here in a few minutes."

"Thank you," we both respond. Before I open the menu, my attention is captured by a warm, clear twinkle light background and several fire pits surrounding the tables; the flames within licking the air in a beautiful dance. Some people are roasting marshmallows over the pits. It looks like fun. And the ambiance is pleasant.

To the side, there is a large dance floor and what I'm assuming must be live music, if the instruments set up on the stage are any indication. The musicians must be taking a break at the moment, because other than the constant stream of chatter, and the crackling from the fires, there's no music.

I look back at Rixton and find him watching me. I hurriedly regard the menu. "So what would you suggest?"

"Well, I've only been here once before with Luke, but they are known for excellent steaks and steak burgers." His eyes alight with mischief. "Hopefully that's something that is in your diet?"

I look at him over the top of my menu, "What are you trying to say?"

"Only that you look like a wine, cheese, and grapes kind of woman. Either before or after the caviar."

"If you thought that was true, then why bring me here?"

"Maybe I wanted to see how you'd fare."

"Oh, really?"

"No, not really," he leans toward me and lowers his voice, "I just want to see you on the tractor." He laughs and I join him, loving the sound. When our waitress, Missy, comes to our table, we order beers and burgers. Rixton raises his eyebrows when I order a burger loaded with everything with a side of French fries, but doesn't say a word.

"Do you miss it?"

His brows lower at my question and he scratches his nose, "Miss what?"

"Texas."

A smile slowly spreads across his face and his eyes take on a faraway look for a minute before he focuses back on me. "Yes. I miss the sunrises, my horse Gunnar, and of course, my family. I miss how it feels after a day of hard, purposeful labor and having a home cooked meal in my belly at the end of every night."

"Luke told me that the two of you met in college. I'm surprised you went from Texas to Illinois, and then back again. I guess I'm surprised you returned to Texas so quickly."

"To work on a farm you mean?"

"Well, I guess, but I don't know what brought you to college in Illinois in the first place."

"A few things. Like many people that age, I wanted to get away from home. I didn't want to stay local, I wanted to escape, and the University of Illinois was one of the colleges that accepted me. Plus, I always wanted to visit Chicago. When I visited the campus and drove into Chicago afterwards, I was sold. Luke and I met my sophomore year in college when he transferred in from Loyola."

"If you loved it here so much, then why go back to Texas after you graduated?"

"I didn't graduate."

Before he can elaborate, our waitress returns again, this time with our drinks. She places them before us and says our food will be out soon. I look down and can't help but stare momentarily at the red plastic solo cups. Of course. Rixton looks at me with a raised eyebrow and suddenly it hits me – this whole date night is more than him just seeing how I'd fare, it's a test. Does he think I'm some stuck-up bitch or something? And if so, why even ask me out? For a moment, I can't decide what to do. Should I be the prissy bitch he thinks I am, or should I be myself? I may come from money, but he's assuming I'm a snob. I don't get him, but I'm not going to take the bait – I'm being myself all the way. He can take it or leave it, the ass.

I pick up my cup and take a big gulp, wiping my mouth with the back of my hand when I'm done. Smirking at the look of surprise on his face, I pick my drink back up in the gesture of a toast. He toasts me back as well with a smile on his face.

"So, how come you didn't graduate?" His smile instantly falls off his face and I almost feel bad for bringing our conversation back up. "I'm sorry. You don't have to answer that."

He makes a shooing gesture with his hand, "No, it's okay. I ended up withdrawing from college because my dad ended up getting sick and my mom needed my help at the ranch. I have two brothers, one that still lives there, but it was too much for him to handle on his own."

"I'm sorry. I hope your dad is doing better now."

"Actually, he passed away almost a year ago."

"Oh hell, Rixton. I'm so sorry."

His smile is sad. "Me too. He was a great man and I miss him a lot."

My heart aches at the look on his face, "Your mom, is she doing okay?"

"She's taking it one day at a time. My older brother and his wife ended up moving into the guesthouse, so she's got two sons and my nephew, Tyler, to keep her busy and happy. She loves having them there."

"I bet she misses you, though. Was it hard for her to see you move away again?"

"It was, but she understands. I love it there, but this is where I need to be."

Missy returns to the table with our burgers and places them before us. The portions are huge. She asks if we need anything else and we simultaneously shake our heads no. We start eating in companionable silence. The food is really good. I don't realize how hungry I am until I begin eating.

Rixton wipes his mouth on a napkin, takes a drink and then looks at me, "Food good?"

"Yes. Definitely one of the best burgers I've ever had."

"Good. So enough about me, tell me your story."

I set my burger down and wipe my hands on my napkin, "Hm, there isn't really much to tell."

"Sure there is. I know you've known Olivia for a long time. And Luke and I kept in touch, so I know all about their history. How are you doing after Olivia's ex intruded into your life?"

My heart starts beating faster at the thought. Deacon is not a subject I like to think about often. Olivia's ex-husband was an abusive asshole that didn't deal well with their divorce. After tying me up and holding me hostage in my own condo, he kidnapped Olivia. We went crazy with worry during her absence, and I still have nightmares sometimes over the whole experience.

"Doing better, taking it day by day. Frankly, therapy helped. That was an experience that took some help dealing with."

"I'm sure. Luke said he's still awaiting trial but is locked up until then."

I nod, "Yes and thank God for that."

"And you own your own spa?"

I laugh, "Why are you asking about me if you already know everything?"

Chuckling, he dips a fry in ketchup, "I just know the gist, but of course I asked Luke for the deets on you!"

"Well you are correct, I've had Shimmer & Soothe Salon and Spa since I graduated from college, and have been running it ever since."

"Wow, that's quite an accomplishment right out of college to own your own business."

"You are correct, but I can't take all the credit. The spa was a very surprising gift from my father. He bought the space, I designed it and run it."

Rixton's eyes widen, "Whoa. That's some graduation gift."

"Believe me, I know. My father has a tendency to always go overboard. I've learned to deal with his generosity because he's going to do it whether I want him to or not."

"Must be nice."

"It is, and I appreciate it very much. But, as they say, nothing in life is free, so it also came with certain strings. I know he doesn't mean it in a manipulative sort of way. I don't expect it, nor do I take it for granted. But, there isn't anything he can ask of me, that I wouldn't give in return. It's hard sometimes to know how to repay his kindness. So, I work really hard to keep the spa in the black. The first year was tough, but I refused to ask for help. I wanted to do it on my own."

The band has started playing and I have to raise my voice to be heard over it, but it isn't horrible, like a night club where you have to scream in the person's ear to be heard. "I figure my success is another way to honor his gift. I want very much to make him proud of me."

"I can imagine that he *is* very proud of you."

"Well, I certainly hope so."

"That's great that your business is doing so well. I would love to come by and see it some time."

"I'll give you my card. You should schedule a massage." I know that isn't exactly what he meant, but he really should get a treatment – I mean I wouldn't be doing my job if I didn't suggest it.

"Mmm, will you be the masseuse? I mean, darlin' if you want me naked under a sheet again, all you have to do is ask. Massage not mandatory."

"Ha. Ha." I roll my eyes at him, but really the thought of all that long and lean muscle naked flashes through my mind, making me feel heat that has nothing to do with the fire pit that's close to our table. Who would blame me though? The man is freaking built.

His smile widens as if he knows what just went through my mind, the cocky bastard. "I don't think I've ever seen a girl eat like you do?"

My brow furrows, "What do you mean?" I look down at my nearly empty plate.

"I like that you aren't afraid to eat on a date. I hate chicks that order salads and pick at their food."

"Oh no, that's not me. In fact, I was thinking we should find out where everyone got those marshmallows. Roasting them would be fun. And who can resist their sweet taste? Though s'mores might be even better."

He signals to our waitress and orders just that, then turns back to me, "They are on the menu. Your wish is my command."

"Oh, that's dangerous. You may be sorry you said that."

His eyes twinkle, "I seriously doubt that."

A busboy takes our empty plates and Rixton leans toward me, "Want to go dance while we wait for our s'mores kit to arrive?"

I look at the dance floor and once again take in everyone and what they are wearing, and then look down at myself. "Well, I didn't exactly dress the part for line dancing or whatever that is they're doing. Someone didn't tell me jeans would be a good idea."

He raises his eyebrows in pure challenge, "Wow, I'm surprised at you. I didn't think you would let something like a dress and heels get in your way."

I stare at him, taking in his smirking face and devilish grin. I don't know what he expects me to do here and I don't care. Fact is, he's right. I stand up, and stare at him as I take off my shoes. "Let's go."

He laughs, stands and takes my hand leading me to the dance floor. I try to follow along and do the line dancing steps they are doing. I pick it up after a few tries and Rixton? Hell the man moves like he has sex. Sinfully.

A slow song begins and Rixton wordlessly takes me into his arms, keeping a little bit of distance between us. The distance is just enough to make our bodies brush against each other now and then as we move. His thighs bump against mine, and my breasts graze his chest. The subtle contact makes me breathe faster, and my body temperature starts to rise with the need to be closer. I step into him, pressing my body to his. We fit together like puzzle pieces – made to be connected.

He feels good. Nothing else exists but the two of us. My head on his shoulder, one of his hands at my waist, the other wrapped around the nape of my neck as if he's staking a claim. I close my eyes and enjoy the moment of pure peace. There's a soft wind in the air and it rustles my hair and feels like a cool whisper on my heated skin. I make myself let go of thoughts of what's right for me, and what isn't. I let go of thinking about what would make my parents happy, versus what I truly want. I let go of the worry that I'm leading Rixton on, regardless of my true feelings of wanting to see where this could lead. Somewhere, in the middle of chaos, I get lost in the simple pleasure of not feeling alone. Of feeling safe and cared for. Surprisingly, after letting go of all of the things that I thought make up who I am – I still find me.

chapter
8

MAKING OUR WAY OFF THE DANCE floor, Rixton holds onto my hand. When we return to our table, we find our s'mores kit waiting for us. I slip my shoes back on and we head over to one of the unoccupied fire pits. There are chairs surrounding it and we pull ours closer to each other.

Rixton laughs as we roast our dessert because I keep burning my marshmallows. "Another one?"

"Dammit, that's like the third one." Trying to remove my marshmallow far too soon from the poker, I shake out my hand trying to ease the pain from my burning fingertips. My fingers are now burned and chocolaty.

Reaching for my hand, then putting my fingers one at a time in his mouth, both soothing the burn and eliminating the messiness, Rixton laughs, "Do you know how to cook at all?"

"Does pasta count?"

"Um, no."

"Oh! I can work the grill. You know, burgers and steaks! Bam! Why don't I have one of those kiss the cook aprons? I should get one."

He laughs and takes my hand that's holding the poker and puts a new marshmallow on the end. He keeps his hand over mine as we hold it over the flame. "I'm going to show you the proper way to roast marshmallows. The key is to turn it so you create a shield around the gooey center."

"Wow, I had no idea there was such a science to this."

"It's a good thing you met me. Think of all the marshmallow lives we are saving."

It's cheesy but I laugh, pull my marshmallow out of the fire and blow on it to cool it down. I look at Rixton to see how his is fairing and catch him looking at me. Actually, he's looking at my mouth. I involuntarily lick my lips in response, and I can't be sure if it's heat I see enter his eyes, or just the reflection from the fire.

"Oh shit!" He pulls his marshmallow away from the pit to find that it actually caught on fire.

"I thought you were a professional! Marshmallow killer!" I happily take a bite of mine, plain and yummy, and moan, attempting to tease him. "Oh! You should be jealous. It's soooo good. Too bad you burned yours." I lick my fingers slowly, trying to get the stickiness off and look over at Rixton, ready to tease him a bit more, only to find him watching me again. He stares at me for a moment, then reaches out and brushes what must be marshmallow out of the corner of my mouth. He brings his finger to his mouth, and keeping his eyes locked on mine, he licks his finger. The act feels shockingly intimate and before I realize what I'm doing, I lean forward, making my intent to kiss him clear.

His mouth closes over mine without hesitation, and his tongue is at the seam of my mouth immediately, begging entrance. I open for him and then moan softly as his tongue brushes mine as he licks deeply inside my mouth. Rixton is an amazing kisser and I could easily get addicted to his kisses. He cups my face in his hands, pulls away, biting my lip gently, then smiles at me. I can't help but smile back, his happiness is addicting.

"You ready to get out of here, darlin'?" He emphasizes his drawl, his voice sounding full of promise.

"Yes, definitely."

The angel on my shoulder starts telling me that what I'm thinking isn't right. I shouldn't have Rixton over like I'm intending. I need to calm the hormones and kiss him goodnight, thank him for the evening and go inside with him on the other side of the door. It isn't right to lead him on.

The devil on my opposite shoulder has me relive the kiss we just shared over and over, and the ones we shared before that. I again feel his mouth on my fingers and feel his fingers stroking my cheek. My mind flashes back to our night together, and I see his hands trailing the contours of my body exploring. I remember the feel of his lips and tongue all over me from head to toe. Remembering his ability to communicate that he obviously knows his way over a woman's body makes me shudder. He knew just when to bring me high, and how to keep me there, drawing out the feeling until I couldn't take it anymore. I once again hear our breathless sighs, our heated moans, and gasps of pleasure. Right then I decide the devil on my shoulder is smart as hell, and I give the angel on the other side a kick in the ass.

As soon as Rixton pays the bill I'm ready to go. He walks me to the door of the restaurant and then without forewarning, jumps in front of me and throws me over his shoulder, causing me to laugh in unending giggles all the way back to his truck. We make small talk as we drive back to my place. We talk about everything; about our favorite color – his red, mine yellow, to our favorite time of year – his spring, mine autumn.

When we reach my building I immediately ask, "Do you want to come up for a bit?"

He looks at me in surprise. "Well I was going to park and escort you up to your door, but I could stand to come in for a drink, or to just hang out a little bit more."

"Great, I'd like that." I look down, feeling shy, but confident in my decision to ask him in.

He parks his truck, helps me out and we walk to the elevator, each of us glancing at the other out of the corner of our eyes. I smile to myself, liking the way my stomach flutters and my heart races. As soon as the doors to the elevator close behind us, we make eye contact. I don't know who moves first, but suddenly we are on each other. Our lips fuse together hard, seeking and demanding. My hands move up his shirt and I groan at the feel of his firm stomach and chest. His hands are buried in my hair, slightly pulling, putting my head where he wants it so he can easily devour my lips. I move my hands to his back and run them up, while his hands go down to my ass, pulling me closer – fusing my hips with his. I can feel his excitement and it only serves to enhance mine.

When we reach my floor the loud ding makes us break apart with a laugh. We practically race to my door, hands entwined. Laughing and anxious to get inside, I quickly unlock the door, turn off the alarm and decide I don't want to play games. No watching TV until things heat up on the couch, no getting a drink and waiting until the sexual tension is unbearable. No. We are both adults and it's obvious what we both want. I lock the front door behind us, grab Rixton's hand, and lead him into my bedroom.

"You sure about this, Red? I can't promise I won't leave something here again," he teases me while his hands run up and down my arms, making me break out in goose bumps.

"I don't want to dissect this okay? For once, I just want to act impulsively."

He pulls back and looks at me, smirk on his face. "Okay fine. I want to act impulsively *again*, okay? I want to go with what I'm feeling. It's nice to not have it all thought out first. Is that so bad? I'm being spontaneous here."

His grin turns wickedly hot, "I'm not complaining."

I shut my bedroom door and when I turn around, he grabs me by my arms and pushes me against it, attacking my mouth again. I groan at the feeling and then boldly reach behind him and grab his ass, this time pulling him to me. He groans when our bodies touch, and I gasp from the feeling. He takes my breath as his own and sweeps his tongue in my mouth before pulling away to look at me. "God, I want you."

"Then stop talking. More doing." He chuckles at my words, but it quickly dies as I begin unbuttoning his shirt. I remove it in record time and throw it on the floor, not caring where it lands. He's pulling on the zipper at my back, and moves it down at a pace so slow I want to scream. I just want to feel my bare skin against his. I push him away from me a little and attack his belt, wanting to release him from his pants. I make a sound of triumph when I get him unbuckled, his zipper down and thrust my hand down his briefs. I revel in the sound he makes when I stroke him and watch as he throws his head back and swallows hard.

He pushes my dress off my shoulders and it falls to the ground. Just as I start to use my other hand to pull his pants off his hips, I'm startled when I feel a buzzing sound at his front pocket. I pull away, "What is that?"

He stares at me, eyes half-mast and full of lust, desire and need as he eloquently asks, "Huh?"

I giggle but it's drowned out when music that I can't decipher starts blaring from his pocket while continuing its buzzing at the same time. Clarity comes to him, and he pulls his phone from his pocket, but his eyes are on me. Assuming he's going to toss it aside, I walk over to my bed, reach behind me and unfasten my bra, letting it fall to the floor. I can't mistake the undeniable heat in Rixton's beautiful eyes as they rake over my skin. His phone stops ringing and he takes a step toward me, groaning in want as I hook my fingers in my panties, ready to pull them down my legs. He stops when his phone starts ringing and buzzing again. He glances at it in frustration, and his face freezes as he looks at the screen.

"Excuse me, Red. I have to take this."

My mouth drops open. "Seriously?"

"I'm sorry, I have to. Just a second." I run my hands through my hair in frustration as he says, "Hello?" Immediately his brows furrow and a concerned look comes over his face. Whatever it is he's hearing on the other end must not be good. "Okay. It's okay. No. No, you're not bothering me. I understand. I'm glad you called. Yes, you should have called. I'll be right there. I already said it's okay." His eyes flicker too briefly, "No, nothing important. I'll be there in fifteen minutes tops. Okay, bye."

His comment "nothing important" burns my stomach, even though I don't know for sure what he's referring to. His look however makes me certain it's me. He obviously doesn't want someone to know he's with me. I look at him in disbelief, anger and confusion.

"I'm sorry, I have to go."

"Okay," I draw out the word because I'm feeling at a loss for words. "Is everything alright?"

"Yeah, fine," he replies shortly.

"It didn't sound fine," I push.

"It will be."

"Do you need me to come with you?" I grab my bra and hurriedly put it back on in case he needs just that.

"No!" His fierceness startles me. He doesn't make eye contact as he quickly puts on his shirt and buckles his belt. I briskly walk to my closet, grab my robe off the back of the door, and cover myself, suddenly feeling very exposed in only my bra and panties. He barely spares me a look before he's moving toward my bedroom door and opening it. He looks over his shoulder briefly, "I will call you later, okay?"

"Yeah. Sure. Okay."

Left alone in my room, I pause for a moment in utter confusion. By the time I get down the hallway and look toward the front door, he's already unlocked it. Stepping out into the hallway, he closes the door with a soft click, not even sparing a look behind him. I approach the door, turn the lock, and set the alarm. Leaning against the door, I try to understand what just happened. That was... odd. He obviously didn't want to tell me what that was all about and for some reason that hurts.

I feel a little like a tennis ball. My emotions have whacked back and forth all night long and it has left me feeling out of sorts. I was determined to go on a date with him because he wouldn't leave me alone about it. Even if I felt torn, knowing that he is not the type I'm seeking. But, once with him, I relaxed and really had fun. I was even able to let go and just be. Sighing, I feel frustrated with myself. This is just a casual thing that isn't going anywhere anyway. I know that. So, why do I feel so hurt? And why am I not able to just be concerned with him, and for him, and whatever the crisis was? Am I that selfish? What is going on with me?

chapter
9

"SO HE JUST LEFT? WITHOUT GIVING you a kiss, or even commenting on the night? Without so much as a brief explanation?" Olivia is just as surprised as I am by Rixton's strange behavior.

When she called me this morning asking if I could go to her gown fitting and bridesmaid dress shopping with her, I gladly accepted. Not only was I excited to see her in her gown, but I was hoping it would distract me from thinking about Rixton. I should have known better.

We started out visiting a nearby florist so Olivia could see samples of their work. She's having trouble deciding between two and thought additional visits to their stores would help her decide. We'd barely left the shop before she was asking me for details about the date. I love her because she didn't even blink twice when I told her I had invited Rixton up to my place and we started getting hot and heavy again. Not for the first time I realize how lucky I am to have her in my life and what a treasure of a friend she truly is.

She's standing before me and I'm almost breathless at the sight. On a platform in front of a three-way mirror, she's adorned in her one-shouldered wedding gown and beautiful bridal shoes. The gown is made for her – formfitting to about mid-thigh it showcases her curves and small waist perfectly, until it flares out just a little on the bottom. There is an overlay of lace over the whole gown, but it becomes transparent at the top of her breast and hugs over her left shoulder until it meets the top of her gown again at her back. A champagne sash ties around her waist to complete the look. It's gorgeous and couldn't be more perfect. She is simply a vision. I can't even imagine what she will look like on her actual wedding day if she is this gorgeous at a simple fitting without makeup or her hair styled.

"Sorry, first things first, you know you have to do an up-do with this dress right? To show off your shoulders, collarbone and the lace over your shoulder."

Olivia smiles and holds up her hair, turning her head back and forth while looking in the mirror. "That's what I was thinking too."

The three-way mirror she stands before projects her image from all angles. Luke would be in heaven. The seamstress at her feet works quickly going around the bottom of the dress, pinning where her gown needs to be a little higher, just a whisper away from touching the ground.

"Back to Rixton, yes, he just left without an explanation. I tried to ask him if everything was okay, but he told me it was fine. He seriously couldn't get out of there fast enough. And his behavior – I don't know – it was this odd mix of concern and annoyance or irritation...it was really hard to read. " I shrug feeling at a loss.

Olivia drops her hair and gives me a look of sympathy, "I can ask Luke if he knows anything if you want me to."

"No, please don't do that. If he had wanted me to know, he would have told me. I don't want to invade his privacy through Luke." I sigh, "It was just really odd. And he didn't call me later or this morning to say that things were okay or to apologize for leaving so abruptly or anything." I shrug again, then stand and pace back and forth a little bit, feeling annoyed with myself. "At the same time, why do I even care? He doesn't owe me anything. And, not only is it not my business, I don't really know him all that well anyway. So why does it matter and why is it bothering me?"

Olivia frowns at me, "Is that a rhetorical question, because you and I both know why. I don't understand why you are asking the question or pretending that you shouldn't care."

I stand still and look at her, feeling exasperated, "Well then, miss smarty pants, tell me, why it matters."

Olivia rolls her eyes at me, "Because you like him. Duh."

"Yes. I like him. I'm attracted to him. In an I-want-to-constantly-hump-his-leg kind of way." Olivia laughs. "Truth is, I would love to have a no strings attached, hang out with him until Mr. Right comes along kind of relationship with him, but that's it."

Olivia sighs, "Oh, here we go with this again. And please tell me, you red-headed brat, how it is you know that Rixton isn't your Mr. Right?"

I laugh. Loudly. "Oh please. Rixton is no more my Mr. Right than I'm a champion bull wrangler."

"Now that I would like to see."

"Ha. Ha. You know what I mean. Anyway, his running last night was probably for the best, I guess."

"Whatever you say," the seamstress looks up at Olivia and they grin at each other. It's like one big conspiracy. I want to pull their hair like a six-year-old having a tantrum.

"You and I both know this isn't going anywhere. Rixton is a fun distraction. That's all."

"Are you sure about that Pyper?"

"Yes, of course. Liv, come on seriously. Can you see me bringing Rixton home to meet my mom? My dad? You, of all people, know how ridiculous that would be."

"I think you are underestimating just how much your parents want you to be happy. That is all they care about."

"Yeah, right. I get why you think that. And it's true, they may not have ever come out and said the type of man they expect me to be with, but the men they've tried to set me up with are an example of their expectations. The sons of the men my dad works with, or the guys my mom has introduced me to at the country club, make their expectations and standards pretty clear."

"Did you ever consider that maybe it's because that's the kind of guy they've seen you date and so they assume that's what you want? I mean my God, Pyper, have you ever talked to them about it to verify your presumptions?"

I scoff at the suggestion, "Of course not. Why upset them? I mean, really, it's so obvious and I guess their expectations aren't really all that bad. For example, I have to go to the country club tomorrow night in order to entertain the son of one of my dad's business associates. I'm meeting him there for dinner."

"What? How did that happen? Is it like a blind date or something?"

"No, not a blind date. I actually met him at dinner with my folks the other day."

"Dinner with the folks and I wasn't invited? What the hell? It's been a while. I could seriously go for some of Mrs. B's homemade rolls and honey butter. Then again, I should probably stay away. I can't afford to gain weight and then need Debbie here to take out my dress."

"Oh please. You could afford a few pounds. You still haven't gained back all the weight you lost a year ago."

Olivia gives me a look, "I'm doing much better, but you've convinced me. Not that it was very hard."

Sitting back down, I cross my legs and try to calm my racing mind. "We will plan it. My mom will be thrilled. Anyway, when I got to dinner they had guests I wasn't expecting. A man my dad works with and his son, R.J. Right in front of them my dad suggests we go to dinner at the club. It wasn't like I could say no. I mean, he was needing to do something with the father and needed someone to entertain the son during that time, so I was, of course, the obvious choice."

"I get it, you were put on the spot. What I don't get is why you said yes; why you didn't say you had a conflict or why you didn't speak to your dad privately later and tell him that wasn't okay. You didn't do that, did you?"

"Well, no, but you know that's not an easy thing for me to do. He always does stuff for me. I have a hard time not doing little things for him now and again. Or telling him no. Besides, it makes him happy when I just go with whatever he wants."

It bothers me that Olivia is shaking her head at me like she's so disappointed. "It's still your life and you need to live it the way you want to. Not the way you think you are expected to." Debbie, the seamstress, stands up with pins in her mouth and I wonder how she isn't scared to do that. I would be afraid I would swallow them. Or what if someone accidentally bumped into her or she fell or something? Game over. She gathers the material at Olivia's back and starts pinning the places where the dress needs to be taken in.

"Oh boy, I know you laugh but I really do need to make sure I keep my weight in check. Maybe I should rethink dinner at your parent's place after all. I've been nervous eating like crazy. You don't even know!"

I laugh at the thought of Olivia stuffing her face with chocolates. Though, come to think of it, Luke probably hand feeds them to her. In bed. He could care less what she weighs, he just loves her. I'm totally jealous, but the image that presents in my mind makes me laugh out loud.

"What's so funny?"

"I was just thinking that Luke probably hand feeds you chocolates."

She puts a finger to her chin, "Hmm, he hasn't but I'm thinking he could be persuaded to do just that." She smiles wickedly and it's clear she's got dirty thoughts running through her mind.

"Oh please. Spare me the details."

I'm left to my own thoughts while Olivia starts telling a bridal consultant what kind of bridesmaid dresses she has in mind so they can start bringing in samples for her to look at.

I wish this stuff with Rixton wasn't bothering me. I feel like an idiot that it's getting to me so much. We had one night together. That certainly doesn't mean I have some claim to him or have a right to anything but what we shared – and that was certainly limited. For some reason though, I can't get him out of my mind. I've never had a one-night-stand before. Ever. I certainly was no virgin, but usually I have to date a guy for a little while before I give it up to him. The fact that I just hooked up with Rixton without thinking first is pretty crazy. It's like he's mesmerized me with his golden eyes and Texas drawl. Those things combined make me not able to think straight when he's around. All my rational thoughts go out the window.

Thoughts of him have consumed my mind since our night together, and it's gotten even worse since our date. I really hadn't expected to invite him into my life. In fact, I told myself I wouldn't do it, no matter what. I just find that I can't get enough.

"You sooo like him, don't you?"

It takes me a minute to realize Olivia was talking to me again, "Like who?"

"You know who. Rixton."

"What makes you say that?"

"I can tell you're thinking about him right now. It's all over your face."

I groan, stalling, deciding how honest I want to be, but then the fact that I can tell her anything and I know she never judges me wins. "Fine. Yes, I like him. I don't know why and it doesn't matter, I guess. I've decided that I should just ask him if he wants to have a no strings relationship. You know, friends with benefits. I mean, why not hang out with him in between dating other people. I doubt he's looking for anything serious either. Anything more would be a waste of both of our time." I quit talking about it as dresses and more dresses, are brought in for Olivia to approve, and for me to try on. We happily get lost in the madness of wedding planning.

chapter
10

I WAS TRYING TO REMIND MYSELF that I liked Rixton a few hours later. Not long after I came home from trying on dress after dress for Olivia, I received a text from him.

Rixton: Hi darlin'. I'm sorry I had to run out on you like that. I had a great time. Would love to take you out again soon. How about Saturday night?

Instead of responding right away, I throw my phone on the bed and jump in the shower. It's still early in the evening but a night of vegging out and maybe eating pizza sounds like the perfect evening to me.

While washing my hair, I think about how to respond to Rixton. I can't go out with him Saturday because I'm going out with R.J. I vacillate between wanting to plan a future date with him and just telling him no and ending this now. One thing's for sure, making him wait for a little while for a response is good for him. For his personal growth. Manage his ego a little bit. Especially with him bailing on me the way he did. Almost any dating advice article I've ever read says not to respond immediately after a date because you don't want to appear too eager. The people that write them, with my luck, probably have zero experience, but it sounds like what I should do nevertheless.

I finish my shower and throw my hair up into a towel and dress in pajama shorts and a tank top. Looking at my nail polish collection, I can't decide what color I want to choose to paint my fingernails. I know the girls could just give me a manicure at the spa, but sometimes I enjoy doing them myself. It's relaxing and sometimes, secretly I like to try out various designs and patterns on my nails that I find online. It's fun.

Picking up my phone off the bed, I see that Rixton continued to text me while I was in the shower.

Rixton: You can't be mad at me, I'm too sexy.

Rixton: I will make it up to you, I promise. Let me show you ALL the ways on Saturday night.

Rixton: I will get down on my knees and beg – with my mouth.

Rixton: I keep thinking about the marshmallow on your lips. You tasted so sweet. I want more.

Rixton: Seriously, Red, I'm sorry. Walking away killed me.

Each text sends a thrill through me that I can't contain. He's so cocky and sure of himself and it makes me crazy. But underneath, he's vulnerable and that's the part that makes me want to relent. I'm just about to type out a response when my doorbell rings. I'm surprised to find Henry, the doorman, at my door. "Hello. These were delivered for you earlier. I tried dropping them off, but you must have been out."

"Thank you so much, Henry."

He smiles and hands me a large bouquet of sunflowers. "No problem, Miss. Lexington. Have a nice evening now."

"Thank you. You too."

As soon as I get inside, I set the flowers on the kitchen island and pull out the card. A scratchy barely decipherable scribble says, "I'm so sorry I had to cut our evening short. Let me make it up to you. R."

I head back to my bedroom, intending to text him, then decide I'd like to have the flowers with me, so I pick up the vase and bring them to my room. Sitting on my bed, I grab my phone and type out a reply.

Me: Thank you for the flowers. They're beautiful.

Not even a full minute later, the texts start coming in again.

Rixton: Not as beautiful as you.

Rixton: Do you forgive me? Say you'll go out with me again.

Rixton: I want another chance to kiss those lips of yours. They're haunting my dreams. What are you doing to me?

Biting my lip, I ignore his texts and decide it's a good night for a facial mask. I pull my hair into a bun on the top of my head. Then, I spread my favorite green goo all over my face. Leaving it to dry, I return to my room and stand there, hands on my hips staring at my phone. Giving in, I quickly tap out a reply.

Me: I can't go out with you Saturday night. I have plans, sorry. Thanks again for the flowers.

There. I was nice and thanked him again. Grabbing the polish I selected earlier, I begin painting my nails. The polish is deep purple and I add a silver sparkly accent to the ring finger of each hand. I'm admiring my work when my phone dings again… then again…. and again.

Carefully, so I don't smudge my polish, I push in my password and view the texts I've received.

Rixton: Plans? Break them! I promise I will make it worth your while.

Rixton: I want to see you.

Mixed in is a text from Olivia: Thanks again for coming with me today! I love the bridesmaid dress we picked out. I wouldn't want to do all of this with anyone but you. Love you!

Not knowing what to say to Rixton, I ignore him for now. I use my voice command to send a reply to Olivia telling her I love her too. Then I go into the kitchen and carefully pull out a frozen pizza from the freezer and preheat the oven. Walking into my living room, I pick up the remote and flick on the TV. A new episode of Supernatural is on tonight and I'm excited to watch!

Flopping back on my couch, I wait for my show to start. I miss watching it with Olivia. Really… I just plain miss Olivia. She's been spending more and more time at Luke's place. I mean… of course she has. I wouldn't expect anything less, but I still feel her absence. The only reason she still comes here is because she's indulging me. She doesn't want to leave me alone. I need to have a talk with her because I know she's going to move into Luke's after the wedding, if not before. I need to tell her it's okay. I've loved having her here the last year. I still remember how excited I was when she finally moved back after her nasty divorce. So excited that I completely decorated a room just for her. When she arrived, we were inseparable and I find myself missing her a lot sometimes. But still, her happiness is much more important. I need to tell her it's okay if she wants to move out now. I've just been avoiding the conversation for selfish reasons and it's not right for me to have done that.

After hearing the oven beep its readiness, I check my nails making sure they are dry, then happily put a pizza in the oven and set the timer. I'm taken off guard when the doorbell rings again. Looking through the peephole, I see Henry standing there again. When I open the door and see his eyes widen, it occurs to me that I still have the green gunk all over my face. Awesome. "Uh, hi again Henry. Please ignore the sea monster you see before you."

Henry clears his throat trying to remain professional, but I swear I see his lips twitch as if he's trying to suppress a smile. "Miss Lexington. These were delivered for you."

He hands me a huge bundle of bright red balloons. With a wink, he does smile this time and walks away. "Until next time, Miss."

"Goodbye," I murmur wondering if my face is flaming as red as the balloons in my hand under the green facial. I see a card attached to the balloon's ribbon, so I pull it off.

Here are some balloons to convey how high you make me feel. Your eyes captivate me, your smile brings me to my knees, and your kisses own me. Maybe on our next date I can take you to a saloon. You know... because it rhymes with balloons. Oh hell, I suck at this. Call me! R.

I smile and laugh. He's ridiculous. I mean, balloons! What are we? Six? I don't think he's going to give up. Staring at the balloons, I have no clue what the hell to do with them. Shaking my head in amusement, I take them to my room and tie them to my door handle. Picking up my phone I send him a text as I make my way back into my kitchen. "Thank you for the balloons, but I think I'll pass on the saloon."

With a ding, Rixton texts back as I'm getting the pizza out of the oven.

Rixton: I will take you anywhere else. A platoon? Buy an antique spittoon? We can dance a jig while someone slaps spoons? We can listen to some tunes? Gaze at the moon....

Laughing, I reply, "Please stop. You are so cheesy!"

Rixton: I can't help it. You better just agree to a date so that I'll quit!

Me: Okay fine, I'll think about it okay? But really, it would have to be another day. I can't go out Saturday night.

Rixton: Darlin' I will take you any way I can get you.

I think a long time before sending my next text because I'm not sure I want to hear the answer. Will he have one? Will it just draw me in more? For the thousandth time I ask myself why I even care, then I type, "Why are you being so persistent? Why me? I don't get it."

He doesn't text me back. He calls me.

"Hello?"

"Hello, beautiful."

His voice brings an involuntary smile to my face. "Hi, yourself."

"I really am sorry about last night."

I grab the pizza cutter from the drawer and cut my pizza in even triangles. My stomach is growling. "I know you are. You've made that pretty clear between the flowers, texts and balloons."

"Good. That was the point." I hear rustling on the other end of the line and I wonder where he is. What he's wearing. How much he may *not* be wearing. I am totally thinking like a dude. "You asked me why you. I feel that my response warrants a phone call and not a text."

My brow furrows at how serious he sounds. I lick my fingers after placing a couple of pieces of pizza on my plate. "Okay... sounds serious."

He chuckles, "Don't sound so nervous. Look, Red, all I can say is that there's something about you. I'm still figuring out what it is exactly, but you create a fire in my blood that started the minute my lips met yours. It won't let go. It won't die out. It's raging and burning and refuses to be extinguished. It's clear that one night with you, wasn't enough. I want more."

"I don't know how much more I can give you, Rixton. You and I… we aren't… what I mean is… this relationship or whatever it is, isn't going to go anywhere."

"What do you mean by that?"

"I mean the same thing I've been saying. I don't know how to get you to hear me. I have a specific plan for my life and I'm not sure there's room for a detour with you."

"Wow," he laughs, "you sure are great for a guy's ego. A detour, huh?"

"Hey, you asked. I'm just trying to be honest."

"You're right I did ask."

My throat feels dry. I feel myself wanting to relent, to give in to his words and admit to him that I feel a need for him screaming inside of me as well, but I can't. This is hopeless. "Rixton, I had fun with you that night. It was definitely… a night to remember. And our date at the steakhouse was a lot of fun. Truth is, I'd be lying if I didn't say that I'm attracted to you and a huge part of me wants to get to know you better. But, I just don't think this is going to work."

"How can you say that? You haven't even given it a chance."

"I just know, okay?" I walk to the living room and set my pizza on the coffee table, but then walk to the window and look out. I can see the magnificent mile, Navy Pier and Lake Michigan from this window – at night, the view is simply stunning.

"Fuck that. What kind of answer is that?"

I sigh and try to shake the feeling of sadness that wants to emerge from my heart, "The one you are getting."

"No, Pyper. I don't accept that."

I think that's the first time he's used my name. It makes me realize how serious he is about this. "Well, you have to." He's not listening and it's making me angry. "Besides, you aren't even my type." I throw that out there because I want to push him away. Because making him angry is easier to deal with.

He laughs deep and dark, "That sure is funny, because I seemed like just your type when you were writhing around breathless with me inside you."

Now he's done it. I can hear the growl and anger in his voice and now I just want to lash out. "I can't go out with you Saturday, Rixton, because I have another date. Sorry. That's all I have to say about this."

There is complete silence on the other end and for a moment I think he's hung up.

"A date?" He spits out the word like it's a curse – fierce and sharp.

"Yes, a date. Thanks again for the flowers and balloons. I'm sure I will see you around again because of Luke and Olivia. I want to be friends, okay? Seriously. I don't want what happened between us to make things awkward. No hard feelings, okay?"

"Oh darlin', there is going to be lots of *hard* feelings. With you, naked. Just you wait and see. I'm not going away. You want me – just as much as I want you. That fire between us isn't normal, and I'll get you to admit it. I can't wait. I'll see you soon."

He hangs up the phone, leaving me to stare into the night contemplating his words. The view blurs before me, and all I can think is 'shit.' That doesn't sound good.

chapter 11

THE WAITRESS LEADS R.J. and me to our reserved table. The restaurant is packed. The club restaurant is opened to the public on the weekend and it's always this way. It's a good thing we have reservations.

Our table is near a large glass window, overlooking the pool. The Italian restaurant is lovely and serves great food. The club, however, remains a bit old fashioned, requiring all men to wear jackets. The décor is a soft cream with Old World gold accents everywhere. The Tuscan influence is evident. Gold candle sticks, gold gilded picture frames on the walls, even cream flowers with gold accents. Crisp linens and candles dress every table and the lights are purposefully kept low, creating an intimate ambiance. It always reminds me of a wedding reception type locale, as it feels a bit romantic – and certainly more than I care for tonight, but I'm choosing to ignore those sensations and get through this night of obligation.

The hostess hands us our menus, then recites the featured wine and entrée specials. "I would love a glass, please." I'm going to need some alcohol to get through this evening. That's for sure.

"I'll take some too, thank you," R.J. tells her. The hostess pours a tasting glass for R.J., he nods, and then she fills our glasses. Meanwhile, I take in R.J. He's not bad looking by any means. With blonde hair and blue eyes, he has what some would call all American good looks. His nose is a bit too large for his face, but it isn't horrible. He lacks significant symmetry and his coloring is a bit bland. I pause my thoughts, aware I'm being overly critical, recognizing I'm totally comparing him to an amber-eyed man that takes my breath away without even trying.

Dressed in a well-tailored, navy blue suit, he certainly looks nice. He put an effort into his appearance, which is evident by the meticulously styled hair, complete with just the right amount of gel. Too bad I don't feel one iota of attraction for him. At all.

Taking a sip of my wine, I browse the menu to decide what I'd like to order. "I don't come here too often, but pretty much everything I've had, has been good. I'm partial to their lasagna; their alfredo is good too."

"I'm surprised to hear you don't come here very much. We rarely miss a weekend at the California country club where we belong. I enjoy golf and they have one of the best courses in the state. Plus, it seems they have a different party every weekend for one reason or another. It's usually a pretty good time. A lot of younger people attend."

"That's cool," I respond, taking a sip of my wine. It's crisp and has a slight after taste of apples. Delicious.

"Yeah it is."

He proceeds to name drop various celebrities and sports athletes he says he hangs out with at the club. I'm not sure if he's expecting me to be impressed, or maybe just interested in the conversation. I'm neither. I couldn't care less. "My parents socialize with most of their friends there and my mom has a ladies luncheon every two weeks, so they frequent it much more than I do."

"Hi, I'm Holly. I'll be your waitress this evening. Do you have any questions about the menu?" R.J. and I shake our heads no, so she takes our orders. R.J., who orders before me – such a gentleman – goes with the lasagna I suggested, and I decide to try their ravioli.

When Holly leaves, R.J. and I look at each other in awkward silence. I sip my wine trying to fill in the quiet, not having a clue what to discuss with him. "So, you said California, huh? Do you like it there? I mean other than the country club?"

"It's great. I really like being so close to the ocean. Our home is right on the water in Malibu. I enjoy surfing when I'm not working, so it works out well."

"Our home? You have roommates? That's cool."

"No." He clears his throat, "I still live with my father."

"Oh. Cool." Seriously? He has to be at least my age, twenty-six, if not older.

"My dad wants me as close as possible. He's teaching me all the ins and outs of his business, fully intending for me to take over one day." He leans forward across the table and lowers his voice, "Between us, it will likely be sooner rather than later. I think my dad is approaching retirement. He and his new wife want to travel, and that's hard to do when you're running a software company."

"I imagine that would be the case. New wife, huh?"

"Yes, his fifth."

I choke on my wine, "Oh, wow."

"Yes. Not many women can handle the demands of my father's career. He has very specific expectations; therefore, he doesn't have a lot of tolerance for women that aren't able to support him the way he expects."

Seriously? I'd like to tell him his father sounds like an asshole. "What are your views on that? Do you think having a busy career makes having a relationship difficult?" Could this conversation be any more boring?

"I understand where my father is coming from. I think it's important to find a woman that understands that the needs and demands of the business will often come before her own. I'm sure you understand what that's like. Your father must stay very busy."

"Yes, he is very busy. Yet somehow he's managed to find a balance and stay married to the same woman for twenty years."

"That is definitely impressive, but I'm sure that it's just because your mother knows exactly how to do what your father wants. Most likely as long as she follows his rules, then they are fine."

"I'm sorry, what? Rules?"

"Yes, you know. Hosting his work associates at a moment's notice. Dressing appropriately to support his image. Being loyal. Attending all kinds of events. Being understanding of his long hours and that the job comes before her."

We hold eye contact, my annoyance with him clearly displayed on my face, I'm sure. We are interrupted by Holly, "Here are your salads." I'm thankful for the interruption, because a moment more and I may have said something I wouldn't be able to take back."

I pick up my fork and take a bite, chewing slowing, using the time to calm down. I decide a change of subject is the smartest idea, "What do you like to do for fun besides surf?"

"I don't really have a whole lot of time for fun."

"You see that's something that I just don't understand. I get that running a business is oftentimes maddening and time consuming, but I think if you don't take time to take care of yourself that you'll just get burned out. And we all know that burn out lends to inefficiency and ineffectiveness, let alone a grumpy attitude." I smile slightly.

"The money motivates me to care more about my business than having fun."

"Well that's too bad for you. Life is more than just work. And money. And yours will pass by in no time and you'll wish you had enjoyed it while you could. Plus, haven't you ever heard the term that money can't buy happiness?"

He scoffs, "I'm sorry, but what do you know about it? A woman's place is to care for her husband and help run the household. I know you aren't married yet, but surely your father has already taught you that much."

It takes everything I have in me not to pick up my fork and stab him in the eye with it. I am going to kill my father for doing this to me. Is this really the kind of man my father wants me to marry? Is this the kind of man I'm going to end up with because I'm so determined to marry a successful businessman, an entrepreneur? One that cares more about how deep his pockets are, and how smoothly his business runs, than about nurturing a loving relationship with me? I know my father loves my mom. I can see it in the way he looks at her. I'm not stupid enough to believe that every successful man is like the wannabe sitting before me, but in the circles my father moves in, how likely am I to find a good one? One that has values that I can share and possesses qualities I want to support?

Our food arrives and we continue to make small talk throughout the meal. All the while I have to prevent myself from scarfing down my meal so I can run to the exit. The sooner I can get the hell out of here, the better – for me and for his safety.

I'm contemplating if there are any other topics of conversation that are less toxic when I'm startled by a smooth voice that sounds like honey in my ear. A voice that makes my body respond to it immediately. "Fancy meeting you here, darlin'."

My breath catches as my mouth falls open, my eyes widen, and my fork clatters to my plate. I look up to find Rixton standing at my table staring at me with eyes like fire. The look on his face is intense and hard. "Rixton?" I look around to try to see who he's with, how he is here.

"How's your dinner so far? I heard this was a really great place to eat so I thought I would come and check it out." Speechless, I engulf him in one look. He's wearing jeans, a plaid shirt, his cowboy hat and I know without looking he has his boots on too. Not exactly country club attire. What really catches my attention is the hideous lime green jacket with the country club insignia on the breast pocket he's wearing. It was clearly given to him at the door of the club. If circumstances were different, I would likely laugh at that, but I can't find it within me to laugh at this situation at all.

"It's… um… it's fine. You are here… to eat? By yourself?"

"Yeah, why not? A mutual friend of ours told me about this place."

Instant fire ignites in my stomach and moves up to my chest. Olivia. She's the only one besides my parents that knew I would be here. Oh. Just wait until I get my hands around her tiny neck.

"Pyper, are you going to introduce me to your friend?"

Rixton and I continue staring at each other, completely ignoring R.J. No way in hell am I going to introduce Rixton to R.J. "So this is the reason you were busy tonight, huh?" His drawl is heavier than usual.

"I told you I had plans," I express with shortness, feeling my face burn under his scrutiny.

"So you did." A wicked smile appears on his full lips, "Do you remember what I told you?"

"Excuse me, sir? If you'd just follow me, I will seat you at your table."

Rixton looks toward the table the hostess is trying to lead him to. Looking around he points at a different table right across from mine. "I'd prefer to sit right there please, honey."

"Oh, um, okay." The hostess flushes at his comment, which makes me feel aggravated. Rixton looks back to me, "Enjoy the rest of your… dinner."

"Thanks," I mutter, watching as he heads to his table and chooses the seat facing me. I turn away from him, determined not to let him get to me.

R.J. is staring at me, then at Rixton, then back at me again. "Friend of yours?"

"Yes. Sort of. He actually works at the club my best friend's fiancé owns."

"Oh yeah?" R.J. takes another bite of his lasagna, and then talks to me with his mouth full. Gross. How has his father not corrected that yet? "What kind of club?"

Without looking, I can feel Rixton's gaze burning into me. My body feels it too. My neck tingles, my breasts feel heavier, my breathing becomes more difficult. I shift in my seat to try to soothe the unsettling feeling. "Um, it's a dance club."

"That sounds fun. We should go there. I'm still going to be in town for a few more days. I'd love to grab some drinks and go out and dance. Sounds like fun. What do you say?"

I chance a glance at Rixton out of the corner of my eye. He looks larger than life sitting with his arms across his chest, hunched in his seat. His hat is so low over his eyes I can't actually see them, but I know they're fixed my way.

"You like to dance?" I am struggling with continuing this conversation. I've never been so uncomfortable in my life. I can't believe Rixton is doing this. I move my purse to my lap, open it and pretend to seek something inside. Taking my phone, I tap out a text to Olivia – *you are sooo dead to me* – and feel a teensy bit better.

"Sure. One time in LA I was at a club with some friends and we totally saw…"

Sighing, I completely tune out. He really likes to drop names. Apparently, this has worked for him in the past. I feel my phone buzz and look at it seeing Olivia has responded to me. *Did you think I wouldn't pay you back for sending Luke to mine? Payback's a bitch, huh?* I'm still going to kill her. She may have a point. I gleefully interfered in her dates, telling Luke where she would be so he could interrupt them – more than once. But, in my defense, she and Luke were so clearly right for each other. Meant to be together. They just needed a little help.

"… so it would be fun. Don't you think?"

"Um, sure. Whatever." I have no clue what he said. "Will you please excuse me? I'll be back."

"Of course." He partially rises as I stand to go to the ladies room. I try to smile, but I'm afraid it comes off as more of a grimace. Grabbing my purse, I make my way, ensuring I make eye contact with no one. As soon as I'm inside, I grip the sink with both hands and look at myself in the mirror. I can't believe Rixton is here. I can't believe how uncomfortable I am with this, and I can't believe Olivia did this to me. I'm focusing on taking deep breaths in and out, trying to calm my nerves when the door slams open. I jump, startled, but it's nothing compared to how I feel when I see Rixton's reflection behind mine in the mirror.

"What are you doing?! You can't be in here!" He ignores me and stalks toward me. I turn, facing him, my back against the sink. He stands before me and moves intensely close to me. Placing a hand on the sink, on either side of my hips, it brings us eye to eye. He doesn't say a word. He looks from my eyes, to my mouth, to my eyes again. I gasp in a breath at the look of possession in his eyes. Without saying a word, he aggressively pushes his mouth against mine.

At first I'm taken off guard, but when his mouth starts moving against mine, pressing, demanding, and searching, all thoughts flee my mind. I want to get closer to him. Need to. I press my body against his and wrap my arms around his neck. I want to climb him like a damn monkey. His hands cup my ass and he lifts, propping me up on the sink. I wrap my legs around his waist and dig my heels into his ass, wanting him closer. When his hips align with mine, we both groan.

He devours my mouth. His hands are in my hair, fingers pressing softly against my scalp. My hands move from his neck, to his back, nails digging. The only thought in my mind is more, more, more. I'm past caring where we are, what he does for a living, what's expected of me or what I expect of myself. Pure carnal feelings take me over and all I care about is the man wrapped around me.

Pushing away from me, he maneuvers his hand between our bodies, fingers brushing the lace of my panties, making me thank the gods that I wore a skirt tonight. I hear a tearing sound and realize the scrap of panties I had on, are no more. I'm bared to his finger's manipulations and all I can think about is chasing the feelings he's pulling from me. Tearing his mouth away from me, his eyes blaze as they stare into mine. "Do you feel that? The fire in your blood? The way your body responds to mine? Tell me now that I'm not your type."

I can't. He knows I can't.

"Tell me that the douche at the dinner table can make you feel this way. That some guy in a stuffy suit, that cares more about his bank account than you, can make you feel like this."

I throw my head back, gasping for air. I move my body against his hand, rocking against him, seeking euphoria. He has me so hot for him. All I can think, feel and breathe is him. I want this. I want him. Not just now. Not just in this moment. I want lots of moments like this. I want to keep feeling like this. He kisses behind my ear and licks down the line of my neck. Just as his teeth gently bite at the tendon in my neck I can't hold it anymore. I'm flying and seeing stars from my release, crying out from the feeling.

Panting, I pull away from Rixton and look into his face. I decide to be honest with him. Maybe it's the emotions my release has just brought forth, but I find myself being boldly honest with him, "I want more."

His smile is slow and devilish. He gives me a lingering kiss on the lips then pulls away. "You are going to go back to that table, excuse yourself and then get your pretty ass out the door. We are getting out of here. "

"Rixton, I can't. Bailing on him wouldn't be good. He's the son of my father's business associate."

"I don't give a fuck who he is, Pyper. You are not going back to dinner with him. You were mine the moment I had you screaming my name. I'm not about to let you anywhere near that guy again. You have two choices. You can go give him the courtesy of telling him you're leaving, or we just leave without you saying anything. He's a grown man, he can get back to his hotel. Choose."

He's in complete alpha mode right now, bossing me around. Looking in his heated eyes, seeing the firm set of his mouth, the look on his face daring me to argue – it's hot. Still feeling the after effects of his touch, I find myself nodding my head in agreement, excited to leave with him.

chapter 12

I SHOULD FEEL BAD ABOUT LEAVING R.J. at the country club. The look on his face was pure confusion when he saw me walk up to his table -no doubt looking man handled- with Rixton at my side. I should also feel bad about the wine I spilled on him accidentally on purpose in order to make my escape. And of course, I should also worry about how pissed off my father is going to be when he hears about it. But, lying naked on my bed, while I watch Rixton remove his clothes, I find it difficult to find it within me to care.

When we got to the parking lot of the restaurant, he had me pressed against the door of my car, kissing me in a way that should be illegal. Time and place became obscure. All that mattered was the immediate minute – the lustful needs we had. And I could not get enough. When we finally broke away from one another, I breathlessly asked, "Your place?"

He hesitated for a moment and murmured, "Let's go back to yours. Great memories there." The tease in his voice balanced with the intensity and hunger in his eyes, would have caused me to agree to anything.

We raced back as fast as we could. He followed me in his truck, all the way into the parking garage. Being apart felt nearly unbearable. We each bounded from our cars. Immediately, we were on each other – first beside my car, then in the elevator ---kissing as though our next breaths depended on appealing to the gods of desire. Once inside my condo, we left a trail of clothing from the front door to my bedroom – the majority, mine.

Now, watching him take off his clothes is a treat. Feeling my eyes on him, he purposefully slows down so I can enjoy the show. We already lost his hat and boots on the way to the room. He then begins what seems like an excruciatingly slow production of unbuttoning his shirt, eyes fixated on me the whole time. I'm sporting nothing but a smile watching him. With legs crossed at the ankles, I get up on my elbows, paying rapt attention with a look of what I'm sure passes for pure glee on my face. It makes him laugh out loud and I chuckle at his response. Once his jeans fall from his hips, the laughter dies, and I bite my lips instead. He's all lean lines, taut muscles, and hardness. His six-pack is actually an eight-pack, which is just plain sinful. His erection stands tall and proud against his stomach, making me feel excited at the blatant indication of his craving for me, and I feel my own body ready itself in response. What an exciting and powerful feeling knowing I can cause someone to feel that way about me.

Crawling onto the bed like an animal stalking its prey, he stops when he gets in-between my legs, spreading them wide before him. With a wicked smile he begins kissing up my thighs, behind my knees, over my belly, on my hipbones and then places his mouth to my most sensitive part. I groan in response and grip the sheets at my side, my eyes close at the intense feeling. He takes his time ravishing me, pleasing me and I arch my back in response, murmuring, nearly purring his name like a prayer. When I fall off the cliff, my whole body clenches tight from the feeling, goose bumps breaking out all over my body and contented sighs streaming from my lips.

He kisses his way up my body and I grip his hands in my hair pulling his mouth towards mine. Just before our lips touch he whispers, "I love the noises you make for me, Red." Then his lips claim mine, kissing me deeply. I can feel him pressing against my belly, ready and eager to become one. I lift my hips, a silent invitation making it clear that I want him too. When we come together, we both gasp from the feeling and there is nothing but him. Nothing but this moment. I remember our first night together and how we had the birth control conversation. I've been on the pill for years and right now, I'm grateful. The feeling of us skin to skin is amazing.

We find a comfortable rhythm and move together, creating our own dance. His mouth is all over me – from my lips and neck, to my chest and breasts. For a brief moment, I worry my nails dig a little too hard, but the sounds he's making tell me he loves it. He makes me lose control and forget myself, each reaction instinctual. Stoke by stroke, move by move, I get higher and higher. In no time, he's got me falling off the edge again, the spasms of my body bringing him to completion as well.

He collapses on me, careful not to relax his entire weight on me. "Red, you are going to kill me. What is it about you? About us?"

I shrug I think, but movement feels difficult, "I don't know. Wish I did."

He rolls next to me and pulls me into his side. I rest my head on his heart and feel it pounding underneath my cheek, the sound making me know he's just as affected as I am. His embrace and fingers running up and down my spine, soothe something inside me I don't quite understand. My eyes feel heavy, and a smile touches my lips as I succumb to sleep.

Waking up with Rixton in my bed is completely different than the last time. I am immediately aware of his presence; our legs and bodies are entwined together. It's still dark outside. I don't know how long I was asleep. An hour? Two? His breathing is deep and I just lay there quietly, enjoying his restfulness, not wanting to wake him.

My room is almost pitch black and I can just make out the outline of his body in the dark. I feel contentment with him next to me, until my mind starts racing and running turning and the reality of the moment overtakes me. I feel panicky and begin easing my body away from his, needing space. I exit the bed and stand watching this man – this man I have craved – sleep. Soundly. Peacefully. While the rage is roaring inside me.

What am I doing? I've slept with him again. Sure, his actions at the restaurant were a turn on but I can't keep doing this – to me, to us. It isn't right. This isn't going to go anywhere – it can't. Right? He's the exact opposite of what I'm expected to be with. He works at a bar for God's sake and appears to just take life as it comes his way. I would be surprised if he had a direction, a purpose, goals. That… that doesn't work for me.

Trying not to hyperventilate, consumed by my thoughts, I grab my robe from the back of my closet door and quietly leave the room, looking back at the threshold to make sure he's still asleep. Sighing and in near tears, I pour myself a glass of wine and sit in the living room, thankful that Luke and Olivia are not here. The last thing I need is either one of them to pay witness to this, again. Not that I won't tell Olivia anyway, but telling and seeing are two very different things.

What am I doing? I can't believe I gave into my stupid hormones again. A daughter of a man like my father is supposed to act a certain way. I was raised differently than this. I remember the etiquette and proper speech classes I had when I was younger. Most kids had music or soccer practice on the weekends, while I was learning which utensil to use first during meal time and how to properly shake hands when you meet someone.

When I was younger, acting out was not tolerated. My mom once told me I threw a tantrum at a restaurant due to a combination of being tired and not liking the twisted noodles of my macaroni and cheese instead of the half-moons Mrs. B made for me. There happened to be a photographer at the restaurant we were at and at the time, my father was on one of those stupid 'Sexiest Entrepreneurs in America' lists. I guess a newspaper article came out with a picture of me at the table mid-cry and my father's stern face looking at me across the table. They published an article where the context was about if men that are successful in the boardroom can be successful in the household – as a father and husband. The picture of me taking center stage. I don't remember the incident at all, but I do remember my time with my father in public places was less frequent for some time. It was preached to me that my father was a powerful man, with a lot to lose, so each and every move in public with him was eventually orchestrated. I hated it.

I'm startled out of my thoughts when Rixton clears his throat. I look up to find him standing in the doorway, arms crossed over his chest. My eyes trail over his body, taking in the jeans that are hanging so low on his hips, it's obvious he's not wearing anything underneath them. "What's wrong?"

I shake my head at him, "Nothing's wrong. Just thinking."

His brow furrows, "Thinking about what?"

Deciding to be truthful I blurt, "I don't know what I'm doing."

"What do you mean? Doing about what?"

I gesture between the two of us, "I mean with us."

He walks over to the couch, and sits next to me. He looks in my face and his eyes flash to my lips then back again. He pushes a lock of hair behind my ear. "You're regretting being with me?" I don't answer. I just stare at him, trying to work out in my mind how exactly I want to answer his question. Being with him is the most divergent experience of my life. On one hand, he makes me feel wonderful. I feel safe, sexy, and am able and comfortable with being myself. But, on the other hand, everything about him and us contradicts with what I'm supposed to be doing. How I should be feeling is messing with my head. I never anticipated this. That I could find myself – allow myself to be found – in this situation. He sighs and grabs my hands, "If nothing else, I think we should always be honest with each other, do you agree?"

"I agree, but I've always been honest with you."

"Fair enough. And now, I'm going to be honest with you." He stares in my eyes for a few beats before continuing, "I want you, Pyper. I think, especially after tonight at the restaurant, I've made that very clear. I've wanted you from the moment I first saw you. I don't care if that makes me sound like some jackass, it's the fucking truth. You see… I've figured something out about you."

"What do you mean?"

"I mean, I see you, Red. You were born and raised to be this high society girl. You live in this fancy condo high rise; go to all your family's fancy dinners and parties. I can't even imagine what sort of expectations were established for you as a child – maybe still are – I don't know." I make an unladylike snort at his comment. He has no idea. "But the thing is – I see *you*. You dress up and play the part perfectly, but I think you feel most comfortable when you're wearing jeans and one of your sexy come-and-get-me tops. When your hair is down around your shoulders, and blowing in the wind. You feel wild and free in those moments. But mostly, I think it's when you are most content – closest and real with the person who lives in your heart, when you are doing what you want and not what you think you should do; when you're happiest. Because it's what you want, and not what's expected from others."

His comments hit home more than he realizes. They invoke emotions in me I'm not sure how to interpret or manage at the moment, so I set them aside to evaluate later, in private. I push them into a box in my mind for now. "And you were able to get all of that from our flirting over the last several months?"

"Sure. Not to sound like a stalker," I laugh and so does he, "but I've been watching you since I got here. I'll never forget the first time I saw you." He gets a far off look on his face and in his eyes and I can tell he's seeing it play out in his mind. "It was a busy night

95

at the club. I was working behind the bar and it was really crowded. I was asking a customer at the bar what she wanted to drink when a flash of red caught my eyes."

A light shines in his eyes and a smile pushes up his lips, "It was like the freaking Red Sea parted. Pun intended. People seemed to just move out of your way as you walked toward the bar. I even remember what you were wearing."

"You do?"

"It was this royal blue dress. It had a low v in the front and was short enough that it looked like you had legs for miles. The dress had a shimmer or something to it because as you walked it looked like you were sparkling."

I know just the dress he's talking about. "I love that dress. And I do look good in it." I laugh, making him chuckle.

"I remember thinking to myself, Rixton, that girl is going to make you want things you didn't even know you wanted. You should probably stay away from her."

"Hey!" I smack him on the chest.

He squeezes me, "Yeah well, I didn't listen. I asked Luke about you. Made excuses to talk to you when you came into the club, and even asked Olivia a question or two now and then when I thought I could get away with it. I still want to get to know you, and I'm not just talking about sex. I want to know everything about you – what you do, who you are, what your hair looks like in the sunlight and if your skin tans in the summer. I want to know what makes you happy and sad and even stupid shit like... what your favorite subject was in school and how you found out Santa Claus wasn't real." That makes me smile. "I'm not willing to take your reasoning that I don't fit into some bullshit plan you have for your life. You don't know me, not really. How do you know I can't fit?" I open my mouth to try to respond, but he puts his fingers on my lips, quieting me and continues, "What I'm trying to say is, give me a chance. Give *us* a chance. Let's just take this one day at a time. Let's have fun together and not make any promises and see where this goes. Can you do that?"

I don't even think about it before I find myself nodding my head. "I can try."

A small smile touches his lips, "All I ask is that when something doesn't feel right, or you think you can't do this for whatever reason, you talk to me about it. Be honest with me. All we have is honesty." A smirk now lifts his lips, "Well, that and fucking fantastic sex." I laugh.

"Okay," I whisper. "I can try this."

"If this doesn't work, then it doesn't. If this ends up working, then it does, and that would be amazing. But I'm not willing to end it without at least trying. Are you?"

I pull my bottom lip into my mouth and bite it, contemplating his words. He's basically offering me a friendship with benefits. No promises, no illusions of forever. I can do that. "Okay – one day at a time. With no long-term promises."

"No promises," he repeats.

This is probably the strangest conversation I've ever had. He pulls me into his arms and we lay down together on the couch. It feels good. It feels right. My heart beats faster and I can feel some doubt creeping in, but I push it away and tell myself, *one day at a time.*

chapter
13

WHEN I WAKE UP THE FOLLOWING morning, Rixton is gone. The pleasant exhaustion caused me to sleep soundly. He left a note on the pillow beside me telling me he went to his place to clean up before going to work. I understand, but I wish he had woken me and said goodbye.

With a sigh, I grudgingly get up to get ready for work. I might as well. Once I arrive, I say hi to my employees and a few clients as I saunter back to my office to get some work done.

I'm just putting my pen down and stretching my neck, realizing I've been at it for a few hours when my phone rings. I look at the screen and see it's Rixton. I'm smiling without thought and pushing the green dot on my screen to answer his call.

"Hello?"

"Hi, yourself, darlin'." My smile grows wider at the sound of his voice. "What are you doing?"

"I'm working. Nothing exciting."

"Everything about you is exciting," he rasps, making my body instantly respond and all I can think about is how it felt to have his hands on me last night. "I'm calling because I wanted to hear your voice, but also because I have an idea."

"Oh yeah? Well color me intrigued."

He laughs and the gruff sound makes me clench my thighs together, "I want to take you horseback riding."

And immediately that feeling dries up like a raisin. "What?" I barely hold myself back from screaming. Me? On a horse? No way in hell. "No way. Nuh uh. Not happening."

"Oh come on, Red. There is nothing to be afraid of."

"I'm not afraid," I scoff. "It's called mutual respect. I respect the horse enough to stay away from it, and they can stay away from me and just do its horsey things."

"Horsey things?" I can hear the smile in his voice, but I'm serious.

"Shut up. You know what I mean."

"It will be fun, I promise! I found this great place only an hour and a half outside of the city. We can make a day of it. Horseback ride, maybe have a picnic or something? It will be great."

"Not happening, Rixton. I appreciate the obvious time and thought you put into this idea, but I'm just not the horseback riding kind of gal."

"Okay, then tell me, what kind of date would you have us go on?"

"There are some great restaurants here in the city. We can spend a day at the History museum and maybe go to lunch. We can always go to Navy Pier, or even the aquarium."

I hear him exaggerate a loud yawn in my ear. "Boring," he sings.

"How is any of that boring? The aquarium has really big fish. What's not great about that?"

He laughs. "How about we go for a bike ride along the lake? Or, maybe there is a good country singer or band coming to concert. I can look for some tickets!"

I sigh, "Clearly we have different ideas about this." I instantly start wondering what the hell I'm doing. Maybe this is proof that a relationship between us won't work. Maybe we aren't compatible, other than in the bedroom. We can't even agree on what to do for a date!

"Don't even think it, darlin'."

"What are you talking about? Think what?"

"I know you well enough already to know you have a million thoughts running through your head about our preferences being evidence of why this won't work. Don't even go there. It's okay that we like different things. What's important is that each of us is willing to try something new. We are, aren't we? I mean, I know I am," he challenges.

There is no way I'm backing down from that. "Of course I am."

"Good. Here is what I propose. You plan a date doing things around the city that you like to do. We will go out and do that together – even if that means we go to a museum." I can tell by his tone that's the last thing he wants to do. "The next date, I will plan our activities, which I'm not going to lie, may include horseback riding."

"You know, the difference between my date ideas and yours?"

"That mine are awesome and yours are... well, not?"

"No. The difference is that yours could get me killed."

Rixton laughs into the phone and the sound automatically brings a smile to my face. I love his laugh. It's husky and raspy and makes him sound so sexy. "I promise I would never let anything happen to you, okay? Trust me."

"Famous last words."

It's Saturday, and I'm getting ready for a date in the city with Rixton. Somehow, he managed to get the day off of work, but has to go in tonight to tend bar. I feel comfortable in jeans, blue top, knee high boots, and a scarf wrapped around my neck. I think I look cute and stylish – perfect for my day of fun. Rixton is in for a surprise. He's expecting me to take him to uppity places that will

Jennifer Miller

bore the hell out of him – I know it. Not going to happen. Sure, we could go to one of my favorite fancy restaurants, or shop my favorite stores, or even do a romantic carriage ride – I do love all those things, but that's not what I want to do today.

Since this is my date day, I insisted on picking up Rixton. He balked at the idea, telling me he would just pick me up at my place, but I stood firm. I expected him to tell me where he lives, finally, I'm really curious about his place. What better look at who Rixton is than to see his home, the things he deems important that he keeps around him, how he decorates, and what he loves? A glimpse into more of who he is, is something I would really enjoy. Disappointed is a good word for how I felt when he told me he had to be at the club that morning to do an inventory order, so I could pick him up there. I guess I will see his place another time. I hope.

Instead of pulling into the parking lot, I park alongside the curb outside the club, since I don't expect to be there long. When I hop out of the car and start walking to the door, a woman comes flying out of the club door before I reach it. "Oh, excuse me", I say, slightly startled." I wasn't expecting the door to swing open so wildly nor to nearly hit me. I hold the door open and wait for her to exit, so I can go inside. She stands with legs slightly apart, hands on her hips and doesn't have a pleasant look on her face. She seems to look me up and down in disgust. Maybe she just got turned down for a waitressing job or something. Hesitantly, I smile at her thinking maybe she just needs a little kindness in her day. "Have a nice day," I add just because being kind doesn't mean I can't also cap it off with a little orneriness.

Smiling to myself, I finally walk through the door and seek out Rixton. He's behind the bar with his fingers pinching the bridge of his nose with his eyes closed. I'm guessing his expression is a reaction from the woman I just saw leaving here. "Hey. You okay?"

His head snaps up and he looks behind me before his eyes focus on mine. I can see him visibly shake off whatever is bothering

him as he walks out from behind the bar. "Hi yourself, beautiful."
He gives me a kiss on my cheek, making me smile up at him.

"Bad meeting or something?" I ask, gesturing to the door in
reference to the woman that just left.

"Oh, um, yeah I guess. Just give me a second to tell Luke I'm
headed out, okay?"

"Okay, sure." He gives me a squeeze on my arm, and a smile, then
takes the stairs two at a time to Luke's office. My brow furrows,
wondering again briefly what that was all about, but when he quickly
reappears and gives me a heart stopping smile, my thoughts focus only
on him and the fun day I know we are about to have.

On our way to my surprise, we ask each other questions ranging
from silly to serious. "Favorite pizza topping?" he asks.

"Pepperoni. What about yours?"

He claps his hands together exuberantly and says, "Me too,"
making me laugh.

"How about… what's something you can't live without?" I ask
him. He doesn't respond at first, which makes me look at him
briefly to see him give me a disarming smile and a lift of his brow. I
giggle at him, "Pervert!"

"Hey! You asked. What about you?"

"My friends and family," I say without hesitation.

"You really love Olivia, don't you?"

I smile, "I do. I didn't realize how much I missed her when she
moved away for college until she wasn't here anymore. After seven
years of being away, I didn't think she would ever move back.
Especially when she married her ex-husband. So I tried to accept
that." I shudder involuntarily, because all thoughts of that man
make me do so. Rixton rubs my knee soothingly. "Things have just
been, I don't know, better since she's been back."

"You are lucky to have a friend like that."

"Do you have friends in Texas that you miss seeing?"

"I do. There were a bunch of us from high school that still
hung out together and sometimes I miss our guys' nights and how I

enjoyed watching games with them and that kind of thing. It's nice being back here and hanging out with Luke though. He's a great guy and he's introduced me to some friends of his and they all seem cool." He's quiet for a minute and we are both lost in thoughts about our friends. Rubbing his hands on his thighs he asks, "Where do you see yourself in ten years?"

"Hmmm... well hopefully I will have opened another spa. It would be a dream come true to have a chain of them other than just the one I have now." I see him nod encouragingly out of the corner of my eye, "Hopefully I will be married with children by then too." I add somewhat shyly. It seems weird to say that, even if it's the truth.

"You want children?"

"Well sure. I mean... I guess I've never given it much thought, other than some day in the far, far, far off future in another galaxy perhaps...but yes, I'd like to have them."

"That far, huh?"

I laugh, "Well yeah. I can't imagine having them now. I'm not ready for that. I feel like there are still a lot of things I want to accomplish in my life before I'd have children. Plus, I always thought I'd be married for a little while before I'd have kids. You know... spending time with my husband just one-on-one before taking on the responsibility that comes with parenting."

We're at a stoplight and I look over at Rixton to see him intently staring at me. He scratches his chin and shrugs, "Well... there goes my plan of impregnating you to make you marry me."

I gasp and he laughs. "Rixton! That's not even funny!"

He laughs and gives me a push on the shoulder, "The thought of being stuck with me is that bad huh?"

I laugh too, but the truth is, it doesn't sound bad at all – and that scares me. In fact, when he said the words "marry me," my heart almost burst and my body tingled with pleasure, liking the way that sounds.

I'm distracted by my thoughts when Rixton says, "The zoo?" He looks at me like I'm crazy as we pull into the parking lot of the Lincoln Park Zoo.

"Yep," I respond popping the 'p' with a big smile.

"Well, I wasn't expecting this at all."

"That's kind of the point. You don't like the zoo?"

"I like the zoo."

"Good! Are you ready?"

"Yes, definitely!"

"Perfect," I smile.

We head inside and map out which way we want to go. We have a great time looking at all the animals, imitating some, feeding a few. The elephants are my favorite and Rixton likes the tigers. We laugh at the giraffes and their long tongues, and Rixton makes a crude comment about what he would do with a tongue like that. I flat out refuse to go into the small mammal and reptile house, making Rixton laugh, and when I try to go into the monkey house he stops me with his refusal.

"Do we have to go see the monkeys?"

I look at him in confusion, "Why wouldn't we?"

He looks to the side and bites his lip before he looks back at me. "I don't like them."

I choke on an unexpected laugh, "You don't like monkeys?"

"Don't you dare laugh," he tells me, face serious. "No. I don't like monkeys."

"Okay. I will try not to laugh. Can you at least tell me why you don't like monkeys? I mean… I guess people have stuff they don't like, but monkeys? They are so…cute. I've never heard of someone that doesn't like monkeys before."

He sighs, "They freak me out."

"Freak you out?"

"Yes. They watch you with their freaky eyes and they are like humans, but not. And…"

I bite my lip trying really hard to relate to his explanation, but it's proving difficult. "And?"

"Well, they aren't really cute. In fact, they are conniving and malicious and all they are good for is throwing poop at you and stealing your backpack."

It's all over. The laugh I'm trying to hold in bursts from my lips and tears form in my eyes. "Steal your backpack?"

"Yes," he replies. I can see a small smile curving his lips as he watches me laugh at him and wipe my eyes. "They are sneaky. I don't like them."

We walk away from the monkey house and start making our way to a different destination when it occurs to me, "Did you ever watch *The Wizard of Oz*?"

He starts shaking his head obviously thinking about the flying monkeys in the movie. "I don't want to talk about it. Too traumatizing."

I giggle and he shoulder bumps me. "Stop laughing."

"I'm trying. It's really hard." I look at him out of the corner of my eye. "What about Curious George?"

He shudders, "Okay enough. Curious George is horrifying. I don't want to ever speak of this moment again. Promise me."

"I promise I shall never speak of monkeys that throw poop, steal backpacks, fly, talk, and monkeys that hang out with dudes in yellow hats ever again." He nods his head, happy with my promise.

My laughter is loud and often during our time together and I don't think I've ever had so much fun at the zoo.

After a few hours spent staring at animals, we are in the car when Rixton asks, "So where are we headed next?"

"Are you sure you're up for more? Not ready to call it a day yet? Especially after your near run-in with monkeys?"

Rixton gives me a look because already I've broken our 'never speak of this again' pact. "I'm game for anything you are."

"Okay, you might regret you said that."

Two hours later, I'm laughing as I look at Rixton's canvas. The stop after grabbing a quick bite to eat was a painting class. Saying it was a great idea, before we began, Rixton wanted to make a deal. I had to promise we would choose the same picture to paint and at the end of class we would exchange them. He would bring home mine, and I, his. I readily agreed, thinking it a fun idea.

Our choice was to paint a wine glass and bottle. His painting looks more like an early impressionist work of some sort – or perhaps an impressionist's weakly talented apprentice. If one squints, you can almost make out a glass and larger blob sort of a thing sitting next to it on what is supposed to be a covered tabletop. If I turn my head sideways a bit and squint with one eye closed, that is.

I can't resist teasing him, "Is that a bottle or a penis?"

"A penis?"

"Yeah, it looks like a wine glass sitting next to a penis."

His mouth opens and closes a few times. He even tilts his head to the side contemplating my comment, and it takes everything I have in me not to laugh. I said it so seriously that he's really trying to see if it resembles a penis. Hell, I am finding myself falling for him moment by moment.

He makes me laugh, he's fun, he's sweet, he's so much more than I expected. For a moment I want to smack myself. I've been telling myself that I need to stick to my life plan, but in some ways, I was judging Rixton. There is so much more to him than what is on the outside and that is so clear to me after the time I've spent with him. I feel ashamed. It's wrong to judge people on the outside, and that is what I did. It was easy for me, and likely others to look at him and think he's just cowboy candy, but he's much more than that. Although, the outside package is mighty fine.

Deciding to quit teasing him, I finally laugh out loud, making Rixton give me an exasperated look. He looks away from me to hide his smile, but I see it. Truth is, my painting is no better. It looks like an eight year old painted it. Taking my art very seriously and being true to my personality, I followed the teacher's instruction to the letter. That doesn't change the fact that no matter how hard I tried, it still looks cartoonish. Not exactly the look I was going for. I wanted it to look like you could reach inside my painting and pour yourself a glass of wine. Oh well. Rixton will be forced to look at mine in the future and at least I will have a great conversation starter and something sure to bring a smile, if not a laugh or two.

Before I can read into the evil look that suddenly appears on Rixton's face and in his eyes, I'm shocked when his brush swipes across my nose and I feel the cold pile of paint he's left there. I blink a few times and stare at him, open mouthed, while he starts laughing. "You did *not* just do that."

"What are you going to do about it, darlin'?"

My answer is to take my paint brush and flick red paint all over his gorgeous face. Precisely fifteen minutes later, we get our asses kicked out of class and are told we can never return. We should probably be embarrassed, but I'm way too busy giggling as we drive away covered in paint, our masterpieces proudly sitting in the back seat.

chapter

14

VISIONS OF DEATH BY HORSE trampling after being thrown from a bucking, rearing steed run through my mind as I get ready for another date with Rixton. The thought of seeing him again makes me giddy. Our zoo date was just a few days ago, but I find myself thinking of him and missing him when I'm not with him. I'm choosing not to read into that.

I'm seriously regretting telling him I would do this whole horseback riding thing. I'd probably agree to anything he asks me to truth be told – which is interesting in itself. I'm doomed. I've never been horseback riding in my life. One time my parents asked me if I wanted to take riding lessons. My school friend, Susan, had begun lessons and she loved it and talked about it incessantly. I heard all about her horse, Trigger, and how beautiful he was and how she learned various riding techniques. Susan expressed her plans to being an expert rider, even participating in jumping and barrel events. In fact, she preferred it to the dance classes we had attended together since we were four. Horseback riding, she explained had become her life. Oh, to be nine-years-old again.

My mom, after listening to me complain about Susan's new hobby, privately asked me if I wanted to take riding lessons. She told me how it would be great for my posture and was a great sport. When she told me that only those with discipline and hard work ethic could be a good equestrian professional, she nearly had me convinced. She and my father were happy to find the best stable and private instructor, she said. However, a picture of large quarter horse formed in my mind and my answer was a loud resounding, "No way." And that was that. I've never even thought about it again.

It isn't that I don't like horses, I guess. I'm able to appreciate their magnificence and I've seen *My Friend Flicka*. Who hasn't? I even cried! That has to mean something. But, getting on the back of one, and allowing myself to be at its mercy – um, no.

Sitting on the couch, waiting for Rixton to pick me up, watching my leg swinging violently, I'm beginning to think a couple cups of coffee may not have been the smartest way to calm my nerves. When my leg is still, I can't seem to stop bouncing my knee, or tapping my fingers over and over. Yeah… not smart of me. I'm zero for zero here.

When Rixton finally shows up, he takes one look at me and laughs out loud. "Why Pyper," his lips are curved in a wicked smirk and his eyes are twinkling with amusement, "you aren't nervous, are you?"

Ignoring his question, I plaster myself to his body thinking that maybe he can be persuaded to do something else today instead. I didn't miss the way his eyes took in my attire. I wore a tight pair of jeans, a low cut tank top, and my hair is in braided pig tails on either side of my neck. I don't have cowboy boots, so my sneakers will have to do. I may not have ever gone riding before, but I sure as hell know how to dress the part to impress my man. Oh hell. Did I just think *my man*?

To distract myself, as well as him, I kiss his neck. "What do you say you and I just stay in today instead?" I fiddle with the buttons on his plaid button down shirt, making it clear what I'm suggesting. I even bite his earlobe for good measure and when I hear him groan, I smile to myself, thinking I've totally gotten my way. That is, until he takes my hands off his body, takes a step back and brings my hands to his mouth for a kiss. Looking me in the eyes, he smiles, "This will be fun. I promise."

Tugging my hands out of his with a sigh, and making my best pouty face, which brings a chuckle from him, I grab my jacket. "Fine," I barely keep myself from stomping my foot, "let's go."

He laughs and I grumble as I follow him out the door. As we ride the elevator down to the parking garage, I quickly say a prayer to God, asking him that today not be the day that he decides to call me home.

"What are you thinking so hard about?"

I look at Rixton, "Oh nothing. I'm just praying to God, asking that I not die in a horse stampede." He laughs, making me frown, which only makes him laugh harder.

Once we arrive, I find myself standing in the barn, looking at the horse I've been assigned for our trail ride. I just know my eyes are as huge as they feel. My horse is named Speedy. Speedy! Seriously? While staring Speedy down, I'm convinced his name is a bad omen, given the fact he's staring right back and snorting. I tilt my head to the side, narrowing my eyes, trying to show the horse that I won't tolerate any funny stuff. I'm totally trying to transmit to him via telepathy who's boss.

"Should I be jealous of the fact you're staring at that horse with greater intensity and interest than you stare at me?" I turn my stare to Rixton instead. He holds his hands up, "Never mind. I'm glad you don't stare at me that way. I take it back."

"I'm trying to make sure he knows who's boss here."

I'm pretty sure I hear Rixton choke on a laugh, which makes me cross my arms over my chest, "Red, all you have to do is be confident. You'll be fine."

Yeah, I ignore that. "Have you seen how big their teeth are? I mean, one bite and I could bleed out and be a goner. I just don't know about this."

He puts a calming hand on my back. "If you really don't want to do this, I won't force you, but I promise it will be okay. Who knows," he whispers in my ear, "you might even like it." When I look at him in disbelief, he chuckles, "I asked them for the sweetest and calmest horse they have, just for you."

"They gave me a horse named Speedy, Rixton! They may as well have just told me his name is death."

He laughs but tries to stop quickly when he sees I'm not amused, and clears his throat. "It will be great. Really. I'm going to ride right behind you and next to you as I can, and if anything even remotely looks off, I will be right there, okay? But it won't be," he quickly reassures when my eyes widen.

Chad, the horse groomer and man in charge of our ride, opens the stall door. "Let's get you up in the saddle, missy."

I don't move. Just stand there and stare at him. "Miss?"

Uncrossing my arms, I sigh and walk into the stall and stand stupidly next to the horse. The groomer puts a small step stool next to the horse and shows me how to get in the saddle, but before he has a chance, Rixton walks into the stall too, gestures for the groomer to get out then turns to me. I think it's rather bold, considering Rixton has no business taking over, but I like it. It tells me he really is serious about taking care of me. He wordlessly lifts me from the ground, gives me a boost by pushing on my ass, and helps me get in the saddle. Once on top, I start taking deep breaths, trying to keep myself from having a panic attack. I can't believe I'm doing this.

Rixton mounts his horse, Silver, like he's a champion cowboy. Is there such a thing? When we start moving, I unconsciously let out a squeal in surprise, and jerk in my seat. "Now, now, calm down, darlin'," Rixton says calmly, but with a heavy drawl. I wonder if being around horses is stimulating his roots. It's sexy and if I wasn't so freaked out, I'd actually enjoy it. "Speedy can feel all your emotions. If you're scared, it's going to make him nervous. Calm down and trust your horse. He's done this trail a thousand times with a thousand other riders. He can probably walk it on pure instinct alone at this point. Relax, okay?"

Mouth tight, and muscles tighter, I give him a bob of my head, acknowledging his words. I don't realize I'm gripping the bridle super close and tight until Rixton comes up next to me and shows me how to loosen it, giving the horse plenty of room to maneuver his head.

Without much pomp and circumstance, we start off on what will be a two-hour ride. Rixton is right behind me since at the moment, the trail only allows for single file. Knowing he's there, I start to calm down a little. My back is still ramrod straight, but I lose some of the tension in my neck and shoulders.

The ride goes by surprisingly fast and I'm starting to feel comfortable, smiling at myself, and seriously considering patting myself on the back over how brave I have been. I can't believe I was nervous about this. It's been a piece of cake.

When the horses get to a part of the ride where they all start to trot, I initially pull the bridle a little tighter and closer to my abdomen in apprehension, but quickly force myself to relax and allow my body to move naturally with the horse's movement. I bounce up and down, but notice others are as well and decide to enjoy the feeling of the wind in my hair and the warm sun on my face. Who knows, I could actually start to like this. I really am good at handing this beast. I may want to do this again sometime. It's... nice.

The horse – or maybe it's me – is really bouncing now so I tighten my legs around the horse to gain a feeling of control and settle a bit of the increased nervousness that has suddenly returned. I also think it will help me improve my balance. An open field lies ahead. I glance toward Rixton as he moves his horse up next to me and gives me a smile so gorgeous, my breath catches at the sight. He really is something on top of a horse. Strong thigh muscles move under his tight jeans with each movement, and his strong shoulders and back are evident under his shirt. He has his cowboy hat on and he looks so completely in his element, so happy, that the sight is breathtaking. It makes me understand why he misses Texas – being a cowboy to some extent must be in his blood.

Finding myself enraptured with him yet again, I look away hastily in embarrassment just as he discovers me staring. A sexy smile touches his lips. Looking his direction again, our eyes connect and without any provocation or notice, my horse suddenly takes off in a fast run. My legs stiffen tightly around his midsection and I grab tight while starting to freak out. I give a blood-curdling scream then yell "Whoa, whoa." I struggle to stay astride, loosening my leg hold, somehow aware that it may only make him run faster, while pulling back on the reins. Oh shit, I really am going to die. I'm totally going to die. I'll never be able to realize all my dreams and I totally should have bought those amazing boots I saw in the store window the other day and enjoyed them while I could. You really do only live once – I shouldn't have been so practical. And who cares about the money – I really can't take it with me.

I squeeze my eyes closed and wait for the feeling of weightlessness as I'm thrown from the horse, wondering if those cute little hats equestrians wear would protect them in such a fall, when suddenly, the horse slows and comes to a stop. "It's okay darlin', I got you. I told you I wouldn't let anything happen."

I slowly open one eye at a time to be sure I'm not merely awakening from a coma that I suffered from getting a head injury, and see Rixton , still sitting on his horse, with a look of concern and compassion. My hero. My breaths are coming in quick, rapid succession, and it takes me a moment to calm down. Focusing on the return of my blood pressure and pulse to within normal limits, I hear Chad apologizing over and over on the other side of me. "So, so sorry. Speedy saw me take off and he was just trying to follow. I'm so sorry about that. Glad you are okay. You are okay, right?"

"Okay. I'm okay. Yes, okay."

"You are doing so great. And you handled that perfectly," Rixton compliments and as we begin a slow walk again his eyes stroll leisurely down my body resting at my breasts and the juncture of my thighs, before he meets my eyes again. The look in his eyes makes me automatically forget all about the damn horse. Yeah, I did manage that wild stallion…and I'm not sure if I'm thinking about the horse or Rixton. Regardless, his attention has diverted mine, which was likely his intent. And it is *so* working. "I gotta say, darlin', you on a horse…incredibly hot. I'm so turned on right now."

I feel my cheeks heat and automatically look around hoping he wasn't over heard. When I see no one is paying us any attention, I look back at him, "Oh yeah?"

"Definitely. It's making me anxious to get off of these damn horses. Maybe I should have taken you up on your offer to just stay home after all." He thinks for a minute and then shakes his head, "Actually no, I take that back. The picture you make right now is worth it."

"Well I confess… I may be having a little bit of fun – that scary moment excluded."

"Only a little bit?" His brow furrows, "Let's bring your horse to a stop."

Instantly I tense up, "Why is something wrong?"

"No, nothing's wrong."

I give Speedy the command and he slows to a stop, prompting those that were behind us to go around us. A couple of people give us funny looks but continue on their way. Completely oblivious to anyone else, Rixton puts his horse right up next to mine so that our legs are touching. He leans toward me, "Come here." I lean toward him thinking he wants to tell me something until he cups the side of my face, and places his lips on mine. His kiss is sweet, slow and incredibly sexy. His tongue strokes mine with long strokes, making me moan in response. He gently nibbles my bottom lip between his teeth as he pulls away.

It takes a moment for my head to clear and for me to focus on his smiling face, "What was that for?"

"Well you said you were only having a little bit of fun, so I figured it was my duty to bump that up a notch for you."

"Well, Mr. Andrews, mission accomplished."

He gives me a smile that can only be called panty-melting, and if I didn't already know I was falling for him, in that moment, it's crystal clear.

It isn't long before we're returning to the stables. As scared as I was for this whole experience, it was really fun. Leading Speedy into his assigned stall, where apparently he's going to be brushed down, I swing my leg over and get down from the horse, nearly falling flat on my ass.

I'm not prepared for the fact that my legs feel like jelly. "Whoa there, darlin'." Rixton catches me in his arms. I don't know where he came from, but I'm certainly glad he's there.

"What the hell is wrong with me?"

"It's normal for those that have never ridden before, or if it's been a long time since they've last ridden, to feel funny when they get off their horse."

"Feel funny?" Rixton holds onto my arms as we walk a few steps and I know I have to look absolutely ridiculous practically tripping over my feet. "I feel like I'm still on the horse. And what the hell is wrong with my ass?"

He laughs, "Your ass is fine, but you do look pretty funny. Your legs are apart and you're walking with an adorable waddle. Maybe I just need to put something back between them for you," he drawls.

"Shut up!" I'm so embarrassed. I swat Rixton on the arm, but he just laughs and swoops me up into his arms. "What are you doing? Put me down! I can walk."

"Not a chance. I made you come with me horseback riding. The least I can do is carry you to the car until your body adjusts to you being off the horse."

All the muscles in my legs feel sore. Cradled in his arms I can feel that my back feels a little sore too and oh my hell, I think my ass is going to fall off. There are muscles that hurt that I didn't even know I had. When we are in the car, I have an idea. I get my cell phone and make a call.

"This isn't what I had planned you know. And this is supposed to be my date idea today." Rixton grumbles.

"Yeah, well too bad. You should have thought of this when you knew you were bringing a novice horseback riding."

As we walk into my spa, some of my employees' eyes appear to pop out of their heads as they catch a view of Rixton. I guess I can't blame them. Not only is he ridiculously hot, but they've never seen me with a man before. It's pure luck I was able to get us in for a massage appointment. God bless the person who cancelled today. Rixton, however, is not as delighted. Rather, he has been complaining ever since I suggested this detour.

"I feel fine. I don't really need a massage."

"Are you seriously telling me you don't want a massage?"

"Yes, that's what I'm telling you. I've never had one before, I don't need one now." Rixton is looking around the place, taking it all in. I want to know what he thinks about the spa. I wish I could see in his mind and know his thoughts and if he likes what he sees. I can't help but feel pride in my business and for reasons I don't understand, it's important to me that Rixton like it too. His opinion matters to me.

I walk up to him, albeit somewhat awkwardly since my legs still feel like I participated in a triathlon and whisper in his ear, "So what you're saying is that you don't want to be naked, in a room with me, also naked, while another woman rubs me down and you get to watch?"

He pulls back and stares at me, mouth slightly open, "Well, when you put it that way, where do I change?"

I laugh and point him in the direction of the men's changing room.

Considering that Rixton and I have been naked together and have done extremely intimate things to one another, it's funny to me that being naked in a massage room should feel so awkward. We're both lying on our stomachs, heads turned, facing one another. When we walked into the room together and needed to drop our robes to get on the tables, I wanted to forget the massage right there and just jump on him instead. And by the look in his eyes, he thought the same thing.

Instead, I saw him swallow hard, move to the table, and get situated for our therapists.

My licensed therapists only talk when needed; otherwise they just let clients enjoy the experience. I imagine the thoughts running through their minds and the likely gossip among the other employees. Oh well. If they want to keep their jobs, they will keep their mouths closed at least around me.

A few times when Rachel, my masseuse, hits a sore spot, moans escape my mouth because I can't hold them in. Each time heat flashes in Rixton's eyes and it somehow relocates itself between my legs. He keeps his head turned toward me and eyes fixated on me the entire time. It's an intensely intimate situation and with each passing minute, the sexual tension builds – so thick, as they say, I could cut it with a knife. I have never had to work to keep my breathing steady during a massage before and all I can think about is how I want to press my body and lips against his. Who knew a massage could be so provocative?

When our massages are over, and the therapists leave the room, Rixton is off his table and on mine immediately. "God, Pyper, I want you," he whispers moments before his lips are on mine. He kisses me like he's drowning and I'm water. Like he can't get enough, like he will never get enough. I put my hands in his hair and squeeze. I can't get enough either.

Ripping my mouth from him takes extreme effort, "We can't do this here," I whisper. "This is my company, my employees… I can't."

"I know, I know. I just want you. Bad." He keeps talking in between placing kisses all over me – my mouth, jaw, behind my ears, my neck and chest. "Let's get out of here, okay? I want to get you home. Now."

I've never gotten dressed so fast in my life.

chapter
15

RIXTON DRIVES FAST AND FURIOUS back to my place. I don't even think until later about the fact that he didn't take me to his, but chose mine again. As we pull into the parking garage of the condo, I'm practically panting with want and need.

Rixton is already out of his car and has come to collect me, obviously as eager as I am and not wanting to waste another second before we ascend in the elevator to my condo. We stand as close as possible in the elevator, waiting for the car to stop on the designated floor. We hustle out, and after fumbling a bit with my key, open the door.

Once we're through the door, Rixton tosses his hat in the air and as it floats to the floor. He starts tugging at my tank and I begin unbuttoning his shirt. He walks me backwards toward the living room couch. "I want you," he murmurs with his lips against my jaw after throwing my tank on the floor.

"Less talking, more kissing."

He laughs and opens my jeans with a flick of his fingers. I get impatient with his buttons and have to force myself not to rip the shirt and pop all the buttons. Completing that task, I make a sound of joy as I remove his shirt just as he removes my bra and we smile as we go skin to skin, celebrating our success with a firm, deep kiss.

My zipper slides down like a scream in the room and his hand immediately descends the front of my jeans making me moan in response. Feeling the couch behind us, he smashes his lips to mine in a hard, passion-filled kiss. "This is going to be fast, darlin'."

"I like fast. And hard," I find myself brazenly responding, unencumbered with pretense or formality. Rixton groans and turns me around. With my back pressed against his front, he takes my breasts in both of his hands and squeezes my nipples. I throw my head back onto his shoulder and moan again when his teeth nibble on my neck. "Now," I command.

He bends me over the arm of the couch and eases my jeans down my legs. "Lift your feet one at a time," he instructs, then helps me step out of them. I hear his zipper and look over my shoulder to see him tugging his jeans down just far enough to free himself from them. With a hand on my back and another on himself, steadying, he eases into me. When he's completely inside, we both groan together at the amazing feeling.

"Yes," I shout and plant my feet wider apart. He finds a rhythm, slowly easing out and then back in quickly. "Faster," I instruct him as I feel the need within me start to rise in my belly. He reaches a hand to the front of me and runs the tips of his fingers over my most sensitive spot bringing me higher. I find myself rocking back to meet his thrusts, and simultaneously grinding against his fingers.

"Come for me, darlin'," he pants, almost begging me, both eager to satisfy me and anxious to obtain his own release.

"I'm almost there," I pant, loving the feeling of him wanting more, needing more. When I come, I scream with my release, the feeling so intense, remaining quiet not even an option.

"Yes, that's it," he continues to stroke me. "Fuck, yes." He pulls out every sensation he can until his movements pick up, become choppy, and then he loses himself too.

119

Both of us panting and slightly shivering, his body collapses on top of mine and we start laughing breathlessly at how desperately anxious we were and at how astoundingly remarkable we feel. Basking in the afterglow, we're alarmed as we hear, "Ummm. Wow. Uh. So yeah. This is a bit awkward."

Our heads jerk to the side to see Luke standing there, gawking at us. "DUDE," Rixton yells and covers as much of me as he can while Luke turns to face the wall.

"Oh my God!" I yell.

"Geez. Get out. Privacy, man." Rixton tells Luke who is already hurrying away.

If I wasn't so satisfied right now, I'd be completely mortified. I'm not sure if I will ever be able to look Luke in the face again, but I do know a talk with Olivia is very overdue.

I've had so much fun with Rixton these past few weeks. We've continued to date and get to know each other better. Each and every encounter tops the one before. Every date reveals something new about Rixton and he continues to surprise me. Moreover, I continue to open up to him and am at ease, able to be exactly who I am. In one brief interaction he can make me laugh, swoon, and get me all hot and bothered. He's informed, can carry an intelligent conversation, and is exceedingly silly. He is so much more complex than I ever would have thought, and yet so very simple and sweet. I enjoy him. And I really do like him. He's all I think about and he's nothing and everything I expected. But mostly, he's everything that I want.

The thought has been torturing me. I'm ashamed to admit that at twenty-six years old I'm still afraid of what my parents think and feel. I don't want to disappoint them and I know that everything I do is a reflection on them. They have made me aware of that since I was young. And mostly, I know that my behavior and desires are directly opposed with their expectations of and for me and that I am willfully defying them – with glee. The moments of angst and guilt are becoming fewer. And when I look in the mirror these days, I see a stronger, more confident, more aware me. Mostly.

"I think you are wrong, and I don't know how many times I have to tell you this." Olivia, who made a surprising solo appearance for breakfast this morning, is giving me the look she should patent. It tells me she's exasperated. And I'm the target of her annoyance this time.

Trying to determine how I want to respond, I replay what she told me this morning, sorting out fact from fiction. Apparently, Luke had a late night at the club and an early morning this morning. Olivia decided to come here instead of waiting at his place alone. She said she just wanted to be in her old room, but I'm fairly certain that's only part of the story. Regardless, when she walked into the kitchen as I stood at the table pouring my first cup of coffee while holding my bowl of granola, I shrieked and practically tossed my entire bowlful of cereal onto the table and floor, prompting her to apologize profusely. Given the mutual hyper sensitivity we have about such surprises after what we both went through, even if it had to be worse for her at the hand of Deacon, her excessive apologies are understandable. Horrors like he caused take time to get over. A lot of time. We clean the mess up, then sit down to enjoy breakfast together. Something we haven't done for quite some time, and something I've missed.

"I just don't know if you're right, Olivia. I think my parents want me happy too – don't get me wrong – but that happiness has a price – and several conditions. *Their* conditions, to be more specific." I take a sip of coffee and pause for a minute, enjoying its sweetness. "I've never done anything contrary to their wishes – certainly not anything of substance. I've never rebelled, never got into drugs, drinking, partying, or any of that stuff. I've been their model little daughter. A perfect little soldier." Scratching my head, I tuck my hair behind my ear then grab the hair tie off my wrist and drag it to the top of my head and tie it into a high bun. "They do not expect – nor do I think they will tolerate – me doing anything contrary to their wants, beliefs, or desires. And I never have. Frankly, I can hardly imagine what it will be like for them – or me – when that happens the first time. And it is about to happen."

"I think you are crazy to think they have expectations as far as your long-term happiness goes, Pyper. They want you to have the fairy tale. They want you to find someone and fall in love and be happy ever after." She sits across from me cupping her coffee cup in her hands, blowing on the contents between her words. "I mean really, it isn't a big deal is it? So you fell in love with a cowboy and not an executive or entrepreneur. Who really cares? It isn't like he isn't supporting himself or that he's some felon or druggie or something. Give me a break."

"First of all, I didn't say anything about love." She makes a noise that I ignore. She doesn't get it. And I hate thinking that because she is my best friend. "Secondly, it doesn't matter, Livvie, none of that matters. My dad wants me to be with someone that either has a ridiculous amount of money on his own, has inherited money, or at the very least has the potential to make a lot of money. And he has a standard for how he wants me to live. And it's not about what I should have, really. It's about him not being able to settle for having a son-in-law that doesn't fit the image. He is also concerned that someone will use me to get to his money or that someone will only want to be with me to get to my inheritance. That, Livvie, is his criteria for the fairy tale as you call it. And, frankly, for the first time, maybe, I see it as a bit sick. No matter how much he loves me."

"How do you know that?"

"Because he's said as much. Maybe not in those exact words, but I can certainly read between the lines. The messages have been loud and clear through the years."

"Maybe you have misunderstood. I still think they want more for you – true love, happiness, contentment. Surely, they care more about those things than money shit. And if you are right, when they see how happy someone makes you, none of that other stuff is going to matter."

"It's a nice thought," I sigh. "I'm just not confident it's my reality."

"All I know is that I watched your dad spend a crazy amount of money making sure that you have everything and anything that you want. And I've seen his expression when he has given you things. He likes to see you happy. There is no way that he would not accept – and respect – a person that makes you happy too. No way."

I think a change of subject is in order. We aren't going to agree on this right now and it's starting to give me a headache. "I'd like to hope you are right. We will certainly see. Now, speaking of being happy, how are things with you and Luke?"

"Wonderful," she smiles, the change in conversation not even phasing her given its subject. "Why do you ask?"

I take a deep breath – here we go. "Because I'm just wondering why it is you haven't finally moved in with him yet?"

Her face falls, "Are you trying to kick me out? Does this have to do with Luke walking in when you and Rixton… because he apologized for that profusely. So did I. I didn't know I was going to be running late at the florist…"

"You know better than that. I mean, yes, that was mortifying. And horrifying. Humiliating. Appalling. And I still can't look Luke in the face, but that's not why I ask. The thing is, I know you. I think you forget that while you know me better than anyone, the reverse is also true. And I know you are staying here because you don't want to leave me here alone. You worry about me being here by myself."

"That's not…"

I don't let her continue. "I know you two are practically living together already. What are you waiting for? Is it because you want to wait until you're married before officially living together?"

"No, it isn't that."

"Then tell me what it is, because be honest… how many times has Luke asked you to just finally move into his place? I know you guys already repainted, redecorated, and brought most of your things over. So, what gives?" Olivia shrugs and takes a sip of her coffee prolonging answering me. "Livvie, you need to move in with Luke. You need to start the next chapter of your life. I understand that. You know that, right? As hard as it is to see you go, I need you to take care of yourself and quit being concerned about me. I know that's what you're doing. And I know what you really want."

Tears form in her eyes making the green stand out even more in her pretty face. "It's hard, Pyper."

"Tell me why. Are you having second thoughts? Is the commitment scaring you because of what you went through with asshole?" I ask, referring to Deacon. "Because if it is, you say the word and we can hightail it the hell out of Chicago right now. If something happened and if this is seriously not what you want then tell me and I am here for you, no questions asked. Well… maybe some questions, but mostly what I said before."

She gives me a watery smile, shaking her head, which is what I was going for because I know there is no way in hell she's having second thoughts about marrying Luke. They love each other so much it's palpable. "No, it's nothing like that and you know it. It's just… you're right… I don't want to leave you. Not alone."

I push my coffee cup aside and reach across the table for her hand. She grabs mine and holds on tight. "I'm happy for you. So, so happy, Livvie. And I love you, and am so lucky to be loved by you in return. The fact that the thought of leaving me alone would even give you pause, means so much to me. And yes, I will miss you. Your presence, our late night talks, the lip glosses of yours I find all over, our Supernatural binges, ice cream confessions, but most of all, you. I will miss you. But you know what? More than all of that? I'm so excited and happy for you. And I know that just because you aren't living here, it doesn't mean that anything changes between us or that those things we love to do together, can't still happen. I mean, hello, can you say slumber party?"

She laughs and a tear falls down her face, bringing a smile to my face at its beautiful contradiction. My heart swells with friendship, loyalty and love for my friend. "I'll miss you too. I mean, I know we will still see one another and like you said, I'm over there more than I'm here anymore, but completely moving out is just so *final*, you know? I guess I haven't been wanting to let go."

"Look, you can stay here as long as you want. I'm not telling you that you have to leave. I just want you to know that I will be fine and I'm happy for you, and this is all a great and exciting thing and I'm so honored that I get a front row seat to all of your dreams coming true."

"I love you too. So much."

I laugh joyously, "So now admit it, how many times has Luke asked you to get your butt over there?"

A grin crosses her features and lights up her eyes, "More times than I care to admit. Especially after what we shall now call, 'the couch episode'."

"Ugh. Can we not call it anything? Like banish it from our memories?" She laughs and I find myself laughing in return. "You should call him and tell him the news. I'm sure he's going to be really happy."

"Are you sure about this? He will probably be over here immediately with boxes, helping me pack up the rest of my belongings before I change my mind. How much you want to bet me?"

I stand up from the table, "I'm not taking that bet because I have no doubt you're right." I bring my coffee mug to the sink to rinse it out then turn to her, "Come on then, let's get a head start on gathering your things."

We walk into her bedroom hand and hand to do just that.

Later that evening, I'm alone, enjoying a glass of wine and thinking about the love on Luke and Olivia's faces as they took the last of her boxes to his waiting vehicle. Olivia was right. Luke showed up not only with boxes but with Rixton's borrowed truck to load up her stuff. To say he was enthusiastic is an understatement.

Olivia gave me a significant bear hug, one that nearly fractured my ribs and suffocated me as they readied to leave, while Luke mouthed a thank you behind her back. How he knew I was responsible for giving her the push she needed, I don't know, but I smiled back and gave him a wink. I should make him buy me shoes to show his appreciation. Jimmy Choo's.

When my doorbell rings, I'm surprised and apprehensive. I have no idea who would be coming by. When I look through the peephole, I'm surprised to see Rixton leaning against the doorframe. Opening the door I look at him with surprise, "Hey. What are you doing here?"

"Well, when Luke asked to borrow my truck to move out Olivia, I figured you could maybe use a friend tonight, so as soon as I got off work, I came right over."

Surprised and completely moved, I grab a fistful of his shirt and pull him inside, kissing him as I close the door behind him. I'm pretty sure if I hadn't already been falling, I would have nose-dived into love right then and there.

chapter 16

WE'RE LYING IN MY BED HOLDING each other close. Before returning to bed, Rixton sat on the couch and watched *Supernatural* episodes with me for a while; poking fun at the fact that Olivia and I love the show. He made comments about Dean and Sam, calling them 'pretty boys' and saying that they are probably super prissy in real life. I refuse to believe that and am glad Olivia isn't here because those are fighting words. I must tell Olivia we can never watch this show with both Luke and Rixton around at the same time. It would be ugly. I picture lots of blood, nails scratching, and screaming.

Knowing without words that his closeness is exactly what I needed tonight, when I started yawning Rixton turned off the TV, stood up, reached for my hand and led me to my room. I'm practically purring in his arms, immensely enjoying the feeling of fingers running through my hair. It's like he knows the way to my heart; in fact, it almost feels spiritual. It also shows me that he listens. One night when he asked me what service I most liked to receive at my spa, I told him I'd take a scalp massage over a full body massage any time. It doesn't bother me that I have crazy electrocuted looking or oily messy hair by the time it's finished. The pleasure is well worth it. In addition, Rixton having been with me during my last massage, likely picked up on my enjoyment. I hope he never stops, it's fabulous, and, come to think of it, scratch spiritual and replace with orgasmic.

He's quiet, but I swear I can hear the thoughts turning in his mind. I can't help but ask him, "What are you thinking about?"

He looks down meeting my eyes, "I'm thinking that someday I'd like to take you with me to Texas."

I can tell he's gauging my reaction to his words, but all I feel is intrigued – and special that he would want to share that part of his life with me. Resting my hands on his chest, I throw a leg over his so I'm half lying on top of him. I prop my chin on my hands and get comfortable. Moving has made the scalp manipulations discontinue, but I don't mind. I find equal delight lying like this with him and relish his thought and smile, "You would?"

"Yes," he reaches out and tucks my hair behind my ear. He's always doing that and I love it. "I think you would really like it. No, scratch like, you'd *love* it. I think you'd definitely love it."

"Tell me about your home and why you think that."

He smiles and then closes his eyes. He has that faraway look in his eyes, revealing he's picturing his home in his mind to provide specific details. "The house itself is simply beautiful. There really is no other way to describe it. A combination of white and gray, with beautiful brick details that must have taken hours to perfect. A great architectural design. It has huge picture windows that are surrounded with white shutters, a wraparound porch with a swing, and a lawn so green and lush it almost kills you to mow it. The house sits on 100 acres of land." My eyes widen. I can't picture that, but I know it's a lot. "My daddy helped build it himself with his brothers years ago, not long after he and my mama were married. The land had been in my family for years and neither of my dad's brothers wanted it in light of the associated responsibility. My daddy freely snatched it up and they got to work. He and my mama always wanted a home with a lot of land, and my daddy was

128

determined to make her dreams come true – no matter what. If my granddaddy had told him no, or my uncles would not have wanted to deed their portion, he would no doubt have figured out another way to get her that dream."

"That's extremely sweet. It sounds like he really loved her."

"He did. I still remember hearing the story about when he surprised mama. She, of course knew, the house was being built, and was in on the design plans, but when it was done, he insisted on blindfolding her and taking her to the property."

"Oh! I can picture it in my mind. Your dad, who I imagine to look like you, would be smiling in pure pleasure as he brings his wife to their new home. He would be giddy and smiling, excited and proud of his accomplishment. I picture your mother so excited she could burst, eager to arrive at their destination. Holding hands tightly, she would giggle in anticipation and he would run loving circles over the back of her hand smiling at the sound. It would be true enchantment, exceeding that in any fairy tale."

"Aw Red, I like the picture that creates; and you are right. It likely was like that. And, I do definitely favor my daddy."

I smile, happy that I could put that thought in his mind.

"About a half mile around the house, there's a white fence that encloses the house in a large square. When you drive into the property up a reasonably long road, he built a large gate. The fence ends on either side of the road and there's brick that matches the house built up very high. A gate connects the two sides, and there are words made of metal above that makes an awning. You have to pass under it, to access the house." Now he smiles, no doubt picturing the parents he loves, "He helped my mama out of the truck, and stood her in front of the gate before he took off her blindfold. The metal sign at the top of the gate names the ranch. He named it 'Wild Heart Ranch'. When she saw it, the first thing she asked was why he chose that name. You see, he hadn't asked her opinion; he just chose the name himself. He told her it was because that's how she makes his heart feel. Wild." His soft smile widens and I can see the love he has for his parents in his expression as he opens his eyes even wider, looking at me and for my reaction. "My daddy says she stood and stared at that sign for a long time and then things happened that just weren't any of our business. But I heard once that he said that's when my brother was conceived."

I sigh and smile broadly, "That's really romantic."

"It is, isn't it?" He laughs, "That's the funny thing. I wouldn't say my daddy was a softie by any means, but around her, he became a different person – something better – something more. And that was always the case. Even after all that time."

"How long were they married?"

"They were just shy of their thirtieth wedding anniversary when he died." I can hear the pain in his voice.

"How did he die?" I ask softly a little unsure if I should have asked the question.

"Cancer."

"I hate that word."

He sighs, "Me too, darlin', me too. Looking back, it seemed like it happened so fast. He went from diagnosis to chemotherapy and radiation so quickly. They said the cancer was aggressive and already well advanced and he needed to take action right away. I felt like we barely had time to absorb the diagnosis before we were told that he only had months to live. The cancer was already so far along that by the time they found it treatment did little to help. He was determined to do anything and everything he could to prolong his life, but in the end, it didn't help and I think that was one of the hardest things to swallow."

"What do you mean?"

"We watched him waste away. He would go to appointment after appointment, all of us taking turns to help him. He never complained, never said a word about it. Kept going like it was just part of his daily routine, like brushing his teeth. In the end, it didn't matter and all the treatment did was make him sick, confine him to bed because he was so weak, and took up his time. Time he could have spent doing something he loved. In hindsight, I wish we had spent all that treatment time making memories. Not that we didn't do that too, but it was all for nothing."

"Yes, but he didn't know that. I'm sure he and your mom made the best decision they could given the information they had. And he loved you all and no doubt wanted to do anything he could to be with you as long as possible."

"I know. It's just still hard to swallow. Seeing my bigger-than-life dad so weak and worn away from a vicious disease was something I don't think I will ever forget. And as if watching that wasn't hard enough, one time I couldn't sleep and decided to go check on my dad to see if he needed anything. Toward the end, we all took shifts caring for and watching him. We had a big old bed delivered and placed it in the room that has the big picture window because he loved to stare out that thing. I thought since I couldn't sleep, I'd relieve someone so they could get some rest. When I got to the door of the room, my mama was in with him, even though I know for a fact it wasn't her shift. We had sent her to get some rest earlier. Anyway, I was struck immobile by the two of them staring at each other, talking and looking so intense. I heard him," he pauses and his eyes get glassy. Clearing his throat he continues, "I heard him tell my mama that he didn't want to leave her and then apologized, saying how sorry he was that he couldn't stay with us longer." A tear runs down his temple and he sniffs. I feel tears fall down my face in response. "Anyway, it's something I will never forget. He was fighting to stay with her as long as he could to the very end. They loved each other like nothing I've ever seen and if I ever doubted, that convinced me of how lucky I was to have such loving examples of what it meant to be spouses and how fortunate I was to pay witness to that scene. It still gave me hope and appreciation for life and for love. How could it not?"

"I can't even imagine how hard that had to be, Rixton. I am sure your mom misses him desperately every day."

His fingers are trailing up and down my spine, making me shiver. "We all do, but she most of all." He pauses for a moment, lost in thought. "While the house is as beautiful as I described, it's not my favorite place on the ranch. My favorite place is the barn." He looks at me and smiles, "Don't make fun of me now, darlin', but I'm going to be honest with you."

His smile is infectious and helps shake off the sorrow my heart feels at the loss of his father, "Please do."

"I love the smell of the hay, the welcoming sounds the horses make when you walk inside. I used to spend hours in there reading, dreaming, hiding in the rafters and eavesdropping on others when they would come inside. I would play in there for hours pretending. I was a world champion bull rider, a horse trainer, or a sheriff. It was my special place. Many times, I would fall asleep in there, which always resulted in a scolding from my mama." I giggle at the thought of Rixton getting in trouble. "You though... you would love the sunflower field. The sun sets over it and it makes the flowers look like they're on fire. The prettiest yellow gold you've ever seen with sunflowers reaching toward the sky for what looks like miles."

"It sounds extremely beautiful."

"It is. We have a mini water hole through the woods in the back of the property; my brothers and I spent many a summer swimming and swinging from a rope we hung from a tree. We would have contests over who could do the fanciest jumps and who could jump the farthest. It's a wonder how none of us ever broke our necks."

There's pure longing and something else, maybe loss, in his voice. "It sounds like you miss it."

"I do," he squeezes me closer to him, as if the act will push away the wanting of his home, "more than I thought I would."

"Hearing your description and seeing the way you feel about the place, I'm even more surprised you came back here. It sounds like it's where you love to be. Where your heart is."

"Yes well, I've learned the hard way that things in life don't always go the way that you plan."

I'm curious by his words, but more so, they humble me. I feel ridiculous thinking I can go through life always trying to plan out every last detail. Life isn't supposed to be that way. I mean, look at his father – he sure as hell didn't plan for his life to end that way. It's not about a perfect plan, and having everything all lined up in a pretty little row. It's about love. It's about living life to the fullest with every minute you have. It's about purpose. It's about being fearless.

With sudden clarity, I realize that if I continue trying to make my life fit into this special box that I created, life is going to continue passing me by. It will always be a disappointment. While I've been waiting on perfection, I haven't realized it's been staring me in the face all along in the form of a crazy, wonderful, beautiful, sometimes messy, life.

In a million years I never could have planned that I would be here now, in my bed, with a cowboy bartender, with his fingers running through my hair and heart beating in tune with mine. I never thought that I could feel so happy and complete with a man who, for the most part, is the total opposite of the individual I created as ideal for my future. And isn't that the point? Trying to plan it all out will make me miss out on the beautiful things that an unexpected life has to offer. It won't be easy, but I'm going to try to change – and I know the perfect place to start.

"Rixton, how would you feel about meeting my parents?"

chapter
17

"YOU ASKED HIM WHAT?" Olivia screeches in my ear, causing me to hold the phone several inches away in fear that she will blow my eardrum out.

"I know! What was I thinking?" Olivia starts in but I talk over her, "No! Don't answer that. I know what I was thinking. I was thinking that I can't keep living my life for anyone but me. I was thinking that I don't want to live with regret and that if I don't follow my heart that's exactly what I will do."

"Those are all really good points, and I do seem to remember some red-headed crazy girl giving me the same speech a little more than a year ago too. All these things sound incredibly familiar."

"Yeah, yeah, you've mentioned her before. Sounds like she should be scalped for all her stupid advice."

"You know the thing is... her advice... not so stupid."

I sigh and run my fingers through my hair, needing something to do with my hands, "Livvie... I know this sounds so incredibly ridiculous coming from a grown woman, but I'm scared."

"Do you want Luke and I to go with you when you meet with them? Maybe having another couple with you will help diffuse any potentially uncomfortable situations."

I actually contemplate her idea for a few minutes wondering if that's the exact shield and protection I might need. But I decide to avoid the non-grade school thing and act like the grown up I am; I can't ask my friend to hold my hand and do this with me. After all, staking my claim as an independent adult is in great part what this is all about. "Thanks for offering, but no. I need to do this on my own."

"I really think it will be okay, babe. Hopefully you are going to find out that you needlessly worried.

"I hope you're right." Knowing there is nothing more that can be said on the topic that would be helpful, I change it. "So, what are you up to today? I'm thinking about making a personal lunch delivery to the club for Rixton. Once I'm done doing some things here at work."

"Oh, that's nice. I'm sure he will really appreciate that. You really do *care* for him."

Her words bring Rixton's face to my mind making me smile, "I really do."

"Then you're doing the right thing. You can never go wrong following your heart."

"I hope you're right."

"I am. And since you asked what I'm up to, Luke and I have a cake tasting appointment today, which should be fun. Luke's pretty excited at least."

"A cake tasting appointment? Wow, all of the things I'm learning from you during all this wedding planning are insane. I don't know how you keep up with it all."

"Um, have you seen my wedding magazine collection lately? You'd be afraid. Very, very afraid." I laugh, having no doubt she's correct. "So, has Rixton spoken to you yet about the bachelor and bachelorette party?"

"You mean other than briefly discussing potential venue and food and drink ideas that we were each thinking about? Not really. Only one concrete reservation made by me and none by Rixton that I know of. We did talk about you wanting a low key day at the spa followed by an intimate dinner with a few friends and he was telling me they might go bar hopping or something. He said he had suggested Vegas, but Luke declined and in fact, emphatically so. "

"Yeah, well, Luke convinced me that we should have a joint party."

"Really? How do you feel about that?"

"Fine, I guess. I mean I'd still like to do the day at the spa, but then afterwards we could all meet at the club and drink, dance to the DJ Luke wants to hire and hang out."

"Oh, so basically like every other time we're at the club?"

"Very funny, but yes. Only with close friends though. Not a huge crowd. Actually given its history for us, there's no place we'd rather celebrate our impending nuptials."

"Well, that sounds like fun."

"We always all have fun together so no doubt it will be. Luke told me he would rather spend our parties together than apart and I just couldn't say no. I didn't want to."

"Spoken like two love sick people." She laughs and I can't help but laugh with her. "Well, I have us all booked at the spa. We are starting off with massages, then facials, followed up with manicures and pedicures. Then we can use the beauty bar to get ready to go to the club. Sound good?"

"That sounds perfect! Aside from you obviously, I'm also going to invite my friends Cindy, Lauren, and Tami to join us. Will that be okay?"

"Absolutely. Just let me know if they are in for sure and then I'll make sure we are all booked accordingly."

"Okay, I will get in touch with them today."

"Are you sure you don't want me to call them for you. I feel like I'm not holding up my end of the bargain as your maid of honor."

"No, silly. I really want to ask them personally."

"Ok. Perfect, but I'm going to ask just one more time. Are you sure you want the group party? I mean… I did have the party bus, inappropriate party favors and strippers all planned out."

Olivia's booming laugh comes over the phone line because we both know that's the last thing she would want. She's way too low-key for that. Doing something like that would be so out of character, but certainly would surprise some people I'm sure. "It's really hard to say no to that, but I'm going to go with the party at Zero Gravity instead."

"Okay. Rixton and I take our roles as maid of honor and best man very seriously, so we will be sure to make your party one to remember. I promise."

"We know you will, and thank you for doing this."

"You betcha. I just expect you to return the favor someday."

"You got it!"

"Alright, well I'm going to run. I'm expecting a shipment in of our new skin care line any time and I need to finish up some book work so I can supervise its arrival and display in the gift shop. "

"Okay, talk later."

"Later, toots."

Ending the call, my thoughts turn to bachelorette party ideas. It's only a week away and a party at the club is a lot different than a spa day and relaxing dinner with friends like we had originally planned. I had made reservations at a fondue place that Olivia loves for dinner after the spa sessions, so I pick up the phone and cancel them. Scouring the internet, I start researching wedding, bachelorette, and other party ideas not having a clue about how to best bring this thing together. Hopefully, Rixton will have a few ideas up his sleeve when we put our heads together.

I jump, surprised, when one of my employees pops her head in the door, "Pyper? The shipment just arrived."

"Oh wow, already?" I look at the time and see more has passed than I realized. "Okay, I will be out in a moment. Will you please have them put the boxes on the counter in the shop please? Thank you."

"You got it."

Grabbing my phone, I decide to call Rixton real quick and give him a heads up of my impending arrival. It would be a shame if he has already eaten. When I get his voicemail I change my mind and decide to surprise him instead. "Hey, so Olivia was telling me about this joint bachelor and bachelorette party. Sounds like maybe we have some planning to do. I started doing a little bit of research. You have any ideas? Talk to you later. Bye."

Smiling I hang up and head out to unload some boxes.

Creating the desired display effect and putting all the remaining products in storage doesn't take as long as I anticipate. I'm really excited about this new product line. With the increasing push for more organic products, this line is exactly what our clients have been asking for. It's so much better for their skin, and I'm anxious to try the line myself.

Deciding that a quick trip to the club to see Rixton is just what the doctor ordered, I head to a sandwich shop and pick up a couple of items. Unsure of what Rixton might prefer, I do the obvious. I select one with lots of meat and one veggie and get all the available sides separately so he can add what he wants. Better safe than sorry they always say.

Pulling up to the club, I decide to park in the lot since I'm unsure how long I will be here. Walking into the club, balancing the large bag of food, I immediately search for Rixton behind the bar, but don't see him. My brow furrows wondering where he is. A few people call out hellos as I make my way to the current bartender, Jimmy, and I return the greetings.

It's so unusual to be in the club after hours. I pause and turn in a circle, taking in the atmosphere. It looks and sounds so different. It's a lot brighter with all the lights turned on. Of course, hardly anyone is here and any noise produces a slight echo effect. When the room is really filled up end to end, it's hard to appreciate just how nice the club is. The gorgeous chandeliers glisten and the white, blue and silver décor is even more eye catching. The easy furniture just yells to come, sit down and relax. Yep, how different it all looks when bodies aren't draped all over everything.

Smiling at Jimmy, I watch him clean a glass with a towel. "Hi Jimmy. Is Rixton around?" I gesture to the food in my hands as I place it on the bar. "I brought him lunch. Thought I could join him on break, but I don't see him."

Jimmy hesitates for a minute, "He's uh, in a meeting or something in Luke's office."

"Oh, okay. Shoot!" I tap my fingers on the bar wondering if I should wait around to see if he finishes up any time soon or just take my sandwich and head out. Would it look all stalkery weird of me to eat here at the bar like I'm just waiting around for him? Talk about looking desperate. That makes up my mind. "Do you have a paper and pen, Jimmy? I'll just leave him a note and this sandwich here if you wouldn't mind passing it on to him?"

"Sure, that's fine." He grabs a pad of paper and searches for a pen behind the bar making a triumphant noise when he locates one.

I'm in the middle of scribbling out a note when I hear a door slam at the top of the stairs, which catches my attention. I turn and see the same woman that almost ran me down the other day, angrily stomping down the stairs. I stare at her wide-eyed, shocked by her livid expression and angry eyes that are currently drilling into my own. She is seriously giving me a look of death. I get the distinct feeling I've done something to piss her off, but for the life of me I have no idea. She continues to hold my stare all the way down the stairs, until she passes me and heads toward the door to leave.

Confused, I look to the top of the stairs and see Rixton standing there, massaging his temples. Walking over to the bottom of the stairs, note and food forgotten, I hesitantly call his name, "Rixton?"

His head snaps up and his eyes widen when he sees me. I get the feeling he's not sure if he should approach me, as I see a look of uncertainty cross his face. I begin walking up the stairs, and he eventually walks half way to meet me, touching the side of my face with a small, sad smile. "What's wrong?' I don't know what the hell happened and I'm not sure what rights I have to ask, and certainly have no rights to demand that I'm told, but he's the one who said he wanted honesty. So again I prompt, "Are you okay?"

He holds my eyes for a few beats, then looks down and nervously wipes his hands on his pants. He gestures behind him, "Let's go into Luke's office." I silently follow him, worry churning in my tummy and making me feel nauseous. We take a seat on the couch and face one another. I stay silent, waiting for him to tell me what's going on. He holds my eyes for a few beats, looks away, then back again. The look on his face is indecipherable and I feel my own hands start to sweat in nervousness. His eyes are churning pools of emotion. I'm about to ask him again what's going on, but he finally asks, "Remember when I told you I would never lie to you?"

I nod my head, "Yes, I remember."

"I won't." He grabs hold of my hands and squeezes them tightly. "If there is one thing that I can promise you, it's that I will not lie to you. When I said that I want there to at least be that between us, it's because honestly is important to me. I need you to know that."

I nod my head, not sure if there is anything else to say to that.

He hesitates, but doesn't let go of my hands. If anything, he's squeezing them tighter. "I know you are curious about the woman that left here. I know you saw her the other day, and I don't know if you overheard anything…"

"I didn't really hear anything. I just heard the door slam when I was down at the bar and it drew my attention."

A look that can only be described as relief crosses his face, but it's short lived. He swallows a few times in clear uneasiness and at this point, I don't know what to think. "I need to ask something of you, and I recognize that it may not be easy for you to give, but I'm going to ask it anyway."

"Okay," I respond drawing out the word, sure my expression is clearly displaying the apprehension, if not near panic, I'm feeling.

"I promise that eventually I will answer your questions. I will explain, and share, and answer anything you want me to, but I'm not ready to do that yet. Not today. Maybe not tomorrow. But soon."

"Rixton, I don't understand," I respond, pulling my hands away from his.

He runs his hands through his hair in exasperation. It's something I've never seen him do. It's clear he's distressed, and I have no clue not only why, but what I can do about it – if anything. He blows out a breath and looks back at me, "I'm sorry, Red. I know you don't. Believe me, I know. But I need you to try and understand that for now, I have something going on, and when I'm ready, I will talk to you about it, okay?"

Watching him, I take in the pleading look on his face, the tiny bit of sweat I see on his brow. This is really bothering him; is serious for him. He's watching every move I make, taking in every expression. Before I realize it, I'm nodding my head in agreement. "Okay. I can respect that. For now."

"You can?"

I almost laugh at the disbelief in his voice. It's clear that is not how he expected me to answer. "Yes, I can. I appreciate you being honest and telling me right now you can't or won't tell me about this. I mean, we are still getting to know each other, right? How do you even know you can trust me? You don't have to tell me everything. I get it."

His face falls, "No, darlin', no. It's not about that. I trust you. I really do. I just… I can't talk about this with you yet. You'll understand when I explain, but please, please don't think it's because I'm still trying to figure out how I feel about you or that I don't want this. It has *nothing* to do with that."

"Okay. I trust you. We'll talk about it when you're ready. Just… can you answer one thing?" His look holds trepidation but he nods his head. "Are you married?"

He blows out a breath he must have been holding and a laugh bursts out of him. "No. No, darlin', it's nothing like that. I'm not married."

"Not drugs either, right? Because I can't handle that."

"Not drugs," he smiles.

"Okay then."

"Okay?"

"Yes. I just needed to make sure, because if that was your wife or something, I don't want any part of that what so ever. No matter how much I may like you."

Rixton laughs, but it sounds forced, "Understood." He cups the side of my face, does his signature move of putting my hair behind my ear, then places a soft kiss on my mouth. "You're amazing. You know that right?"

"That's what I've heard," I tell him with a smile trying to wipe away the worry that's festering in my mind.

chapter
18

WE CRUMBLE UP OUR SANDWICH WRAPPERS, and toss the trash away. Rixton went and grabbed the bag from Happy's from the bar, pleased and impressed with my thoughtfulness. While we were eating, Luke came back and saw us eating in his office, but didn't seem to even notice. He came in, grabbed something off his desk, and left again. Or perhaps he has merely learned not to look in our direction, I think, as a smile crosses my face.

"Thanks again, for bringing these. It was really kind of you to even think about doing something like this for me."

"Well, it wasn't just for you. I admit to having an alternative motive."

"Oh?"

I smile shyly, "Yes. I wanted to see you."

A slow, lazy smile crosses his face. Patting his leg in an invitation for me to sit there, I look him up and down and take in how scrumptious he looks today. The man should be illegal. With a smile, I pop up off the couch, and sit in his lap, making myself comfortable. He puts my legs across his lap and snuggles my side up against him. Running his hand up and down my back, he asks, "How has your day been so far?"

I tell him about the shipment that arrived at the spa and other boring stuff that I'm surprised isn't putting him to sleep, but instead he listens with rapt attention. I can't help but think about how nice this is. Not only the affection he's showing me but also sharing my life like this with someone is extremely intimate and nice.

"Oh! By the way…"

Rixton raises an eyebrow, "Yes?"

"I spoke to Olivia today and she mentioned that the separate parties we were planning for the fools have now become a joint bachelor and bachelorette party?"

"That's what I hear. Luke told me the same thing."

"Well I was thinking it probably makes the most sense for us to just plan this thing together."

"Yeah, I agree," he starts running his hand through my hair. "It will make things easier now too I suppose. I mean, Luke said he'll make sure the bar is fully stocked, which is awesome. So, we can have a cash bar and everyone can pay for their drinks just as they would have if we went out. Wouldn't be right for Luke to pick up the tab at his own party. And if he doesn't sell the stock that night, he will during business hours."

"Yes, I agree. Plus, it will likely be less expensive for the guests per drink and with no bar cover charge now. We can select a menu that will appeal to both the girls and guys, and we can use one of the regular bands if they are willing. It should be enjoyable, still a bit more low-key in harmony with Olivia's preference, while meeting the objective of a joint party. And not that expensive or difficult for us."

Rixton nods in agreement. "Good thing we were going to work together to figure this out," he says with his drawl and a bit of sarcasm.

"Oops. Sorry. Habit. Bad habit. So, what would you suggest we do? Those were all merely thoughts."

He laughs. "Sounds like a plan to me. I guess. Just giving you a rough time."

We both pause, looking at each other in that familiar way. "Are you sure you're okay with this? Do you think this is a bad idea?"

"Well not exactly, but, yeah, kind of. From a guy's point of view, anyway. I mean the point of a bachelor party is to have one night out with the guys. The last day of being single, to cause trouble and get in trouble. Having girls around kind of ruins it. No offense."

I raise an eyebrow giving him a dirty look, "Oh, I take offense alright. I think it is a stupid old fashioned out dated tradition. I hate the idea. I mean, what? A guy decides that since he is going to be," I use air quotes to accent my next point, "tied down with one wonderful girl – and especially in this situation, with one the guy is very fortunate to be marrying – that they need one night of freedom to" – and my air quotes get turned on again, "act single? News flash, they aren't. They haven't been since they made the commitment in the first place. That whole bad boy bachelor party shit is seriously lame."

"Oh, so you don't have any opinion on this, huh?" mocking my usage of air quotes by providing his version when he says the word opinion. "Maybe it's dumb – excuse me, lame," and his hands do air quotes again, "to you, but that's the way it is. The way it's been for generations. All of my married friends had bachelor parties that were freaking epic. And, respectfully, I do not say that merely because I helped plan many of them either. "

"You are such an arrogant ass."

"What's your point? You know I try my best to be the image of arrogance. And you love it."

Rolling my eyes, I decide it's best not to comment. "So just what kind of *entertainment* were you going to do when you thought you were planning Luke's party with just the guys?" I avoid making air quotes by holding tightly onto my hands.

"I can't tell you all my secrets."

"Yes, clearly," I let slip before I think twice. I shouldn't have said that. I told him I understand. So instead, I try to give him my best sexy look, "I have ways to get them out of you."

A wicked grin crosses his face making me happy, "You think so, huh? I wouldn't mind seeing some of these ways of yours."

Deciding it is best to leave this topic behind, taking him by surprise, I turn toward him, straddling his lap. I teasingly run my lips up and down his neck, and nibble on his ear, smiling when he groans. I kiss my way up his jaw, then kiss him, putting everything I have into it. I grab fistfuls of his hair, yank his head to the side, and give him all I've got. My lips are firm and demanding, taking control of the kiss and his pleasure. I rake my nails down his chest, making him gasp, then I claim his breath as my own before breaking off the kiss with a smile.

He slowly opens his eyes, tries to talk and it comes out as a squeak. He clears his throat and tries again. "Well, of course I was going to take him to a stripper joint. That's like the way it should be."

"Well how about we do this? I will be in charge of the entertainment for the bridesmaids and you can be in charge for the entertainment for the groomsmen. Sound like a deal?

"Sounds like a good idea to me."

I look him in the face and laugh in it. "Plus you wouldn't be able to handle my level of fun anyway," I tease.

"Are you sure about that, darlin'?"

"Oh, absolutely," I reply, smiling, "I'm totally right and you are definitely wrong on this one."

"We'll see about that. In fact, care to place a wager on that?"

"What do you mean," I hesitate.

"I bet you, my entertainment will go over better than yours. Much better than yours. If I'm right and I win, then you have to do anything I want."

"Anything you want?"

"For a whole day."

This makes me nervous, "What exactly will that consist of?"

"You'll have to wait and see."

"Fine. I will take that bet. And the same goes if I win."

"Okay. Challenge accepted." We reach for each other's hands and shake on it with a laugh. Then Rixton pulls me in for a kiss. "It's only good if we seal the deal with a kiss." I laugh indulging in his request.

Later at home I smile, thinking of what a surprise Rixton has been. He's everything I never thought I wanted, and I can't wait to continue to find more out about him. And even more amazing is the fact that I'm not panicking about how I feel. I'm not second guessing it. For the first time in forever, I'm going with what I want to do. No help, no expectations, no requirements – just one day at a time.

I'm distracted from my thoughts by a knock on my door. After looking through the peep hole, I open it to my father standing on the other side. Swinging the door fully open, I look at him in confusion. My father doesn't come by very often. I usually go to his place. "Daddy?"

"Pyper," he says with a slight nod, his mouth in a straight line, and I know immediately by his tone, he's not happy. "May I come in, please?

"Of course. You are always welcome to come here. You know that, daddy."

Stepping into my condo, he takes a quick look around and I immediately feel intimidated by his larger than life presence. Giving him a hug, that he returns stiffly, I offer to take his coat. He looks me up and down with clear loathing and I instantly regret the sweats and t-shirt I'm wearing. My oversized, comfortable, lounging clothes. Then I push that thought aside as silly. I'm in my own home, I can dress how I want to.

As I hang his coat in the hall closet, he walks past me into the living room and stands. Legs slightly apart, straight back, in front of the large window, overlooking the city below. I hesitantly walk into the room, recognizing the tension in his posture, readying myself for whatever he's here for. I know his excessively annoyed posture when I see it. Without turning, he addresses me, "Would you care to tell me why it is you thought it was okay to abandon the son of one of my best clients at the country club?" When he slowly turns to look at me, my stomach drops as his eyes, stormy as thunderclouds, bore into my own. "I'm sure you have a sensible explanation, because let me assure you, I refuse to believe the reason I was given."

My stomach drops. I shouldn't be surprised. What did I think was going to happen when he found out? And I knew he would find out.

Without giving me a chance to respond to his question, he barrels on. "I was told that you left R.J. at the table, presumably to use the restroom, only to come back with another man." He pauses here and gives me a look that screams disbelief and displeasure. "Another man that you then proceeded to leave the restaurant with; leaving my client's son to fend for himself. But only after creating a mess and a scene."

Feeling his words like a punch in the gut, I swallow before replying, "Dad, I can explain."

"You bet you're going to explain this to me, Pyper, because for the life of me, I have no goddamn clue what the hell you were thinking."

Wringing my hands together, I have no idea how to begin to explain. I know that each explanation running through my mind will be viewed as inadequate justification, implausible, and mere rationalization. No answer would be good enough for him. "I didn't intend for that to happen... you see..."

Interrupting, my father continues, "You've been instructed from the time you were a little girl how to behave around my clients, and you know damn well what is expected of you. What *I* expect of you. Care to explain to me why you seem to have forgotten the rules?"

God, I'm actually cringing and cowering like a child at him, an abused child. How pathetic am I? "Father, I didn't mean to-"

"That doesn't change the fact that you did. Now tell me, who is this man that had to borrow a jacket from the club and who you allowed to practically kidnap you from dinner according to R.J.?"

"Rixton didn't kidnap-"

"Rixton? That's his name? What kind of a name is that? Who is he? I don't recall any of my associates having a son by that name, and I'm certain I would remember. And they would certainly all know better. How did you meet?"

"He's a friend of Olivia and Luke's," I lie throwing in the Olivia part because of how much he and my mother love her. "He was just surprised to see me there with R.J., and-"

"Forget the pitiful attempt at explaining, Pyper. Better yet, I want you to bring Rixton over for dinner so your mother and I can ask him these questions and others."

My stomach immediately tightens into knots. I already asked Rixton to meet my parents, but I didn't know it was going to be under these circumstances. My dad clearly has enough preconceived notions based on what happened at the country club to make that a night to remember. This is a nightmare. "Well actually, I just asked him if he would meet you and mother."

His eyebrows rise as he continues to stare at me, taking in my twisting hands and nervous posture. "Oh, so you think it's that serious is it?"

"Serious?" I stare at him, all thoughts having left me. This is the worst conversation to have – ever.

"No matter," he pulls his phone from his pocket and clicks at it, "I have to be out of town for business, but I would like you to call your mother and schedule dinner sometime after the next week. The sooner, the better."

Anger begins to rise over the humiliation. He's treating me like I'm a mere business associate and this is one of his business meetings, "I will check my calendar and determine if that time frame works for me as well." Two can play at this game, I determine.

He stares me down and I instantly regret the slight defiance, and I hate myself. I become a shadow of myself around him – whether he behaves like this or not. "Make it work." He grabs his coat from the closet and tosses it over his arm. After he gives me an air kiss toward my cheek he breezes out the door, taking all of the tension with him and allowing me to breathe again.

Collapsing onto the couch, I put my head in my hands and feel my eyes fill with tears. I know my father loves me – I really do – but he has a shitty way of showing it. He does things like buy me a spa and car and a freaking condo to show me, but I would rather have the occasional hug just because – not because I'm coming or going. Or a phone call just because.

Suddenly feeling exhausted, I go to my bed and lie down. Staring at the ceiling, I go over the conversation with my father over and over and feel angry with myself for giving into his bullying, and also for not just telling him more about Rixton and getting it over with.

My phone beeps on the table next to my bed and I pick it up, looking at the screen. It's a text from Rixton – "Just spoke to Luke, party in a couple weeks. Also, spoke to him about our challenge – just want to give you one more chance to back out, being the gentleman I am."

Smiling, I immediately type back, "Wow, scared already, cowboy?"

His reply is immediate, "Not a chance, Red."

Setting my phone down, my thoughts are now filled with Rixton. Reflecting on our conversation today I admit I'm nervous about whatever is going on that he doesn't want to talk about. I try to force an understanding of why he doesn't want to tell me right now. But it feels like a bit of an insult. We seemed to be making so much progress. I want him to feel like he can talk to me about anything. And, in truth, I just want to know because I'm flat out curious. It's obviously not good. It is clearly distressing him. And the woman that I keep seeing just looks like trouble. Innumerable possibilities come to mind as my imagination flips into high gear. Considering the plausibility of each, I try to dismiss each one. Nervousness and anxiety consume me. To deflect, I make an effort to turn my thoughts to better things. The way Rixton holds me when he kisses me – tight, like he doesn't want to ever let me go. The way his southern accent can get my blood pumping with just a few words. His different smiles – teasing, flirty, wicked and just plain sexy. Here, in the dark, confronted with nothing but pure self-disclosure and honesty while thoughts of Rixton consume me, I admit that Rixton is worth more than displeasure from my dad – in fact, my heart says he is priceless. My dad can learn how to deal with new facts and a new reality. I'm not so sure at this point, I can deal with being without Rixton. He's already left too much of an impression. My heart wants him more than anything.

chapter 19

"I'M REALLY NOT SURE ABOUT THIS," Olivia looks down at herself, scrutinizing the white body suit she's wearing. It covers all the important parts, and cuts diagonally across one shoulder leaving the other one exposed. It's lined so no one can see through it, but its tight fit certainly doesn't leave anything to the imagination.

After walking over to her, I reach up and make sure the small white veil with crown is pinned tightly to her head. It needs to endure some serious hair whipping. "Stop worrying. You look marvelous. This is going to be great. And fun. We've gone over and over the routine and we've got it down perfectly. Rixton and his band of misfits are soooo going down."

"Hey! One of those misfits is my husband-to-be."

"Yes, I'm aware, and you know he's just as guilty as Rixton."

"Yeah, that's undoubtedly true."

"That's why this is going to be perfect. They are so sure our choice of entertainment is going to suck. Aren't they going to be in for a huge surprise?!" I smile wide when I think about the look that will appear on Rixton's face. No way can he top this. No. Way.

Olivia sighs and fidgets with her hair for a moment before she drops her hands and surveys me from head to toe. "At least yours covers both of your shoulders. What if my boob falls out?"

"Your boob won't fall out."

"We look kind of slutty." She tugs at the top of her bodysuit insecurely.

"Why are you glaring at me when you say that?" My hands are on my hips and I realize I'm in total defensive bitch mode. The thought makes me beam. "We are basically wearing the same thing. Yours is white and only slightly different – more special – because you're the woman of the night."

"Well, we both look slutty then."

"Whatever. That's kind of the point. And we look awesome. The guys are going to love it."

Olivia smiles and I know she's thinking of Luke's reaction to her attire and her upcoming moves. "Yes, that is definitely true."

I turn and smile excitedly at Olivia's other friends, Cindy, Tami and Lauren. I guess they've also become my friends too by association, which is great because I really like them. We've had fun getting together to work on our dance number. "You look great! I'm so glad you are doing this with us!"

"Thanks for asking us!" Cindy responds with a smile and squeeze to my arm.

"Yes, I'm excited. This will be a lot of fun," Tami answers while fixing the pin in Lauren's hair. Their enthusiasm and smiles are infectious. I admire them in their black bodysuits and stilettos, identical to mine. Yep. We are going to rock this.

The engagement party has been a success. Luke closed Zero Gravity for the night, which in itself is amazing and special. The club is always slammed with people, and there is always a line of people waiting to get in all night long, especially on the weekends. There's no doubt he's losing a lot of money tonight, but he would do anything to make Olivia happy. Putting Olivia first is automatic for him. And, I think he is equally happy to be honoring his upcoming nuptials. Nearly everyone we invited was able to attend, so there's a fairly sizable crowd of people for the joint party, and most importantly, everyone seems to be having a really good time.

As planned, Luke supplied all the alcohol via a cash bar, Rixton and I were able to get a well-known and highly admired caterer and the food has been simple, but yummy. They provided an array of food that appealed to both genders: fruit trays, veggie trays, crab puffs, various hot and cold cheese spreads, crackers, mini pizzas, cocktail meatballs and sausages, quiches, shrimp cocktail and varied meat skewers. The desserts and chocolate fountain are insane, and so delicious.

There are no wall flowers here. The conversations and interactions have been non-stop. Both the food and the alcohol have been consumed with abandon. The music has had everyone tapping their foot, swaying, or singing to themselves or their dates. A few brave souls have littered the dance floor. Everyone seems to be truly enjoying the evening and being together. And Luke and Olivia have shared a multitude of giggles, laughs and smiles and seem to be reveling in the spotlight. There's a large table with gifts for Olivia from the girls, but nothing for Luke from the guys. I guess guys don't do that — they're so weird. They must think it uncool or something, although it doesn't appear that Luke's paid for a drink all night. Guess that is how they provide gifts. No doubt most, if not all, of Olivia's presents contain lingerie. She wants to open them at home in private later without all the men around. Can't say I blame her.

Olivia and I elected to forgo the usual bachelorette paraphernalia since the men are here. Somehow lipsticks, candy, suckers, chocolates, and a cake all in the shape of a penis just don't seem as much fun when there are real penises in the room.

Rixton approached me a little while ago and asked if my entertainment vendors were ready and that we could get started anytime. He has no clue that we are the entertainers and will be performing and I can't wait to see the look on his face. He offered me to go first using his best Texas drawl when he twanged "ladies first, darlin'." Seriously, sometimes he doesn't give me enough credit. He was full of conceit and sarcasm, but I am convinced he's just covering up his edginess. He wants to check out the competition and possibly even concede to our awesomeness once he realizes he can't beat us.

Turning back to Olivia, I give her my best confident smile. "This will be fantastic. Besides, we've been practicing practically non-stop – we've totally got this. I'm *so* going to win! I'm going to be legendary. Tonight will be known forever as the night Pyper kicked Rixton's ass." Olivia glares at me, "Uh, I mean we. *We* are so going to win and be famous. Uh, and surprise them for sure!" For good measure, I add in my best optimistic, encouraging manner, "And you will give Luke an engagement present he will never forget."

Walking out onto the stage, we each take our place. Olivia is in the center, with Lauren and I on one side of her, and Cindy and Tami on the other. The band is across the room allowing us full use of the stage. We have plenty of room. Impatiently, we wait for the curtain to rise. When it does, we stand facing the crowd. People – lots of them – appear to be all over the room. Some have plates or beverages in hand. Most stop in mid- activity and gaze up at the stage, appearing to curiously wonder why the music has stopped and what is happening. Some start to whisper. I immediately look for Rixton and find him with Luke, leaning against the bar staring wide-eyed and mouth agape at the stage.

Olivia tosses me a smile and in that instant I know whatever apprehension she had has been replaced with excitement and enthusiasm. No doubt seeing the look on our men's faces has given her a boost of confidence. Our men. Is Rixton mine? Shaking my head, I let go of that thought and focus back on Rixton with a smirk on my face. The look on his face is priceless. All of us are standing here in full hair, makeup, bodysuits that leave little to the imagination, and stilettos. I know damn well we look hot –very hot indeed.

Smiling back at Olivia, I quickly put a serious look on my face as Beyonce's "Single Ladies" starts playing right on queue. We immediately start shaking our hips to the beat and as the song plays, dance our asses off. We may not be Beyonce – I mean who is? – that woman is one of a kind – but we can shake our asses with the best of them. After I had this idea and Olivia concurred, rapidly, I might add, she came to my condo every chance she had and we spent hours learning the dance from the video. Once we got it down, we had Tami, Lauren and Cindy meet us after hours in the yoga room at the spa and taught it to them. It was hard work, but we all mastered it – learned the damn thing to perfection. We incorporated as much of Beyonce's dance as we could, hair flips and all. When things were a bit over the top, we created our own moves, and the result is a piece of art and beauty.

When we get to the part of the song where we are shaking our hands to, "If you liked it then you should've put a ring on it," the crowd raises their voices and are screaming and cheering for us. I look at Rixton whenever possible and giggle to myself. At one point, they seem to have disappeared, but I find them again – right below the stage. They apparently needed an up-close and personal view. Their mouths continue to hang open, which makes me want to shake it harder, shamelessly tantalizing him, and because the dance moves so fast, I have to work hard to keep myself from laughing or I'll mess up.

When the song ends, we are breathless, panting, and laughing. We gather around one another, "We did it!" Olivia yells! "I'm so happy I didn't mess up."

"I know! I was so nervous, but then the music and crowd made it so fun. " Tami says wiping off her sweaty brow with the back of her hand.

"That was so awesome," Cindy gives me a half hug and we all readily agree.

"And look Olivia, your crown stayed on the whole time. I told you it would be perfect," Lauren reminds her.

"Yes, definitely perfect. Mission definitely accomplished," I agree.

I'm smiling and listening to Tami talk to Olivia about a part where she almost lost her balance and was afraid she was going to trip when I feel arms encircle me from behind and lips at my ear, "That was so fucking hot. I think we should leave right the hell now."

Feeling the evidence of his pleasure, I take a second to press into it before turning around. Grinning, I can't help but tease, "Rixton, darlin', you should probably just admit defeat right now. I completely understand that you can't top that. I mean, really… who could? Nothing is better than Beyonce. She's in a class all her own."

"That may be, *darlin'*, but I don't admit defeat that easily." He raises a brow at me and smiles his killer smile and all I can think about is how I want to jump his bones. Badly. Very badly. Now.

"You know… I won't think less of you. We should just leave. Right now. Who knows, maybe we wouldn't even make it all the way home. I haven't had sex in a car in years. That could be a lot of fun."

Rixton growls softly and kisses me, "Stop trying to distract me. That's a game foul. After that number, all I can think about is leaving too, but no. I would never live it down."

Pouting, I pull away a little, "Fine. Party pooper."

"Oh darlin' there will be a party, just not right now." His words excite me. All over. "I have to admit, I'm surprised," Rixton says pulling me out of my racy thoughts.

"Surprised? You mean because you didn't know I could move my hips and flip my hair like that?"

"Now darlin', you know better than that. I've seen you move those hips like that up close and personal. I'm kind of jealous everyone in the room got to see you move like that too."

"Ha. Ha." I roll my eyes but can't keep the smile from my face.

"What I meant was that I'm surprised that you chose that routine as your entertainment. I confess I was expecting a magician or illusionist or some other Vegas type performer. Something a tad more … cheesy."

"A magic show? Really?"

He shrugs his shoulders, "Maybe a nice competitive game of beer pong? Or spin the bottle?"

"Thanks. Thanks a lot. Guess you don't know me all that well after all." I playfully pull away from him, "I need to go change."

Rixton's smile falls from his face, "What? Why? Is that really necessary? You look fine. Better than fine."

"You don't want me to change?"

A wicked smile appears on his lips, "No. No I don't. I quite enjoy the thoughts that getup provides and anyway, I have plans for removing that outfit myself."

I feel a flush come over my cheeks and suddenly, the appropriateness or lack thereof, is not of concern. Rather, my mind is distracted with all kinds of naughty ideas. And teasing him in this costume may add additional fun to this evening. Something that was not a part of my plan. My thoughts briefly turn to the cool temperature awaiting us when we leave the club later, but I only smile, thinking of how that cold air could add to the night. In fact, the assault of cool air may feel good on my flushed skin, especially if Rixton keeps looking at me with such wicked lust.

"I suppose I don't have to change," I give in with a smile that he returns. "When are you guys starting your entertainment?"

"Soon."

"Give me a hint. What do you have planned? Maybe you're the ones going to start a rousing game of beer pong."

His grin widens and he runs his hand through his hair, "I suggest you go get a good seat, Red." He slaps me on the ass, making me release a squeak in surprise. I laugh and turn to find Olivia who is relaxing in Luke's arms with his face buried in her neck. Smiling, I head off the stage entrance and walk to the bar to get a drink.

Drink in hand, I turn to look around the room when Olivia comes up next to me asking the bartender for the same drink I'm enjoying. I turn to look at her and see she's still in her outfit too. I laugh. "Not changing either, huh?"

"Um, no. Luke asked me not to."

I laugh harder, "Rixton asked me to keep it on too."

We laugh and then take our drinks to a table and sit, feeling a little break is deserved after our booty shaking. Who knew shaking your ass could be so tiring? People come up to our table and tell us they liked our performance and congratulate Olivia on her upcoming nuptials. She's full of smiles and happiness and it makes my heart feel full. I never tire of seeing her this way. "Can you believe you and Luke will finally get married in a couple months? Where has the time gone?"

"I know. Some days I feel like it can't get here fast enough and other times I'm afraid there isn't enough time to get the last things finished."

"You know that if I can help with anything…"

"I know and really there isn't anything you can do or rather, need to do. My mom's enjoying helping with all the arrangements and we are thrilled to be doing it all together. It's a little hard with her being long distance, but you'd be surprised what phone calls, emails, and texts can accomplish when it comes to wedding planning."

Before we can say more, the music stops and the stage curtain rises.

chapter 20

ON THE STAGE BEFORE US LUKE is wearing a suit and tie. Their friend Darrin is wearing a fireman outfit, Jimmy the bartender is dressed like a police officer, Sean is wearing a construction worker get up and Rixton – whoa. Rixton is dressed in distressed jeans, a sleeveless flannel with a vest over it, a belt with a large buckle and a cowboy hat and boots. My mouth salivates. Holy shit, it's Rixton in full cowboy get up. All he needs are chaps. Where are the chaps?

"Oh my God," Olivia whispers.

I nod my head in agreement, then look at Olivia, "What is this? Are they going to start lip-synching to the Village People's YMCA?"

Olivia only has eyes for Luke and I look away from her and back at Rixton to find him staring right at me. His thumbs are hooked into the front pockets of his jeans and he looks completely comfortable up there. My gaze rakes him from head-to-toe and I uncross and re-cross my legs, trying to ease the fire between them at the sight of him. He's too far away to know for sure, but I can almost see the heat flashing in his eyes. He knows what he's doing to me.

Like a magnet, our gazes are drawn to one another and we can't look away. I unconsciously lick my lips and he smirks in response.

We are forced to look away from one another when the music starts playing. The music is a far cry from Village People's YMCA – it's "Pour Some Sugar on Me" by Def Leppard. It's pure sex music!

My brows go up automatically, "What are they…" the words fall from my lips as soon as they start dancing. And by dancing I mean sexy dancing. And by sexy dancing, I mean doing things on stage that should only be seen in the bedroom – running hands down their bodies, thrusting their hips, and some of them are starting to unbutton articles of their clothing.

"Oh. My. God." I can't even glance at Olivia to see her reaction because I can't look away from the stage. Physically can't. My eyes are glued to the sight before me.

I hear Olivia comment, "I second that 'oh my God' and raise you a holy fuck."

I make a noise to confirm my agreement to that statement. Rixton is like every girl's wet dream come to life. Well… maybe not every girl, but certainly mine. He swivels his hips from side to side and slowly removes his vest letting it fall to the ground. "Instead of Magic Mike, it's freaking Magic Rixton."

"And Magic Luke," Olivia agrees.

"I can't believe they are doing this."

"I wouldn't either, except for the fact that it is happening right in front of us," Olivia puts her hand over her mouth when Luke's tie hits her lap. "Pyper, I hate to say it, but I think they are going to win the bet."

Rixton takes his hat off and flings it at me with a wink. It lands at my feet and I lean down to pick it up, and then plop it onto my head. "I think you're right about that. And I have to say, it's a bet that I don't mind losing after all."

Olivia and I look at each other and giggle like teenage girls. Quickly looking back up, I do so just in time to find Rixton removing his belt, then watch as his fingers begin working the buttons of his shirt. "No way. No way he's going to seriously take his shirt off. Olivia, are they taking off their clothes?"

"I don't know about anyone else at the moment, but Luke has taken off his suit jacket and is fiddling with the buttons of his shirt." Her voice sounds strained.

"Oh God," I say as a button on Rixton's shirt, then another, and another start coming undone. There are girls throughout the crowd going crazy. I can hear them yelling, "Rixton, over here baby!"

"Take it off!" someone yells.

"Mama loves cowboys," another yells.

"Bring that meat stick over here!" A girl in front with blonde hair and way too much makeup hollers and all I can think is 'ew.' Seriously, what is wrong with people?

There's a small group of women at the bottom of the stage hooting and hollering. They are doing anything short of stripping themselves to get the attention of the men on the stage. A wave of possessiveness washes over me and I'm not sure how to feel about that. I never get this way and it kind of pisses me off. One thing is for sure; I don't like the fact that other women here are looking at Rixton wanting to sex him up. I want to run up on stage and pee on him or something to stake my claim. My brow furrows in annoyance at the thought, but then quickly flees when Rixton undoes the top button of his jeans. "Holy hell."

"I'm going to see your 'holy hell' and raise you...."

"I know, I know." I'd laugh but it would just catch in my throat. "He's really not going to..."

Suddenly, surprisingly, simultaneously... all the guys pull at the front of their pants and they break away, leaving all of them in tight briefs.

Olivia and I look at each other again, mouths hanging open in shock. I can't believe they are doing this. They even bought special costumes for their routine obviously. I love it. The screaming gets louder and even the guys in the audience are heckling the guys too. As one they all turn and put their backs to the crowd and shake their fine asses. Olivia and I giggle, unable to help ourselves. Luke's briefs say 'GROOM' on them and Rixton's say 'BEST MAN' and the other's say 'GROOMSMAN'. It's hilarious.

Thank the lord that the dance ends there. There are women shaking dollars in their hands, but Rixton and Luke ignore them and make their way to us. Darrin, Sean and Jimmy approach the eager women, no doubt going to capitalize on their fifteen minutes and try to score tonight. They are single guys after all, can't say I blame them.

I'm just glad the women are preoccupied with them and no longer after Rixton. Am I possessive? Yes, definitely, and proud of it. Rixton is pure man candy, and he's all mine. I stand when he reaches the table and put my arms around him, "What did you think, darlin'?"

"I think you totally won our bet, that's what I think."

"Yeah?" He has a boyish grin on his face and I just want to climb up him like a freaking monkey and have my way with him. I'm so turned on, it's ridiculous.

"Yes. Definitely."

He gives me a peck on the mouth, but it's not enough. Not nearly enough. I groan in frustration and Rixton chuckles. "You know what that means then, right?"

"What are you talking about?"

"Well you remember the terms of our bet, right?"

"Remind me."

"Anything that I want for a whole day."

"Ah yes, I do seem to remember something about that." I bite my lip my mind turning with thoughts of what his wishes will consist of. "Care to tell me what you have in mind?"

"I will, actually. We are going to spend a whole day together…"

"Yes," I ask breathless waiting for him to end the sentence with 'in bed'.

"At the rodeo."

I swear I hear screeching like a record being scratched by a needle in my mind, whipping me out of my lustful thoughts, "Say what?"

"Oh yes. There is a rodeo competition coming to town about an hour south of here. We're going."

"That is what you want to do with your day? A whole day that I will do anything you want? Emphasis on anything?"

"Yep," he responds popping the 'p'.

"You are a sick, sick man, Rixton Andrews."

He gives me a knock out grin, "You are going to love it. We will have a blast."

Sighing, I look at him doubtfully. "Can I have a condition?"

"No. You lost. I get what I want." I give him my best sexy, pouty face making him smile, "Okay let's hear it but no promises."

Pressing my body against his, I lean close to him and almost touch my lips to his, "Can you wear the same thing you wore on stage to the rodeo? Minus the breakaway jeans of course, replaced with normal ones."

Rixton laughs and places a kiss on my mouth, "I reckon I can do that just for you darlin'," he drawls.

Shivers run over my body at his accent, "How much longer do you want to stay?"

"Ready to leave already?"

"Hell yes. After seeing that dance, I just want to get the hell out of here."

Laughing, we look around the room and realize people are already leaving. Thank God it doesn't take long for them to clear out except for a few stragglers that the bartenders are going to escort out before they lock up. Rixton takes my hand, we turn to Luke and Olivia to tell them goodnight but see they are too wrapped up in each other to pay attention to anything else. Rixton and I get our things and head out.

When we get to my place, we don't waste any time pretending that our intentions are other than the obvious. We eagerly stride directly to my bedroom. We close the door behind us, although with Olivia officially moved out, it's not really necessary. I turn to Rixton, "That was one hell of a show you put on tonight, but I was wondering?"

He raises an eyebrow, "Yeah?"

"Can I get my own private show?"

With a laugh Rixton pushes me to sit on the bed while he slowly does a strip tease for me. Music must be playing in his mind because he rhythmically moves to an obvious beat that only he can hear. It must be one hell of a tune!

I giggle when he throws his shirt at my head, "Woo hoo cowboy, give me more!"

Chuckling, he makes a show out of removing the rest of his clothes and then beckons to me. I stand and walk to him. "Let's get you out of yours now."

Rixton scans every inch of my body again and I feel like I'm already bared before him. He traces the outline of my body with his fingertip making me shiver. "When I saw you in this on stage, all I could think about was getting this off of you. It doesn't leave a lot to the imagination. It forms the full roundness of your breasts, hugs your sweet ass, and shows off those gorgeous legs of yours. My God, do you have any idea what it did to me to see you in this? You're gorgeous, Red. So gorgeous."

As he bares my skin, he places gentle kisses there. I'm shivering with excitement. As he undresses me, he does it with such precision and so much care that it feels like an erotic dance in itself. It isn't easy peeling my bodysuit off, but he doesn't seem to mind. . As he removes my bra and I step into his body, he groans when my skin touches his. He runs the tips of his fingers down my back, stopping to knead in places, and I release a moan of pleasure of my own. I've had probably hundreds of massages but none of them have ever felt as good as the one he's giving me now. This is sheer ecstasy.

Standing in nothing but a black lace thong, I tremble with excitement and need when he hooks his thumbs inside my panties on either side of my hips. He slowly slides them down my body one inch at a time. He places a kiss on my stomach, on the inside of my thigh and even my knee as he lowers himself to help me step out of them. "We're leaving these on," he says referring to my black stilettos, making me laugh.

"Oh yeah? Like them do you?"

"Hell yes, but wait, I forgot one thing." He picks up his cowboy hat off the floor behind him, and places it on my head. "There, that's perfect."

I can't help but giggle at the sight I must create in this get up – me in nothing but a hat and stilettos. "Fantasy of yours?"

"One of many. And I can't wait to experience them all with you."

He eases me back on the bed and I scoot to the top, with him following. Once we reach our destination, I push on his shoulder, telling him to lie on his back. . Straddling his hips, cowboy hat still in place – at least for now – I slide up and down his erection a few times, producing a low moaning sound that pours from his mouth. Without warning, I waste no time bringing my body down on his, making him curse under his breath. We are both ready, no need to pretend otherwise. "I was thinking I should ride my cowboy. What do you think?"

"Yee haw, darlin'."

I giggle but it quickly cuts off into a groan and a sigh as Rixton moves his hips. His hands are all over me. He rubs my breasts, circles my nipples and even runs his hands over my stomach. He grips my thighs and helps me get into a rhythm that works for both of us. "Giddy up," I tease. He laughs then groans and I groan with him. I love feeling this way with him – the mixture of teasing and sexiness is a perfect combination for us. It makes me feel closer to him, it makes it more personal.

It isn't long before I'm so close to coming that all of my concentration centers to what's happening between my legs. It's almost a feeling close to madness, nothing else matters but chasing that feeling that's just slightly eluding me. I lose my inhibitions, throw my head back, reach up and fondle my own breasts as I move on Rixton until I'm hitting my sweet spot over and over until it sends me right over the edge. I see stars as Rixton helps me ride out the feeling, prolonging it as long as possible. "Feel good, Red?" I nod and then collapse on his chest, words beyond me.

"God, that felt so good. You feel so good." His hands are restlessly trailing up and down my back and after he gives me a few more moments to recover, he flips me over. The hat which has miraculously stayed in place, tumbles off my head and lands on my face, but I hardly notice until Rixton chuckles and removes it and places it out of the way. He enters me again and begins moving slow and deep. I never want this feeling to end.

Sighs and whispers of his name leave my lips as he lifts my hips up allowing him to penetrate deeper. He leans forward and places kisses on my mouth over and over. He whispers endearments, compliments, and promises, and when he reaches his last, his eyes lock with mine and it's like a shade lifts and all his hidden emotions flood out, washing all over me. I read so much in his eyes. Happiness, affection, need, desire, and possibly... something more. It thrills me, scares me, and leaves me in awe. I'm afraid, on some level, to admit it to myself. Our fingers are entwined, his face buried in my neck, my name tumbling from his lips like a prayer and in that moment I know that this, what's happening between us, is more than just one moment. More than just us taking it one day at a time. This is both of us silently hoping for much, much more.

"I know this is cliché, but that was amazing," I twirl my finger in circles along his spine.

"I don't think I will ever get enough of you." He kisses my neck and turns his head to the side. I turn mine too and lock eyes with his and he leans forward and kisses my nose. I sigh happily and run my fingers through his hair, enjoying the aftermath. "What are you thinking?"

"Rixton... I...."

Before I can say anything else, his phone rings, startling us both. At first I think he's going to ignore it, but then he slides away from me and off the bed looking for his pants to drag his phone out of his pocket. "Hello?"

The look on his face goes from 'I just had awesome sex,' to concerned in a heartbeat. It makes me sit up, holding the sheet to my chest, waiting to hear what's going on.

"Is it bad? Okay. I understand. I will be there as soon as I can to help. I'm..." he stops and looks at me a moment, "with Pyper. Give me a chance to say goodbye and then I'll head over. No. No. That's not your concern. Bye."

"What was that all about?" I look at him with a mixture of concern and apprehension. "You have to leave?"

"Yes. I'm really sorry, but I have to go."

"Why?"

"Because I..." he stops and looks at me. Takes in my tousled hair, sheet covered breasts and walks to me and places a kiss on my lips. "I'm sorry. I wouldn't leave if it weren't important. Please believe me."

"Can you just tell me what's going on? I hate this, Rixton. We just had..." I want to say we made love but is that right when we haven't even said I love you? Ugh, there needs to be a manual for this shit. "We just had sex and your leaving right after doesn't feel great."

God, I can't believe I even admitted that. Who is this person I'm turning into? I'm Pyper Lexington. I'm not dependent on anyone. I should always have my game face on. I do my best to school my features and like the wind during a Chicago winter, I can feel the coolness washing over me. "You know what? Never mind. It's fine. I have a busy day tomorrow anyway. It's probably best that I sleep alone so I can get a full night's sleep."

Rixton's brow furrows and he grabs hold of my shoulders, "Don't do that."

"Don't do what?"

"Don't close yourself off to me and act like you don't care that I'm leaving."

"Correct me if I'm wrong Rixton, but you are leaving, right?"

"Yes. I'm sorry. I have to."

"Then don't tell me how to feel or how I should act, okay? So you have to go, and you don't want to tell me why – fine. That's your choice. But acting like this is *my* choice. You don't have to like it any more than I have to like yours, so deal with it."

"Pyper-"

"Just go, Rixton."

He sighs and puts on the rest of his clothes and shoes. "Tomorrow night is dinner with your parents. I will be here so we can drive over together, okay?"

"Okay." He walks over to me, and stares into my eyes. Cupping the side of my face, he brushes his thumb across my lips before placing a kiss there, then whispers, "I'll see you tomorrow." I nod my head and as he walks out my bedroom door, a lone tear falls down my cheek.

chapter
21

WAKING UP ALONE AND REMEMBERING what happened the night before, makes me angry all over again the next morning. I'm not ashamed to admit, at least to myself, that I want him with me. I want him to want to be with me too. With a sigh, I drag my ass out of bed and get ready for work. I barely slept, the interaction with Rixton turning in my mind like a broken movie projector doomed to play the same part over, and over, and over. I rolled and tossed all night and now awake, with Olivia gone, the condo is so still and very quiet. There's something to be said in the knowing that someone is physically present even if it's in silence. But this silence is deafening. It only lends to thinking and I do not want to think any more.

Feeling slightly better after downing a cup of coffee and scarfing a granola bar, I leave and head into work. It's early, but I'm anxious to lose myself in my work and distract myself from thinking about Rixton's disappearing act. Again.

I know I told Rixton that he can explain all of this to me in his own time, but thoughts about what could be going on consume me. For the life of me, I can't imagine what it is and when I do, thoughts so ridiculous enter my mind that I can't decide if I'm more amused at my vivid imagination, or worried that I could be right. Drug dealer, loan shark, bookie, pimp, debt issues, all kinds of things have crossed my mind. None of which seem likely, but really, how the hell would I know?

Telling myself that I understand why Rixton would choose not to tell me his secret is starting to fall flat. My mind is refusing to continue to be convinced of the reasoning – and so is my heart. The more intimate we get, not only physically but also emotionally and mentally, contradicts the reasons he gives for keeping quiet. How are we really going to continue to grow in our relationship if we keep secrets from one another? And if he can't tell me, then why doesn't he believe I can be trusted? Do we truly want the same things? Am I over thinking this? Asking too much too soon? Ugh. This all makes my brain ache.

Unlocking the spa, I momentarily pause, realizing I hardly remember driving here. Not a good thing. I step in and lock the doors again behind me then immediately punch in the code to shut off the alarm when it starts its irritating beeping. The spa is just as silent as it is at home, but at least here I can quit brooding and lose myself in my work. Once in my office, I boot up my computer, then head to the thermostat to crank on the heat. The cooler Chicago weather has arrived and it won't be long before we are knee deep in wind and snow. I shudder with the thought. As much as I love this city, sometimes thoughts of moving to a warmer climate are very welcome.

Rubbing my hands together, I dive into work and start paying outstanding invoices and updating our inventory. We also need to hire an additional esthetician and masseuse, so I get those ads placed. Various employees pop their heads in to say hello as they arrive and I greet them all kindly. I'm glad this place pretty much runs itself. I've been lucky to hire responsible people and an assistant manager that keeps things flowing smoothly.

I jump when my phone begins ringing, sounding as loud as a gunshot in the quiet office. I laugh half heartedly at my reaction to the noise and glance at the screen. An uncomfortable feeling slices through my stomach when I see Rixton's name. I don't want to answer his call – not yet. I don't feel like dealing with him or my feelings right now. I don't even know what to say. I let the call go to voicemail and return to my computer, but my phone starts ringing again. I guess avoidance isn't going to work after all.

Sighing, I answer the call. "Hello?"

"Hello. Is this Pyper?"

My brow furrows and I feel confused. Why is there a woman on the other end of the line? I pull the phone away from my ear and look at the screen again confirming that it's Rixton's name that appears on my screen. "Yes. This is Pyper. Who's this?" And then my heart stops, "Is something wrong? Is Rixton okay?"

"Rixton is fine – I took his phone. My name is Joanna. I only have a minute before he comes back, but I needed to call you because I'd like to meet with you. As soon as possible."

"I'm sorry, I'm really confused. Who is this?"

"I'm the woman you've seen with Rixton. I know you want to know who I am and I would like to meet with you to talk. I promise it won't take long."

"And you said Rixton is okay? What is this about? I don't get it. Why are you calling me and not Rixton?"

"I promise I will explain when we meet. Can you meet me at Starbucks? The one right by your spa is fine."

My mind is racing. Who is this woman? How does she know who I am and where I work? Is it smart to even meet with her? Maybe I should talk to Rixton first, but then again, what is the harm of meeting her in a public place? She obviously has Rixton's phone to call from, so that means she's with him. She said he was coming right back. Jealousy and anger fills my heart when I remember him leaving me again after we made love, yes love dammit, last night. "Yes. I can meet you there. What time?"

"Does half an hour work for you?"

"Yes, that's fine."

"Okay, see you then."

After hanging up the phone I sit and stare at it for several minutes, replaying the conversation in my mind. Apprehension and nervousness runs through my body. I have a bad feeling about this, but my desire for answers easily overshadows the feeling.

The clock seems to move at a snail's pace. I can't stop checking the time repeatedly while my mind races about what is awaiting me. I try to dive back into work in order to make the time go faster, but I can't concentrate. Marissa, one of my manicurists, pops in to ask a question about an order and admonishes me for biting my nails. "We need to get you scheduled for a manicure before you don't have any nails left."

I sheepishly agree and transfer my nervousness to knee bouncing instead. When I have five minutes until the longest half hour in history is up, I leave the spa, get in my car and make my way to meet the mysterious Joanna. When I arrive, I nervously look around the room and find her already sitting with a drink in the corner. Giving her a brief nod in acknowledgment, I walk to the counter to order a drink of my own.

"Hi, welcome to Starbucks. What can I get ya?"

Why does that feel like such a loaded question? "A hot mocha please with a shot of espresso."

"You got it. And your name, please?"

"Pyper."

"Okay it will be right up."

I smile and pay for my drink but my motions feel robotic. While I wait for them to prepare my drink, I make myself face forward when all I want to do is look at the lady in the corner to see if I can read her face and figure out what the hell is going on. I swear I can feel her stare on my back and my neck heats in response. I don't know if I've been this uncomfortable since the time in high school, Jesse, a boy I liked told everyone he got to second base with me at his party. Boys would walk by and stare at my chest for weeks.

Coffee in hand, I slowly approach Joanna's table like an apprehensive wild animal. I feel like she's laid some kind of trap and I'm walking right into it. The look she's giving me is not kind, but I can tell she is trying to school her features to be expressionless, probably so I don't turn around and run. Sitting down, I stay silent, waiting for her to tell me why she's called me here.

"Hello, Pyper. Thanks for coming so quickly."

Giving her a brief nod to acknowledge her hello, I cut right to the chase, "Why did you call me? Who are you?"

"I'm the woman that's going to give you some friendly advice. You may not like it, but you'll thank me for it later."

My brow furrows at her words and I take a sip of my coffee, trying to soothe myself, but the knots in my stomach only get tighter. I don't like the tone of her voice, her body language, or the look on her face. It's all very unkind and something about her is rubbing me wrong. Maybe it's the hint of anger I see and hear, I'm not sure. "Friendly advice?"

"Yes. As I mentioned, I took Rixton's phone to call you. He was in the restroom at the time and I just acted. I decided to take matters into my own hands because I think it's way past time we meet."

How in the hell is it possible for a person's stomach to drop so many times? I swallow, trying to loosen my tight throat and resist the urge to wipe the sheen of sweat I feel on my brow. "You and Rixton were together?"

She smiles and it isn't kind, "We are together *all* the time."

"All the time." I repeat like an echo. "Okay, so who are you? Who are you to him?"

"Look, some of this Rixton needs to explain himself. It isn't my place to tell you everything."

I laugh without humor, "How convenient. You call me to give me advice, as you say, however the advice is going to have limitations. Whatever. I'm leaving. It was stupid of me to come here."

"Don't be angry at me because Rixton hasn't been honest with you."

That stops me in my tracks. "How would you know what Rixton has or hasn't been honest with me about?"

"I know that he hasn't told you everything. At least not yet – maybe never."

"I'm aware. He told me that he would tell me when he's ready, not that it is any of your damn business. It seems to me that all you're trying to do is cause problems. It was stupid of me to come here."

I pick up my coffee and scoot my chair back in order to leave. She reaches a hand out and grabs my wrist. "Wait." I stop moving and look at her. "Rixton has other obligations and priorities in his life right now. All you are doing is keeping him from them. Not to mention, getting in the way of what is really important."

"Oh, and I suppose that's you?"

"In a roundabout way, yes. Look, all I'm trying to do is save you some heartache and pain because the truth is, you aren't the priority. If you haven't realized that, you will soon, trust me."

Fury washes over me like lava – it's slow, steady and thick and it's burning everything in its path. My mind, my heart, my stomach... I feel sick. "Your trying to save me heartache and pain is a joke. You don't know shit about me, or about Rixton, or about us together."

"I know more than you think. I also know that Rixton has more important things in his life that he needs to deal with, and like it or not, I'm part of that and am not going away. The last thing he should be doing right now is worrying about some girl he basically just met that has grabbed his attention. For now."

This time I really am done. Standing, I push back my chair and start making my way to the door. Joanna calls out to me, "You should be thanking me, not being a bitch. I'm just trying to help."

Stopping, I turn around and look at her and do a very unladylike thing. I give her the finger. "Fuck you."

Turning on my heel, I stalk to my car and immediately pull my phone from my purse intending to call Olivia. I could use my best friend's advice and comfort, but just as I start call, I change my mind. Olivia has enough going on herself, but more importantly I can and must figure this out on my own. I'm an adult, I can handle this myself. For the time being, I refuse to give in to the emotions suffocating me, and drive back to the spa to bury myself in work once more. I want to call Rixton but if I do, I'll be hysterical. I just want to get through dinner tonight with my parents, and then I will ask him afterwards what the hell is going on. It's time he gives me some answers, like it or not.

chapter 22

I THINK I'VE OFFICIALLY LOST MY MIND. Taking Rixton to meet my parents is a bad idea. I'm still furious over my meeting this morning with Joanna and the thought of exposing Rixton to my parents is terrifying. I've never been embarrassed of my parents before, I mean they are who they are, but I just have a bad feeling about this. Especially since my father already has a negative impression of Rixton, given his limited knowledge based on one incident – albeit a huge one; interfering with my date with R.J. But once he has an opinion of someone, his mind is hard to change.

Besides, don't people my age usually wait to introduce the guy they are with when they are like engaged or something? Or in a committed relationship? I mean, I may know that being with Rixton is what I want, but I have yet to even tell him that. And we certainly have not made any commitments to each other. Yet. Did I just say that?

Before I can give it another thought, there's a knock at my door and I open it to see Rixton standing on the other side. The first thing I notice are his eyes and smile. Then I see that he's wearing jeans, a nice shirt and his boots. He's clearly being himself, and that's good. So why does it also make me feel so nervous? I know why. Because I know what my parents will think. Pushing all of my doubting thoughts aside, I try to smile as he steps forward and kisses my lips.

"Hi, darlin'. You look beautiful."

I smile and look down at myself. I'm dressed for dinner in my typical go to dinner at daddy's house attire. My house uniform. A nice skirt, blouse and heels. He tucks a hair that fell from my loose bun behind my ear. "Thank you. You look nice too."

"Ready to go?"

"Yes. Let me just grab my jacket." I grab my jacket, turn on the alarm and lock the door, wincing as I do, knowing I'd prefer to stay right here. We make our way to his truck and I give him the initial directions to get to their home.

Rixton's hand is on my leg and my hand covers his. I try to come up with conversation, but the words are alluding me as I'm forcing myself to not talk about what I'd really like to. I stare out the window and watch the scenery pass – my thoughts swirling in my head. What will Rixton's reaction be when I tell him about the meeting? Will he be mad that I went to meet her? Mad at her for calling? Maybe he'll be angry because I didn't call him right away.

A squeeze to my hand catches my attention, causing me to look at his face. His brow is furrowed, "Why are you so quiet?" I shrug my shoulders in response. "Are you nervous for me to meet your parents? You don't have to worry. Parents love me." I try to smile, but don't have it in me. "Aw darlin', they can't be that bad."

"About that. I should tell you something." I see him nod out of the corner of my eye. "My father came over the other day. His client had told him that I abandoned R.J. at the country club. Moreover, he told him that I left him there, having left with you."

"Okay…"

"He wasn't very happy and insisted on knowing who you were."

"What did you tell him?"

"In truth, he didn't give me much opportunity to say much. I did tell him that you were important to me and that I wanted you to meet him and my mother. He said that was good because he wanted to meet you too."

"Well that doesn't sound so bad."

"Maybe not. I don't know. I just…" I sigh. I don't know how to tell him about my father's expectations of me. And I don't want to tell him just how livid he was. I don't know how to tell him that his casual dress will be more than enough to offend and disappoint him and magnify his misperceptions. And he's never seen how I deal – or don't deal – with that. I don't know how to tell him that I'm terrified to do this because for the first time in my life, I'm drawing a line in the sand. I'm purposefully not complying, being what he would call 'insubordinate.' Doing something that I know will not gain my father's approval. And I have no experience with how that will shake out.

"What?" he prompts.

"I just don't know how tonight is going to go. My parents have always held me to certain expectations. Standards. I'm just nervous."

"Your parents love you and no doubt just want you to be happy. All parents do. And I want to make you happy, darlin', so I'm sure this is all going to go really well. Don't worry."

Giving him a nod I look out the window once more. "Is that all that's bothering you?"

"Why do you ask?"

"You just don't seem yourself. Is it just your parents that have you so quiet and withdrawn? It's last night, isn't it? I tried to explain that I had no choice. And I really am sorry. "

"How about we talk after dinner, okay? I just need to get through that before we talk about anything else."

"What does that mean? So, I'm right? You're struggling with that, despite our conversation? Or, something else is bothering you?" I remain quiet not answering his question. "Pyper, talk to me. Tell me what's going on."

Before I can control it a sardonic laugh tumbles from my mouth. "That's rich."

"What? I'm confused." He takes his gaze off the road and glances at me, his look also conveying his confusion. "Why are you angry?"

"I just find it ironic that *you* are telling *me* to be honest. Asking me to come clean with what's going on."

"I've always been honest with you. And told you what I can, just as I said. So, what is that supposed to mean?"

"Yeah. So you say."

"I'm not just saying. I'm telling. I don't lie to you. I told you I never would. Now tell me what the hell you're talking about."

"Oh come on, Rixton. You, after all, should understand if I choose not to share something with you right now."

"So, that is what this is all about? You told me that you understand that I'm not ready to talk about that yet. Were *you* lying to *me*?"

"No, of course not."

"Look, Red, I know you are worried about this evening, but let's not get carried away and say things we don't mean. How many ways do you want me to apologize for leaving you last night? Okay, let's see… I'm an asshole, I was thoughtless, I was… whatever you think. But, in fairness, I thought we had an agreement – a deal. So let's keep to the plan, okay?"

Plan? Plan?! He has no idea how I've forced myself to alter the plan. How difficult that has been. And here he is questioning my integrity, my ability to keep my word to him. And what about his integrity? Who is this Joanna person? This is going to be one night to remember… or to forget.

He's approached the gate to my parent's home and I give him the gate code. The gate opens slowly and the truck finds its way to the large circular entrance. He parks and I feel him turn toward me.

Boldly, I look him in the eyes, take a deep breath, and command, "While I want to respond, you are probably right. Perhaps I should stick to the plan. It may not be in either of our best interests for me to comment further right now. Let's just get this night over with."

With that, Rixton turns off the ignition, yanks his door open, rounds to my side and pulls the door as he offers to help me descend onto the pavement. He's obviously irritated. He's practically giving off steam in the cool night air. And I'm a bundle of nerves. Great.

I soften my voice, "Let's just do this, okay? We can talk more afterward."

"Sure," he says without any conviction in his voice.

We make our way to the front door, hand in hand.

My knock is greeted by a smiling Mrs. B, "Pyper, it's good to see you as always, sweet girl."

I give her a hug and as I pull away make introductions, "Mrs. B, I'd like you to meet, Rixton. Rixton, this is Mrs. B., my parent's housekeeper and one of my most favorite people in the world."

Mrs. B looks Rixton up and down and a huge grin comes over her sweet face. Before she can say a word Rixton shocks me by giving her a hug, "Anyone that means so much to Pyper, is a friend of mine. It's nice to meet you ma'am."

"Oh, well aren't you a gentleman? It's nice to meet you too. Please come in. Your parents are already in the dining room dear. Head on in and I will serve the salad right away."

"Thank you, Mrs. B."

Rixton takes her hand and kisses it, prompting something to happen that I've never heard from Mrs. B. ever. She freaking giggles! I look from Rixton to her in shock and back again. She walks away with an extra swing to her hips and I look at Rixton with my mouth hanging open. "What? I told you parentals love me."

"Yeah well, she was easy. Just wait."

I take a deep breath, grab Rixton's hand into my own and lead him into the formal dining room.

Stepping through the threshold, I pause and take it all in. The seating is arranged with my father at one end, while the opposite chair is empty, no doubt for Rixton. My mother is on one side and the place across from her awaits for me to fill it. She is wearing a

181

high collared blouse and her standard pearls with her hair pulled back in a chignon. My father is dressed in one of his three-piece suits and is looking at something on his phone, fully unaware that we are standing here. It dawns on me that I can count on one hand how many times I've ever seen him in anything other than a suit.

I clear my throat to announce our presence and both of their heads whip in our direction.

Smile in place, I walk into the room. "Mother."

Standing, she waits for me to walk to her and give her a hug in greeting. She pulls away from me, smiles and kisses my check. "Hello, darling."

I turn and face my father, but find him staring at the doorway where Rixton waits to enter. I touch his arm, "Daddy." Turning to me, he leans in and gives me a kiss on the cheek but remains silent. I clear my throat again trying to rid myself of nerves, "Mother, Father, I'd like for you to meet Rixton, my…"

"Boyfriend," Rixton says for me and it makes me smile unexpectedly. I like the sound of that, cheesy as it may be. Even if I am mad at him. Or me. Or both.

Rixton steps forward and takes my mother's hand and kisses it, "Nice to meet you, ma'am." His drawl sounds thick and I see my mother's eyes widen as she takes him in.

"Welcome to our home, Rixton." My mother is nothing if not polite.

"Thank you for having me, ma'am." He gives her a killer smile before turning to my father. My heart pounds and my stomach drops. "Sir. It's nice to meet you." Rixton puts his hand out and my father waits a few beats just staring at it, lips in a straight line. Just when I'm afraid my father is going to snub him like an asshole, my father shakes his hand in return and nods his head.

"Rixton," my father says in greeting. It's obvious my father is studying him and formulating God only knows what additional opinions. I start to shuffle my feet, feeling uncomfortable with my father's scrutiny. "Welcome to my home."

"Thank you for having me, sir." Rixton walks to my chair and holds it out for me, waiting for me to sit and I give him a smile in thanks. Then he walks to his own chair and sits.

We've barely been served our salads and I've just taken my first bite when my father dives in and starts the beginning of what is likely to be a long inquisition of Rixton. "So tell me, Rixton, how did someone like you meet my daughter?"

I cringe at his comment and interject before Rixton can, "I told you already, daddy, that Rixton is a college friend of Luke's. We met through Luke and Olivia."

"Ah yes, that's right. I recall that now. You and Luke went to college together – that's great. In what field of study do you have your degree?"

Instantly I freeze, knowing that in my father's eyes, Rixton's lack of education is a major downside. Certainly, this fact is not going to be a good thing. Strike one. Or are we already at two? "I didn't receive my degree."

My father, rather ungentlemanly, chokes on the drink he was sipping, "I'm sorry?"

"I said I didn't receive my degree, sir. My family needed me after my father became ill and I had to leave college and return home. He wasn't able to do things around the ranch that he used to, so I went back to be there for them."

"How unfortunate. It sounds to me like your family put their own needs ahead of your education."

"Daddy! Don't be judgmental; you're making a horrible assumption. You don't have all the information and frankly, it's none of your business."

"I just can't imagine what would be so important that they would pull you out of college. Appendicitis? Gallbladder? Arthritis?"

"My father was dying, sir." Rixton's teeth are gritted, but he's doing his best to remain calm. I know how difficult this topic is for him. "He wasn't able to keep up with things on the ranch and I went home to help them. I chose my family's needs over my education, sir."

Ignoring Rixton's response, he barrels forward, clearly unaware of his behavior and its impact on Rixton. "So, where is this ranch? Is it cattle? How many?"

I look at my mother, but she's avoiding my gaze and studiously looking at the salad before her. She's going to be absolutely no help. When my father acts like this, she never speaks a word. Just rides out his attitude until he gets over it. That's what we've both always done.

"In Texas, sir. I was just telling Pyper the other day how I would love to take her to see it," he looks at me, and smiles. I'm relieved to see some of the stress leave him and his eyes soften. "I think she would really love it."

My father snorts softly as if he finds Rixton's statement humorous. I look at him and quickly inquire, "What's so funny?"

"You, on a ranch. I find that funny," my father laughs again, making me frown.

"You would ruin your silk blouses and pretty shoes, honey," my mom chimes in as if she has a clue. What the hell does she think I would be wearing? A prom dress and heels?

"I wouldn't let that happen, ma'am. I'll get your daughter some sturdy cowboy boots that she can wear on the property." Rixton has a mischievous look in his eyes and I have to stifle a laugh.

My father however, doesn't find it funny. Go figure. "How is it that you're living in Chicago if you left college to go home to Texas? Are you only here temporarily for a visit?"

Rixton nervously meets my eyes and looks away again at his plate. "My father passed away and now my brothers are there to help my mom, so I left to come back here."

My father's brows lower over his eyes and he steeples his fingers under his chin, staring at Rixton. He looks like he's trying to put pieces together and isn't happy with Rixton's answer.

"One would think that now is the time your family would need you, but instead, you chose to leave. That's interesting. What do you have to say about that?"

As if on cue, Mrs. B. comes in to remove our salad plates and to serve the main course. Thank goodness for her timing. Her eye catches mine and I swear I see her wink at me. I wouldn't be surprised if she's perched right around the corner listening in to this conversation. I love her. She places a plate in front of me with a chicken breast, asparagus and rice. When we're all served, Mrs. B. leaves the room and I open my mouth to change the subject, but before I can, my father picks up his round of questioning. "What do you do for a living, Rixton?"

After swallowing his bite of food, Rixton looks my father in the eye and announces, "I'm a bartender."

The room is so quiet you could hear a pin drop a mile away. The fork is paused in front of my father's face and my mother is staring at him, waiting for his reaction. I need to say something. Do something. But I'm not sure what to do – what to say. I can almost read the escalating judgmental thoughts in my father's mind.

"Yeah isn't that great, dad? He and Luke enjoy working together." Looking to my mom, I try a change of subject. "What's new at the country club lately, mother?"

"What exactly are your intentions toward my daughter, young man?"

"Did you seriously just ask that question?" I ask. "Is this the 1960s, for God's sake?"

Rixton stares at my father, not looking away or flinching. "My intentions are whatever Pyper will allow." He looks at me, "I want very much to be with your daughter and I hope she wants that too."

Staring at Rixton, I can't look away. That unreadable look flashes in his eyes again and I wish we were alone so I can talk to him more about that look, his words, my feelings.

"How exactly to you intend on getting by on the salary you make as a bartender?"

Rixton chuckles, "I'm doing just fine, sir."

"Right now, maybe. But if your intentions are what you say, how do you plan on someday supporting my daughter on that kind of salary? Or maybe you haven't thought about that? And what about a family? Do you really think you can adequately take care of a family on a bartender's salary?"

Rixton flinches and stands, "Pyper, where is the bathroom?" I give him directions and he excuses himself from the table. As soon as he's gone, I turn to my father.

"What the hell, daddy?"

"It's a fair question, Pyper. The real question is what are you thinking being with a man like that? Get over whatever the hell this is you think you are doing. Is this some late adolescent, rebellious period? Some desperate attempt because your best friend is getting married? It isn't funny anymore. And you are embarrassing yourself. Let the poor boy go and get on with it. It's time you see the illogic in this."

"You couldn't be more wrong. About everything. I like Rixton, dad. Really care for him. And I want to be with him and this is not something I need to 'get over' as you suggest. In fact, I have no intention of doing so."

My father looks astounded; my mom maintains her disconnected posture and attitude. "Already this boy is a horrible influence on you. You never disagree with me on these kinds of things. On anything. It's time to disconnect from him- now. This behavior is unacceptable."

I stand now, angry. "You don't give a shit about me or what I care about at all, do you?"

"Pyper!" my mother admonishes.

"Oh, now she speaks!" I yell, angry that she has chosen this moment to open her mouth. "Where have you been all evening while daddy has been interrogating Rixton?"

"His questions are valid, Pyper, whether you like them or not, he makes a good point."

"No. He doesn't. You both don't care at all about what makes me happy, do you?"

"Of course we care," my father shakes his head at me like I'm an idiot. "But he is not your kind. He does not fit the criteria you were taught to apply in this arena. You're merely wasting your time."

"Not my kind? Wasting my time? Are you fucking kidding me right now?"

"That's enough with the language young lady."

"How about this for language. Fuck you. I can't believe you care more about criteria and image and that I uphold your made-up standards, than my own happiness. I'm tired of always having to play by your ridiculous rules. I'm tired of not being able to be myself, of being afraid to be who I am, and putting on a show being miss agreeable and happy all the time when the truth is…inside I'm losing myself, bit by bit every day because I'm confusing your expectations of what I'm supposed to be with who I really am. And it is your fault. Well, not anymore. "

"Listen here, young lady, I own you. I own the building you live in. The spa you work in. I can make your life a living hell. Don't you dare speak to your mother or me like that and you will behave the way of a Lexington or we are going to have a problem."

"How dare you! Own me? And by the way, I am behaving like a Lexington – like Pyper Lexington. All the rest of it, you can take and shove up your ass."

I look up and see Rixton standing in the doorway with his mouth wide open. I practically run to him, "We're leaving." He nods his head, turns to my parents and says, "It was nice to meet you ma'am. Sir."

He takes my arm and walks me to the door while I hear my father calling my name behind me.

chapter
23

ONCE IN RIXTON'S TRUCK, we can't get out of there fast enough. Racing down the driveway, buckling our seatbelts as we go, we both breathe sighs of relief as we get through the gates and start our way back to my condo to take me home. I just want to go home.

My eyes are tingling with unshed tears, and my heart aches due to a mixture of sadness, embarrassment and hurt. My father was so far out of line. I couldn't just sit there and let him talk to Rixton like that. The more he tried to insult and emasculate him, the more defensive I felt myself get on his behalf.

Like it or not, Rixton has become a huge part – a very important part of my life; my heart. He's burrowed himself in there so deep, I'm so far past gone. Looking at his profile, seeing his clenched teeth and grip on the wheel, my heart lurches because while I'm not responsible for my father's actions, they are embarrassingly pathetic all the same. They feel like a reflection on me.

As far as my father goes, I've never stood up to him like that before. Not ever. I just couldn't keep my mouth shut any longer. There is no mistaking the fact that my father or mother couldn't care less about my own happiness. Not, at least, if it's discovered outside of the boundaries they've created. I'm allowed to be happy and do what I want to do as long as I stick to his rules, his expectations.

How did I not realize that he purposefully maneuvered certain aspects of my life in order to have control over me? How sick is that? I've never done anything to disappoint him, or to go outside of the boundaries and limitations he's set. Not ever. So why the need for it? I feel foolish, because I guess I never realized how controlling he really is. Yes, I knew he had specific desires and goals for me, certain outcomes and achievement, but not to this extent.

"Are you okay?" Rixton looks at me briefly to ask his question before returning his glance to the road.

I laugh. And I can't stop laughing. Between last night, Joanna earlier today and whatever his damn secret is, to tonight, I'm feeling so far out of control that I want to lose my mind. Is it any wonder I've been so careful about having a plan for my life? I do it because it helps me feel like I'm in control – that I have some say in my life. How stupid of me to think that I ever had any say in anything.

Rixton looks concerned and reaches over to put a hand on my knee, but in frustration I push it off and look out my window. "No. No, I'm not okay."

Rixton never speaks again and I'm strung so tight by the time we get back to the condo, I throw down my jacket and turn to him immediately. "I guess I need to start looking for a new place to live. And maybe I should consult an attorney and see what can be done about the spa. I mean, my father bought it as a gift to me yes, but it's in my name. I wonder if I can somehow set up payments to repay him or do something."

"Pyper, just calm down. Your father will probably call you tomorrow to apologize and it will be like this never happened."

"You don't know my father," I tell him laughingly. "He never apologizes because in his mind he is never wrong. No, he's going to do something to make my life hell in order to try to show me who's in charge and just how much control he has over me."

"That seems a bit extreme. At the end of the day, I'm sure he loves you and wants you to be happy. I'm sure that's why he asked all those questions. He only wants the best for you. I can imagine feeling that way toward a daughter."

"That's hilarious coming from the guy who just sat through that sick inquisition."

"Well that doesn't have anything to do with how he will treat you relating to your condo and business."

"Are you kidding me? It has everything to do with it. Do you know I've never brought a guy to meet my parents before? Never. They know... they *know*, how important you must be to me in order for me to have brought you over there."

His eyes soften at my words and he takes a step toward me running his hand down the side of my face and jaw. "I would have handled your father. You didn't have to get defensive on my behalf. I'm a grown man, I can handle whatever he throws at me."

"That's not the point."

"Pyper—"

"No. You don't get it. I'm tired of this." I look at Rixton with exasperation in my voice and likely all over my face. "I walk around with a happy attitude and with enthusiasm seeping out of my pores. I can give Olivia great advice and tell her to jump and take chances and do what she needs to do to make herself happy. In the meantime, I've been living a lie. Trying to pretend that everything is great, when all I've been doing is suffocating. Suffocating under expectations that make no sense. They make no sense, Rixton," I cry. "I've never done anything for him to be ashamed of. And I would have done well, rules or not. I'm a good person. I deserve more. I deserve to be happy and they – my parents – should want that for me. I just want to be able to be me."

Placing a kiss on my lips, Rixton looks deep into my eyes. "I'm falling in love with the person that you are." He brushes his thumb across my bottom lip and my heart leaps into my throat. In the midst of this impossible situation, I feel overwhelming joy and happiness. He looks at me, but not with expectation. He doesn't expect or even want for me to return his sentiments. He's sharing his feelings with me and if I return them, he will be happy, but I can see he's not waiting for me to tell him the same. There's no demand there. No rule. And it makes me fall that much more in love. When he leans in to kiss me again, I tilt up my chin and feel eager to kiss him back until a rock settles in my stomach and I pull back, and stop him in his tracks with the question that's been plaguing me all day. I'm obviously on a roll tonight, so why not. "Who's Joanna?"

Pulling back from me a little so he can run his eyes over my face in question, his eyes widen and his mouth drops open slightly before he asks, "What did you ask me?"

"Based on the look on your face, you heard me just fine. I asked you who Joanna is?"

He steps back from me completely and pulls at the collar of his shirt. He looks to the side, puts his hands in his pockets, and pulls them out again. He opens and closes his mouth a few times before finally responding. "How do you know Joanna?"

I stare at him so hard that I'm surprised I'm not able to penetrate his brain and read it without words. Obviously, he's not going to outright answer my question. "I received a phone call this morning while I was at work," I begin. His eyes are locked on mine and I can see the uncertainty, worry and fear in his. His fear makes my stomach burn. "I looked at my screen and saw your name. Imagine my surprise when I answered, and a woman's voice asked for me."

Rixton stiffly walks past me and goes into the living room and looks out the window into the black night, before turning back to me. The room is dark, so before continuing, I turn on the lights. The brightness feels as if it's indicative of the light shining onto whatever Rixton's trying to keep in the dark. When he turns back to face me he finally speaks, "What did she say?"

"She said she wanted to meet me. That she had some things to tell me."

Running his hand through his hair, he takes a tentative step toward me, "If you're asking me who she is, it seems you didn't meet her?"

"Oh, I met her alright, but let's just say she wasn't exactly forthcoming. She was purposefully vague, but definitely got her point across nevertheless, which was to stay away from you."

His jaw tightens and his lips form a straight line. I see anger flare in his eyes and he loudly blows out a breath, "I can't fucking believe her."

"Who. Is. She?" He stares at me and his silence pisses me off. "I mean obviously I know she's the woman I keep seeing you with. The woman that is somehow wrapped up in whatever the hell is going on with you. But that's all I know."

"I didn't want to go into this yet. Especially not tonight, after that disaster of a dinner."

"You know, maybe it's the perfect time, darlin'," I mockingly throw his nickname for me back at him. "I really don't think it can get a whole lot worse at this point."

He continues to stare at me, not saying a word and not backing down, I stare back. "Tell me what's going on, Rixton. I told you I would wait for you to tell me. I told you I understood and I tried. But that was before some woman called me from your phone, while you were in the bathroom by the way she said, and insulted me, and made me feel like shit for something I don't know anything about. So, I'm sorry, I think the time for secrets is over."

"I don't even know where to start." I patiently wait while he appears to work it out in his mind. "I met Joanna in college."

That is not what I was expecting. "In college?"

He nods in affirmation. "Yes. We dated for a little while before I left to go back to Texas. We broke up when I left." He looks at me and silently gestures to the couch suggesting we take a seat. I do, and he continues. "There was no point, in my opinion, to continue a relationship with her when I was leaving and not coming back."

"But she didn't want that and now that you're back, she wants to have a relationship again?"

He shakes his head and smiles sadly which makes me tense, my stomach dropping again. I have a bad feeling about this. "She's the reason I came back to Chicago."

I don't think, I just stand and move away from him. "Oh my God, so you've been lying to me all this time?"

He stands and faces me too, anger on his face, "How many times do I have to tell you, I will never lie to you? I haven't."

"Says you! How the hell would I know if you have or not? Just be honest. If she's the reason you came back here, then why are you wasting your time with me?"

"I've never wasted one second with you. Not one. Every second, every minute, every moment with you has mattered to me."

I refuse to let his words affect me, "So what then? You two got in a fight or something and so you thought you'd screw around with me in the interim?"

"God, no. How could you think that?"

I turn around and stare at him. "What am I supposed to think, Rixton? She calls me up, telling me to stay away from you because you have other more important priorities. She said she didn't want you to waste your time with me! So is that what I am? A waste of time?"

"No, of course not-"

"She also said she was actually trying to save me some heartache. I got disgusted and left, flipping her the bird on the way, because I thought she was just being a bitch. Was she?"

"She—"

"Oh God. What did I do? What the hell did I do? I mean, I brought you to meet my parents and just confronted them over a guy that doesn't even want to be with me. This is fucking rich."

"Pyper!" He yells my name so loud that it startles me out of my hysteria. He comes up to me and grabs my arms, strong enough to gain my attention, but not enough to hurt.

"No! Don't touch me! Don't you dare fucking touch me! How dare you do this to me!"

"It isn't what you think!" I start to laugh and even make myself nervous because there's a hysterical edge to it. "Calm down. Please. I'll explain. Take deep breaths, in and out. In and out." I feel ridiculous but it helps. "Better?"

I nod my head, "Yes." I pull away from him, still not wanting him to touch me.

"Darlin', please, please, listen to me," he pleads.

Taking a deep breath, I nod my head again, "Okay."

He takes a deep breath, as if to calm his nerves, then looks me in the eyes. "I have a daughter. A seven-year old daughter."

And just like that, everything changes.

chapter
24

LYING IN BED, BURIED UNDER BLANKETS, I keep asking myself if I did the right thing. The past week has been almost unbearable. Staying away from Rixton has been harder than I thought it would be. His revelation keeps playing out in my mind over and over. "I have a daughter," echoes constantly in my head. And so do all the words we exchanged after.

"A daughter?"

"Yes. About a month before I moved here, Joanna called me at the ranch. Shocked the hell out of me when she told me we have a daughter and that she's kept it from me all this time."

Holding my hand up, silently asking him to stop talking, he does. "That's enough. I can't hear anymore right now."

"What do you mean?"

"I mean that I need time to process this information, okay? I know you want to explain, but I'm not ready to hear everything else. In all honesty, just the fact that you have a daughter and her mother hates me, is a lot to think about. We've been dating for... for what? A couple months? How could you not tell me this?"

"I had a really good reason. You told me during one of our dates that you don't want children for a long, long time. I was afraid to tell you."

"It's kind of an important thing to tell the person you're dating. I mean, I get not telling me at first, I think, but I thought… I thought… "

"You thought what?"

"I thought even though we said we were taking this one day, one moment, at a time, that…" I hesitate again because I feel very vulnerable, but at this point, what does it matter? "I thought we both knew without saying we wanted more. So, that's why I don't understand why you didn't tell me."

He reaches out like he wants to touch me, but drops his hand. "You aren't wrong, darlin'. And I was going to tell you. In time."

"In time," I whisper. "Well, I need some time to think about this, okay?"

"Well first, just let me explain what happened."

"No," he opens his mouth to talk again and I shake my head. "It has been a really awful day. Between my meeting with Joanna and dinner with my father, I'm not in a position to be able to process this thoughtfully, kindly or rationally. At all. I have no doubt you have your reasons for not telling me, and someday, maybe I'll let you tell me what they are. But, for both of our sakes, that time is not right now."

"So, what? You just want me to leave? You can't ask me to do that. Please don't ask me to do that."

Remembering the pleading in his tone brings tears to my eyes. I burrow further into my bed and squeeze my eyes closed, trying to push the thoughts from my mind. A few tears escape when I squeeze my eyes closed and I brush them aside swiftly, trying to pretend they aren't there.

I haven't been worth a damn this past week. I've been lying around feeling sorry for myself. Perhaps I should feel bad about that, but I can't rustle up enough energy to do so. I tried to go into work a day, but my mind was so busy thinking about everything but work. When I signed into our appointment booking account and accidentally pushed a button that cleared everyone's schedules for the day, I decided it was time to get the hell out of dodge. I instructed my assistant manager to call the company that we use for computer back up to restore the information, told her I was taking personal time the rest of the week, then got the hell out. Reminding myself I told her I was only a phone call away if anything came up, made me feel better so I lost the guilt when I went home and burrowed myself in my room.

After I asked Rixton to leave, he did so and remained silent that night, but the phone calls and texts began immediately the next day. They continued to come in constantly the first few days. At first, I couldn't listen to his messages. The last thing I wanted to do was hear his voice. I knew I would cave and call him back when I just needed and wanted time to be angry, and just feel how I want to feel without his influence. Then, I gave in and listened to his messages aside from just reading his texts. He keeps apologizing with everyone. Over and over he repeats how sorry he is and begs me to talk to him. Begs me to hear him out and give us a chance. He wants a chance to explain and tells me he knows we can make this work.

I want to believe him. I want to just pick up the phone, give him a call, and talk about this. I really do. But, I still don't know how to feel about everything. I have such mixed emotions and I feel confused. I find myself longing for the kind of relationship I don't have with my stepmother. I wish I could call her and talk to her about this and get advice. I would think she, better than anyone, would understand some of the thoughts I'm thinking; would understand some of my fears. But, that's not an option.

What I do know is that somehow Rixton has managed to integrate himself into my life. Despite my best intentions to do what's expected of me, I broke all my rules for him. I took a chance, kept going back for more, and couldn't stay away. After the disastrous dinner with my father, in some ways I feel like I gave up everything for him, but in return, he couldn't even be forthcoming with me about one of the most important things in his life, and that hurts. It really hurts.

Closing my eyes, I try to block out the stab of pain my heart feels at my thoughts. I let myself start to succumb to the laziness that envelops me because allowing myself to fall asleep, is better than being awake and tormenting myself with thoughts of what I should do next.

I should have expected that my solitude wouldn't last long. Olivia has been calling me constantly the last couple days as well. Being the awesome friend that I am, I've ignored her calls and messages too. It isn't like me to ignore her and the fact I haven't gotten in touch by now, well I should have known she wouldn't just leave me be.

When I feel the covers pull back from my face, my heart starts racing at first. Unfortunately, remnants from the break-in by Olivia's ex-husband can still surface, making sudden sounds or movements startle me. But, when I feel a body slide in next to mine and a soft hand move the hair from my face, I don't have to open my eyes to know who's there. I would know her anywhere, sight unseen.

"Did you really think I was going to let you keep ignoring me?"

Sighing, I open my eyes a crack and glare at her, "I was hoping."

"Now that's just rude."

"So be it."

"Wow, you sure are cranky. So what's up, bestie? Why have you been hiding out in here? This isn't the Pyper I know and love."

Moaning, I close my eyes again, "Go away."

"Not a chance, Pyper Elizabeth Lexington."

"Oh God, not the middle name."

"Damn straight, the middle name. Now answer my question — what the hell are you doing hiding out in here? It smells, Pyper, seriously. It's musty and gross."

"Feel free to leave. You don't have to be here."

"Not happening."

Sighing, I open my eyes fully and take in my friend's concerned face and it makes me soften my attitude towards her, "I'm fine, Livvie, and I'm not hiding. I decided to relive my childhood memories of fort building. This one just happens to be awesome, so I decided to hunker down for a while. I don't know why that has to be such a big deal."

Olivia snorts, "Very funny. What's that saying? Denial is a river in Egypt?"

"You're an idiot."

"Whatever, you love me."

I can't help but laugh softly, "True that."

Quiet for a moment, Olivia reaches down and grabs hold of my hand, giving me silent love and support in such a simple gesture. I want to cry in response. "He told Luke, and Luke told me. Now tell me honestly, how are you doing?"

"This isn't answer enough in itself?"

"Well yes, I suppose it is, but I still want to hear the words."

Sighing, I roll onto my side, and prop my arm under my head so I can see her better. "I'm angry. I'm hurt. I'm sad. I'm confused." I swallow hard before continuing. "It's only been a week and I miss him, but at the same time, I feel completely at a loss over what to do. How's that for words? I don't know how to make sense of any of this." For not the first time this week, tears begin to trickle out of the corner of my eyes and down the sides of my face.

"What is your heart telling you?"

"My heart is telling me to pick up the damn phone and call him."

"Why do you think that is?"

"I'm in love with him," I whisper. "And I want to believe that maybe he feels the same way, and if so, that we can figure the rest out."

Olivia can't hide the curve of her lips in the corners. She wants to smile at my revelation, not realizing I've already come to this conclusion. "So why don't you do that then?"

"Because this isn't some fairy tale. A princess doesn't fall in love with the prince and then they decide to live happily ever after in the real world. Instead, this is a princess that is in love with a cowboy who not only has a daughter, but an ex that is still very much in the picture. This doesn't sound like the kind of story that gets a happy ending."

"Says who? And he has a daughter, and an ex-girlfriend, so what?!"

"Are you serious? This is a big deal, Livvie. First, he didn't tell me. He chose to keep it from me, and that in itself is hurtful and what does that say about what he thinks of me? You know, despite everything that I have always had planned for myself, I fell for someone that is completely different from my warped life plan. Then, because of that, I actually stood up to my father. When my feelings became obvious, I stood up to him and made it clear that Rixton is important to me. I knew damn well there was a chance my father would try to make my life hell because of it, and while it scared me, part of me welcomed it. You know why?" She shakes her head, "Because it meant that I was fighting for something that I want. I'm so damned sick and tired of living my life according to everyone else, and for once, I chose what I want. And that felt invigorating, even powerful."

"I think that's wonderful and is the reason why I don't understand. Why does Rixton having a daughter have to change any of that?"

"For a couple reasons. First of all, if he couldn't tell me about that, what else isn't he telling me or won't he tell me in the future? Secondly, this means that his life isn't completely his or in his control. It's controlled by his child and by this Joanna person in some way too. Where the hell do I fit into that? And do I want to? Is it right to? He said something about how he didn't know at first that he even had a daughter. And so what? I just bust in on the scene and make her have to deal with sharing the father she just met?"

"That is up to Rixton, Pyper. He wouldn't have pursued a relationship with you if it weren't something that he thought she could handle. I have no doubt that he never intended to keep you a secret from her or vice versa for long. You need to talk to him about all of this."

Sighing, I close my eyes and wish I could just go back to sleep and hide from the emotions I'm having. "Because how do I know he won't say what he thinks I want to hear? And the worst thing… the thing that makes me feel like a complete bitch for even thinking it, is that I don't know if I can share him."

"Pyper, that sounds so-"

"Selfish? Yes, I know. But don't you get it, Livvie? For years I've let what I've really wanted come in last compared to what my parents told me is important. I've lost sight of who I am, and what's important to me because I've been too busy trying to configure to what's expected of me. I'm finally allowing myself to get out of that. To want what I want, need what I need, do what I want to do. How will that be possible if I'm in a relationship with a man that will have to always put me last? Aren't I giving up one box, to just put myself into another? There will be expectations of having a relationship with a man who is a father. His daughter will always come first. Maybe his ex even, because of the fact she's his daughter's mother. For once in my life, Pyper, I want to be first in someone's life. I want my needs, thoughts, and feelings to matter. I don't want to be stuck in a situation again where I have no say in anything."

"But is that really the same thing? Your parents wanted you to act and live your life a certain way. They placed expectations on you of how they think you should be and what you should become. Rixton isn't going to do that. Rixton wants and loves you for you."

"He hasn't said he loves me."

"Well, I guess you're going to have to trust your best friend on this one. He loves you. If he didn't, he wouldn't have bothered trying to continue a relationship with you given the multitude of other things he's dealing with in his life. And think about that. He still made you a priority whenever he could, outside of his responsibility of being a father. The expectations required of you in a situation like this, my friend, would be nothing other than love, understanding, companionship and patience. All things that you have in spades. Think about it – married couples don't put one another last just because they have children. Sure, there are times when the child's needs come before their own, but that doesn't mean their marriage comes last – it just means that life requires some organization and prioritizing."

"What about the fact that his baby mama confronted me? There's something going on there. Do I really want to get in the middle of that?"

"Again I ask you… since when does the Pyper I know back down from a fight when it comes to something she really wants?"

"I can't compete here."

"That's because there is no competition. You're looking at this all wrong. I think that you decide if you want to be with Rixton, child and all. And if you do, then you talk to him. And the two of you will figure the rest out – including the ex."

"Livvie?"

"Hmm?"

"I'm scared."

She squeezes my hand and smiles softly, "I know, my sweet friend. I understand that and I've been there. But you can't go wrong following your heart. Not ever. Don't you dare let fear stop you from happiness."

"My heart lead me to Rixton. I miss him. Imagining myself without him actually makes my chest ache."

"Then stop being without him. You know, Luke could have decided not to try again with me. No, I don't have a child, but I sure as hell have a lot of baggage. Even before Deacon kidnapped me," she pauses and I just know that the memories are overwhelming her for a moment, so I give her hand a squeeze in encouragement. "I had an awful lot of baggage I was carrying because of having an ex-husband and Luke could have decided that he didn't want to deal with it and that I wasn't worth it. Thank goodness he didn't."

"I would have had to kick his ass if he thought any differently." Olivia laughs and it makes me laugh too. Then I sober when I tell her, "Rixton's been calling and texting me a lot."

"I'm not surprised. Luke said he sounded desperate on the phone when he asked for help talking to you."

"You know, that makes me wonder, how did you not know that Rixton has a kid? I bet you anything Luke's known."

"Yes, Luke did know but he chose not to tell me. He loves and trusts me, but he knows the temptation to tell you is too strong. I would have wanted to keep his confidence if he asked me to, but I'm glad he didn't put me, or himself, in that position."

"Yes, that makes sense. I'm glad he didn't do that too."

We lay in silence for a bit, each of us lost in our own thoughts. On some level I think I always knew I would want to call Rixton and work this out, but initially I just needed some space. "I think I'm going to clean up. I may even give Rixton a call later tonight."

"I think that's a good idea about calling him, and an even better one about cleaning yourself up – you freaking stink. When is the last time you even took a shower? And don't even get me started on this room. It smells like you haven't lived anywhere else for a week. My God girl, I'm surprised the musty smell alone hasn't drawn you out by now."

"Ha. Ha. Very funny." As I get out of bed, I grab a pillow and laughingly smack it into her face. She squeals and it makes me laugh and run into the bathroom before she can retaliate. I'm not sure what will happen when I call Rixton. His calls and texts haven't stopped, but they've definitely slowed down. Will he want to talk to me and explain? Or will he be angry because I couldn't deal with this at first? I'm afraid he could tell me that this isn't going to work out between us after all. The thought makes me feel ill. Pushing it aside, I remember that once again, taking it moment by moment is a good idea. Starting with getting cleaned up – relationship domination can wait – for now.

chapter 25

"OH THANK GOODNESS! YOU ACTUALLY look like you belong to the land of the living again." Olivia teases. "Please tell me that you also brushed your teeth." Sticking my tongue out at her, I continue to my closet wrapped in my towel to get some fresh clothes. Pulling on yoga pants and a long sleeved shirt, I walk back out of my closet and see that Olivia has been busy during my twenty-minute shower.

My bed has been stripped and she must have put my sheets in the wash, because she's currently making a fresh bed. The blinds are open, letting light shine through for the first time in a week. I kind of want to make the form of a cross and hiss in pain like a vampire at the sight. It's been too long. All the remnants of food and drink around my bed are gone and so are all the used tissues. Not for the first time I thank the lord for that snotty nosed brat Joey in the second grade that tried to bully Olivia. Angry over the way he was treating her about playing on the monkey bars, I stalked over and took care of business. The note that went home to my parents prompting the lecture from them as a result was totally worth it. Olivia and I have been inseparable ever since. And I'm so glad. And grateful. She's the sister I never had, but always wanted.

"You are such a bitch," I laugh, "but yes, I brushed my teeth." Grabbing a far corner of the fitted bed sheet, I pull it over the mattress to help. We pull up the comforter, fluff the pillows, and then plop on the bed. "Thank you. For everything."

"You don't have to thank me."

"Yes I do. Not just for cleaning, and for coming over here, but for getting me. You know, I've never had to tell you that the face I wear most of the time is the face that hides how I really feel at times. Everyone always thinks I'm constantly happy and positive and clever. They see this confident, in control, and dare I say, high class entrepreneur. Inside, sometimes I feel like no one has a clue of what's really going on. Of who I really am. It's in those moments however, that I realize you do. You've always known and seen the real me, or the potential for the real me, regardless of the script I've used or how I've performed. And you have loved every part of me. And have cautiously and subtlety encouraged me to claim my true identity."

"Of course I see you – and accept and love you. No matter what 'face' you have on, you have always still been you. No matter what. It's just now, you are finally acting on what it is that you really want. Not some ridiculous plan that has everyone's needs and desires fulfilled but your own! I really am proud of you. I know this isn't easy for you, but if it helps, I believe in you and am confident you are doing the right thing and in the end, you will be happy. I know it."

"I know. It was way past time that I took a stand and claimed me and my life. Speaking of that, I hope you don't mind if I come and shack up with you and Luke when I move out of this place. I want to unravel as many attachments to what my dad owns as possible. I expect that I can find a place that is one hundred percent my own, say, within six months or so."

She pauses for a moment open mouthed and I know that she will tell me that it's fine, whatever I need, but I take pity on her. "I'm only kidding. I would never do that to you two soon-to-be newlyweds. Ew. I can just imagine the horror I would likely walk into on a daily basis."

"Oh you mean kind of like the horror Luke walked into with you and Rixton."

If Olivia's laugh is any indication, I know the look on my face is just as horrified as I think it is. "We shall never, ever, speak of that again." Throwing her head back to laugh, she makes me smile too. "In all seriousness, thank you for coming over here, taking care of me, talking everything out with me… it means a lot. I have never and will never take our friendship for granted. I hope you know that."

She smiles with just a small curve of her lips and shrugs, "I do. You've been there for me in the past, and likely will have many chances in the future."

She laughs suddenly prompting me to ask, "What's so funny?"

"Remember when I came face to face with Luke again after all that time, or even before that when I was dating around and trying to make a life for myself again?"

"Yes, I remember. You were taking control of your life again."

She nods, "You were so positive, happy and pushy. Always reminding me that life was about taking chances and I wouldn't be happy unless I just jumped in and tried to be fearless."

"Yes, I do seem to remember something along those lines. Why is that funny and how did you not punch me in the face?"

"It's funny because the advice and laughs always come easily when you're on the other side huh? I know how that is too. Some things are easier said than done, but I know for a fact that all of this is going to work out beautifully."

"And how do you know that?"

"Because as soon as you pick up your phone and call Rixton, he will pounce on it and probably be over here in a hot second. That boy has it bad for you. He will be dying to talk to you."

"I hope you're right and that I didn't mess things up by waiting so long."

"Don't feel bad about that. You took the time you needed for you and in doing so, it made you realize your true feelings and just how much you want to make this work, even though you still have doubts and questions, the two of you will figure them out together."

"You are so positive about all of this."

She shrugs, "It's hard not to be when things worked out so well for me. I have to believe that they will for you too."

Before I can respond with how I hope she's correct, Olivia's phone starts blasting 'Here Comes the Bride' making her giggle. "New ringtone?"

"Yeah," she giggles, "isn't it awesome?" I chuckle to myself while she answers. "Hi babe," she lovingly speaks into the phone. My brow furrows when I see her face fall. "Luke, it's hard to understand you – slow down. An accident?" My heart begins to pound when her eyes cut to me. "What do you mean you don't know? Okay. Okay." She laughs but it's without humor, "Fat chance in that happening, I'm with Pyper right now. We're on the way. If you hear anything in the meantime, call me back. Okay. I love you too. I will, I promise. Bye."

My hands are twisted together in worry, "What happened?"

"Okay, don't freak out, but-"

"You know telling me not to freak out is going to make me freak out, right?"

"Okay fair enough, but that's not going to help anything because I don't have a lot of details because Luke doesn't know exactly what happened."

"Oh God, you're scaring me. Please just spit it out. He doesn't have all the details about what?"

"All I know is that Rixton has been in some kind of accident."

I stand from the bed immediately and run to my closet to get my shoes, "Oh God."

"Calm down, Pyper. I do know that Rixton was well enough to be able to place a phone call to Luke. He called him because he's not going to make it to work because of whatever happened. Luke's concerned because he said Rixton sounded extremely upset and stressed on the phone but had to go before he could give any other details. Instead of waiting around to hear anything, Luke is going to the hospital in order to see if he can help, and at the very least to get more information."

"Well, we are going too."

"Luke said he would call back with any information he gets."

"I don't give a shit. Would you sit around and wait for information about an accident involving the man you love?"

"No way in hell, which is why I told Luke we are on the way."

We race out of the room and I grab my jacket and handbag on the way out. "Let's go. I'm not about to sit here and wait for news."

"I know. I agree. Come on, I'll drive. I'm not going to let you behind the wheel."

On the drive to the hospital I'm quiet with constant thoughts about how stupid I am. I'm thankful Rixton was able to communicate on the phone, so he's not hurt in a life threatening way, but what if he had been? Why did I let fear get in the way of being with Rixton? No matter how large the challenges, we should be able to work them out, if we really want to be together. I'm ashamed that I ran instead of standing up to my fear and insecurities. If you love someone, isn't the love unconditional? I'm not the kind of person to end a relationship with someone I love because he has a child. This child is half of the man I love, therefore just because of that, I love his child already too. How could I be so thoughtless, so impulsive?

"Rixton and I can handle this, right Livvie? We will make sure his daughter knows that I love her dad and I'm not there to take the place of her mother. I can't let him go, I won't. I hope he can forgive me for acting like a scared child. I love him. I love him so much. That's all that matters, right?"

"It matters. This will all work out. Just try to relax."

As soon as we pull into the hospital parking lot, Olivia parks in the first spot she finds and we both race in through the doors of the emergency room. I stand there for a moment, unsure of how the hell I'm going to find him. I don't even know for sure if he's in the emergency room. An irrational part of me wants to yell out his name over and over and see if he responds. That would definitely be one way to find him. Likely not the best, however. Without wasting another second, I go up to the nurse behind the information desk and ask for Rixton.

"Are you family?"

"Yes."

She looks at me doubtfully, "Just a moment."

She walks away and I have no clue what she's doing. I wait a total of two minutes before I ask for the entrance doors to the exam rooms to be opened, and start racing all over the place, peeking in rooms that are open, and asking for him when I see a hospital employee. Finally, some kind nurse takes pity on me and points me into the right direction. She seems to scan the area and has a somewhat guilty look on her face the whole time. I give her a quick thank you and move in the direction she tells me even when I realize she was about to tell me something. I don't want to wait around to hear it or have her change her mind about letting me go.

As I turn a corner, I see Luke standing outside of a curtained area. Olivia, who's right behind me, calls his name. He turns, but I barely spare him a nod before I'm racing into the room already calling out, "Rixton? Oh God, Rixton."

Racing into his arms, I practically knock him over in my relief to see him. I squeeze him tight and murmur words I'm not even aware of, not wanting to ever let him go. I'm so relieved to find him okay that I can't even form a coherent sentence at first. Until it suddenly dawns on me that he's fine, and not really squeezing me back.

Freezing, I pull away from him. He's not in the hospital bed – he doesn't even appear to be hurt. He looks surprised to see me and... and nervous? He reaches out and cups the side of my face and it makes me close my eyes for a moment in relief. It's a loving gesture and I soak it up. "Pyper? What are you doing here?"

I quickly inspect him from head to toe, trying to discern if he's sustained any injury, I look at him in confusion. "I was with Olivia when Luke called saying you had been in an accident. I didn't even think, I couldn't even breathe, Olivia brought me here and I was racing all around to find you. But you look... you look fine. What's going on?"

Rixton's eyes shoot behind me and I immediately turn around and make a noise of surprise when I see a small figure lying in the hospital bed, staring at me wide-eyed. She's adorable with long dark hair, eyes the color of Rixton's and she's wearing a frown upon her small lips. One of her arms is in a sling and there's a doctor next to her, holding an x-ray film in his hand. He's also looking at me like I've lost my mind.

"I'm... oh gosh... I'm so sorry. I thought...I thought." I turn to Rixton, "I'm so sorry, I didn't know."

Rixton steps forward and wraps me in his arms, "It's okay. I'm so glad you're here," he whispers to me. "We can talk later, okay?" I nod against his chest. He pulls me back, and turns me around. "Pyper, I'd like you to meet my daughter, Emily. Emily, this is my very, very good friend, Pyper."

"Hi, Emily, it's very nice to meet you although I wish it wasn't happening for the first time in a hospital room."

"Hello." Emily says quietly, almost shyly, in return. The frown on her lips is still present, but her glassy, heavy eyes make me wonder if she's under the influence of some pain medication.

"Is she okay?" I ask turning to Rixton.

He smiles, "She will be, she gave me quite a scare. We were just being told by Dr. Lewis that Emily did in fact, break her arm when she fell out of a tree at the park. Just what we thought."

Jumping right in, the doctor explains, "That's right, Mr. Andrews. As I was saying, Emily has a clean break in her ulna and a hairline fracture of one of her carpals, one of the bones in her wrist. We are going to have to set the break, and she will be in a cast for six to eight weeks. The cast will keep the bone sturdy and allow the healing process to occur naturally."

"Okay. I understand," Rixton nods.

The doctor turns to Emily, "You are doing a great job, Emily. Tell me, what color would you like your cast to be? We have blue, yellow, orange, red, pink-"

"Blue, please," her small voice requests.

"Okay, blue coming right up!"

The doctor approaches Rixton and lowers his voice, "We will put her to sleep in order to set the break. Once we get it casted, we will send you home with some pain medication for her as well as instructions for cast care. Do you have any questions?"

"No, I don't. Thank you very much Dr. Lewis," he glances at me, "and thank you for your patience."

He gives us a small smile, "No problem. Someone will be here shortly to take Emily to the casting room."

"Okay, thank you."

Once the doctor leaves, Rixton turns to me. "I know this is probably going to take a little time, but will you stay with us? When she's discharged, we can go back to my place and talk. Does that sound okay?"

"Yes. We have a lot to talk about."

He nods, and bends to give me a kiss on the cheek, "Yes we do."

With that, he leads me over to the side of Emily's bed and she looks at me curiously through her drug-induced mind and I try to focus on making sure she's okay and push away all the questions I have spinning through my mind.

Chapter Twenty-Six

While Rixton gets Emily settled in what I see is her very own room in his apartment, I use the opportunity to walk around and take in his place. It's obvious to me now why he never wanted to have me over – Emily's room – plus there are pieces of her all over. A jacket, a child's book, and a few toys scattered about. Clearly, a child resides here some of the time.

Decorated with leather furnishings, and large masculine wood pieces accented with black, this is definitely a guy's pad. Tidy and clean, it could definitely use a woman's touch here and there.

Walking to the bookshelf, curious about the photos I see framed there, I take in his collection. Pictures of what must be his parents, siblings, horses, the ranch and even some of Emily. There are some of them at the park, one of her eating a hot dog with ketchup smeared on her face and another of her at Navy Pier. To my surprise, there's also a picture of me, and another of Rixton and I together. Picking up the one of us together, I see it's a candid shot that someone else must have taken at Luke and Olivia's bachelor and bachelorette party. I have no recollection of it being taken, but I love it. Rixton is leaning toward my ear with a wicked smile on his lips like he whispered something dirty in my ear, and I'm laughing at whatever it is he said. The photo takes my breath away. Our feelings for one another are clearly displayed on our faces. It's ridiculous that it took me so long to realize what I was obviously displaying to everyone else.

The other photo is intimate and brings tears to my eyes. I'm lying in my bed sleeping. It's clear that it was captured by someone lying next to me. My face is soft and relaxed in sleep, but only a person in love with me would find beauty in a shot like this. And to have it so boldly displayed on his bookshelf in his own home, is telling and profound.

I'm startled by Rixton speaking just behind me, "You look so beautiful when you're sleeping. I had to get a photo that I could hold onto forever."

Turning with the photo in my hands, I look at his face. I take in his eyes, tired, but hopeful. "I'm surprised you have this here where anyone can see it."

"Why wouldn't I?"

"Well, with Emily and Joanna-"

He sighs and takes the photo from my hand, placing it back on the shelf. "Come and sit on the couch with me. Let's talk."

"Okay." I sit and shift my body to the side so I can face him. "First, I just want to apologize."

He immediately shakes his head, "You don't owe me an apology."

"Yes, I do. Instead of talking about this with you a week ago, I pushed you away and ran away instead. I'm sorry. I'm sorry I hurt you, I'm sorry I behaved the way I did."

"You were in shock. I can't blame you for that. I'm not sure how I would have reacted if our roles were reversed."

"Fair enough. So, if you're willing, I'm ready to listen now."

He takes a deep breath and begins, "Joanna and I met in college. Like I told you, we dated and obviously slept together. When my mom called and told me about my dad being sick, and I made the decision to go home and help them, I broke things off with Joanna. She didn't want to break things off. She pleaded with me to try and have a long distance relationship with her, telling me she would save money and fly to visit me or vice versa during our breaks. I told her no. In fact, I wasn't exactly kind about it." He wipes his brow and runs his hand through his hair, "Actually, I was an asshole. I was completely stressed over the news about my dad and pissed off too that I had to leave college to go home. When she kept clinging to me and begging me not to break it off, I was mean and told her to leave me the hell alone – that she was the last thing on my mind." He sighs and looks at me with apology in his eyes as if he owes me one. "You see... I never loved Joanna. Her feelings for me were more than mine for her and I knew that, but I didn't respect that at all."

"You mentioned that she called you at the ranch to tell you about Emily?"

He laughs without humor, "Yeah. I hadn't spoken to her in all that time. When I left and went back to Texas, my life became nothing but my responsibility at home. Sure, I went out occasionally and dated here and there but nothing serious. My focus was on helping out at the ranch and assisting in the caring of my father while he was still there. So you can only imagine my surprise when I picked up the phone and Joanna was on the other end."

Rubbing a hand over his face he looks in the distance and I can tell he's reliving that phone call all over again. "She told me that she was only calling me because she had to. That she had never even intended on telling me about Emily. I was so angry. I'm still very angry." He looks at me and I can see the anger flashing in his eyes, "She's almost seven-years-old, Pyper. Seven years old. I missed out on almost seven years of her life because I was an asshole to Joanna and she got back at me by not telling me that I had fathered a child." He shakes his head in pure exasperation. "She found out about the pregnancy not long after I left. She dropped out of school right away and got a job to start saving money for the baby. At first, I didn't believe her. I flew out here before I actually moved out in order to have a paternity test done. The results were positive, Emily is mine."

"I'm glad she told you and she should have from the very beginning, but what made her finally change her mind?"

"Joanna's sick."

"She's sick?" I feel confused. She didn't look sick when I met her at Starbucks that day.

"Yes. She has lupus."

"What's lupus? A form of cancer?"

"No, Lupus is a complicated and unpredictable disease. It constantly changes, as do its symptoms, even within the same person. It's an autoimmune disease. Normally our immune system makes proteins called antibodies that fight against viruses and bacteria. With Lupus, her body's immune system becomes hyperactive and attacks her normal, healthy tissue. Her symptoms are swelling, damage to joints, skin, her kidneys, blood, heart and lungs. So far, her kidneys have taken the worst hit."

"That's horrible. I've never heard of Lupus before."

"It really is hard on her. One day she can feel just fine and have no problems and the next day she can have swelling or fatigue so bad that she can hardly move. Her joints can swell or get so still that movement is hard. Her fever can spike out of nowhere, and her muscles hurt so bad that basic ibuprofen doesn't help. Sometimes she gets skin rashes and sores in her mouth. It's made her life difficult at times and she reached out to me because she was desperate for help."

"Does she have family that can help you guys too?"

"No, she doesn't. Her dad left when she was young and her mom passed away years ago. She finally called me because she needed help and decided to quit being stubborn. As much as I hate this disease for her, I hate to say that I'm grateful for it in a way too because it allowed me to find out about my daughter. I feel like such a douche for even saying that."

"No, I understand what you mean. I get it. You don't wish it on her by any means, but at the same time it's what brought you to your daughter." I pause and look at him, "Wow, Rixton. You have a daughter. I can't imagine how that revelation had to feel."

"Scary, horrifying, amazing, wonderful. So many things. I'm still figuring it out. And we are still figuring out what we think about each other. It hasn't been easy with me just showing up like 'hey, I'm your dad,' but we are figuring it out one day at a time."

"She looks so much like you."

"She does. When I saw her eyes, I knew she was mine, but I still performed the test anyway. After the results came in, I decided to move here immediately to help Joanna out and to get to know Emily. It's been a strange and amazing road so far and the last thing I was expecting, Pyper, was you."

"I can't believe that you've even given me the time of day in the middle of all of this."

"Are you kidding me? How could I not? You came into my life like a fiery angel and no matter how I told myself it wasn't the time or that I wasn't being fair to you, I couldn't help myself. You sucked me into your sexy, flaming vortex and wouldn't let go." I laugh at the image that creates. "I told you, I decided not to tell you about Emily because I was afraid of losing you. There was this moment when you popped out of bed with me after our first night together and you started gesturing madly at me without words. Freaking out about me being in your bed. A sheet was wrapped around your body and your hair looked like it was on fire with the sunlight from the blinds trickling in and setting it ablaze. You looked crazy and beautiful and I knew in that moment I was falling in love with you. We'd been flirting and trading insults for months, and I approached you at that engagement party on a whim, but I've thanked my lucky stars that I did ever since. I wouldn't trade a moment with you, but here's the thing. This last week I realized that I need you to be either in this or out of this."

I open my mouth to say something, feeling tears flood my eyes at his words of when he fell in love with me and all I want to do is tell him I love him too but he holds up his hand silently asking me to stay quiet while he gets out whatever is on his mind.

"I know that's asking a lot and I know that we are still figuring things out here and it's still early in the game. I know all of that. What I'm saying is that if we give this a shot, then we throw it all in. No running away, no hiding or keeping things from one another. I hate, absolutely hate, what Joanna did to you and she and I have already had words about it. I want you in my life, Pyper. I'm in love with you and I want to see where this goes. I know that I'm not part of your plan. I know that I'm not what your parents or maybe even you would prefer for yourself, but I can promise you that I will take good care of you." He laughs and it catches me off guard. "Have you ever heard of the cowboy way?"

"No, what's that?"

"It's a promise a cowboy makes with God. He promises that when God helps him find the one, he will protect her, spoil her, laugh with her, dance with her, make promises of forever with her but mostly, he'll never stop loving her because if he doesn't do all of those things, then someone else will. That's how I feel about you. It's asking a lot. I know I'm a package deal, and maybe you need time to think about this, and I understand. The thing is, I can't have what happened this week with us, happen again. I was useless. I couldn't stop thinking about you, needing you, wanting you. I wanted to fix this and make it right, but I knew I needed to give you space. I'm not saying that you either commit to me forever right now, or damn it all. I'm saying that we go all in and promise to give this everything we have, not caring about what anyone else thinks. If, God forbid, it doesn't work out, then we will part ways amicably. I can't have an unstable environment, though, with Emily involved. She already has that enough with her mom's unpredictable disease. I wasn't expecting you, Pyper, but I believe that there's a reason that I found you now. And I don't' want to let you go."

"Enough. That's enough, Rixton." He looks at me in alarm and I automatically reach out a hand to his face, wanting to soothe him. "Let me talk now, okay?"

He swallows hard. "Okay."

"You are right. I understand everything that you are saying about Emily and I respect that. Look, I'm not going to lie, this Joanna thing and the fact you have a daughter threw me for a huge loop. I never would have expected that in a million years. And I'm not about to lie and say that this will be great and we will all be one big happy family. I'm scared, Rixton. I have no freaking clue how to be a… a… what the hell would I even be to her?" I ask in a panic.

Laughing softly he takes my hands, "You would be the woman her dad loves."

I squeeze his hands, "I don't know if kids like me. I don't know anything about an almost seven-year-old, but I'm willing to try. You see, before I thought you were in an accident, Olivia was over at my place and I had just told her that I was in love with you and was going to tell you. That your child, Emily, was a piece of the man I love, and that's all that matters." He leans toward me as if he wants to kiss me, delight and happiness lighting up his whiskey colored eyes. I laugh and shake my head. "Rixton, you are not at all what I expected. I've had a plan for my life as long as I can remember, I told you that. But, what I've come to learn is that the best things in life aren't planned. How could they be? There is no way in a million years anyone could plan someone like you. You are so smart, sarcastic in a way that makes me crazy and hot at the same time.

You make me laugh, and make me happy. But most of all, I am able to be myself with you. There is only one other person in this world that I feel that way with. My father and his expectations and my own stupid plan be damned. I'm in love with you too, Rixton. You've helped me realize that a plan and life can definitely take you unexpected places, but love… love will bring you home. And you're my home. I want to make this work too."

He can't wait any longer and neither can I. He puts his mouth to mine and the kiss is slow, soft and sweet. It makes my toes curl and I put my arms around his neck pulling him closer. When we pull apart and look at each other, I whisper, "I love you."

A smile that can only be called brilliant lights up his face. "I love you too. And I have a surprise for you. Come with me."

"A surprise?"

He stands and holds out a hand to me, gently pulling me to my feet. He leads me down the hall to his room. "Um, listen here buddy, I've seen that surprise before."

We walk into his room and close the door and he breaks out into a laugh once he's sure it won't wake Emily. "Get your mind out of the gutter, darlin'. I wasn't referring to that, although now that you mention it…"

"No way. I want the other surprise," I tease delight filling my heart.

As he walks into his closet I take in his room. It's a lot of black. A black headboard, black dresser, black easy chair and rug. His comforter is black but he's accented it with red pillows and sheets. Another room that could use the softening touch of a woman. Someday, I promise myself with a smile.

Rixton walks to the bed and places a box upon it. "Here you go. Open it."

I look at him with glee, and walk toward the bed. Lifting the lid, I pull the tissue paper away and break out into a laugh. "Boots?"

"Not just any boots, darlin'. Those are all blinged out just for you. Only the best for my girl."

I take them out of the box and hold them up. They are extraordinary and so me. The brand is Frye and they are a light brown. The foot part of the boot is plain, but the part that goes up my leg is decorated with hundreds of tiny shiny studs. They are boots fit for a princess, for sure. "They are perfect. I love them, thank you."

"So I confess, I have a fantasy that involves those boots?"

My smile grows wider and I take a step closer to him, "You do? Please tell."

"It involves you, and those boots…"

"Uh huh."

"In nothing else."

"Well I think we should work on that fantasy right now."

His eyes light up making me laugh. "Yeah?"

"Absolutely."

We waste no time doing just that. The boots fit perfectly and when Rixton sees me wearing them and nothing else, the lust in his eyes alone is enough to drive me crazy. We come together, fast and then slow. Anxious to stake our claim on one another and confirm our love, but wanting it to last at the same time. He touches me tenderly from head-to-toe, placing kisses all over my body. Just when I think I can't take it any longer, he enters me and everything feels right with the world. We move together, creating a story all our very own. When we find release together, it's with a big sigh, a feeling of contentment and a love so strong, it's amazing it can be contained in my chest.

My eyes open and Rixton's arm is draped over my naked sheet-clad body. He's got my back nestled against his front and I can feel his breath blowing on my temple. Feelings of confusion wash over me, when I'm not sure what it is that woke me up. I'm content, warm, and happy, but something is off. And then I hear it.

"Dad?"

Popping up like a shot out of a cannon, I hold the sheet to my chest. My eyes immediately find Emily standing in the doorway, sleepy-eyed and disheveled. Her blue cast is held close to her body and she frowns at me when she sees me next to her father, in bed. I want to die. "Rixton?"

He's already moving around, my actions having startled him too. He sits up, "What's wrong?"

I look at him, wide-eyed, "Emily's at the door." I briefly wonder if I should have used pig Latin to communicate to him. Wait, do kids already know pig Latin at her age? Maybe I need to learn a new language all together? Or maybe sign language? Oh wait, definitely not. Sign language would make me drop the sheet and that is so not going to happen.

"Emily?" Rixton asks, "What's wrong, honey?"

"I'm thirsty. Can I have a glass of water, please?"

"Of course, honey. Give me just a minute okay?"

"Okay."

She closes the door and Rixton turns to me, "Oops, guess I didn't lock the door. Live and learn I guess. At least it wasn't a few hours earlier, huh?" His face falls when he sees I'm not laughing or smiling, "What's wrong, darlin'?"

"She saw me in your bed. Naked."

"She didn't see you naked, and you know what, seeing you here with me is something she will have to get used to. We will talk to her tomorrow and explain exactly who you are to me, okay?"

"Are you sure that's a good idea?"

He looks at me in his bed, disheveled and worried, "I think it's a great idea. Especially because I plan on having you just like this a lot more. It's a damn fine sight, seeing you in my bed, Red. It's going to happen a lot."

Blushing I momentarily lose myself in his flirting, then snap out of it. "Go get dressed and get your daughter something to drink, you cad."

"Cad? What is that? A western movie?"

"It sometimes feels that way with you."

Laughing, he gets out of bed and I admire his nakedness as he throws some shorts on and leaves the room. I put my head in my hands and try to contain my embarrassment. A rustling at the door draws my attention and I lift my head up. Emily is standing there once again staring at me. I'm shocked when she says, "I'm not sure how I'm going to feel about this."

I open my mouth to respond but don't know exactly what to say. She spins on her heel and heads back in the direction of her room. "You and me both, kid. You and me both."

The End

of Part One

Find out what happens next with *Perfect Little Promise* coming 2015.

Will Pyper be able to ingratiate herself in the lives of Rixton and Emily seamlessly? How will Emily react when she sees Pyper doing things for her that her mother can no longer do, because of her illness? How will Joanna feel about Emily's developing relationship with Pyper? Will Rixton and Pyper's love for one another be enough to weather this new family dynamic, or will it all fall apart?

acknowledgements

THANK YOU SO MUCH FOR READING! I appreciate each and every one of you and if I could hug and meet you all, please know that I would. I write because I love it, but you all help provide the motivation to keep me going when it gets hard at times. Thank you for that. Your facebook comments, tweets, words of encouragement and emails mean more to me than you can imagine.

As always, it takes a team of people to help publish a book. Thank you to my mom, Cindy who is always there for me every step of the way. I've said it before and will say again, I'm so lucky to have someone who knows me as well as you do and is the best content editor I could ask for. Gypsy Rae Choszer, thank you for hashing this story out with me. This book about killed me and because of you, and our many talks, I realized it was because I was trying to write a story other than Pyper wanted me to write. I would honestly be lost without you – you are sooo stuck with me for life. Cora Brent, thank you for all of your support. I live for our weekly writing meetings with Gypsy and am so happy to have found a friend in you. Angela Corbett, there aren't words for my love for you. Thank you for your consistent support and all of the advice you offer. I would be lost without you. Espe, you always ask me how things are going and push me to keep going. Your excitement, encouragement, and proofing as always, is appreciated. Thank you for still loving me even though I totally suck with commas. Robin

Harper, with Wicked by Design, thank you for my gorgeous cover and working with me until it was just right. Kassi Cooper, thank you for being patient with me and making my book so pretty with your formatting.

To all the girls on my street team – I adore you all. You always make me laugh, just when I need it most. Our dinosaur jokes make my day.

To all my fellow InDivas – I'm so lucky to belong to an amazing group of Indie Authors that understand the importance of lifting one another up in this industry. Your advice, suggestions, questions and support are unwavering and I'm blessed to be surrounded by all of you. Thank you for your friendship.

To my family – I love you all. It isn't always easy following your dreams. It takes hard work, time, patience and understanding. Thank you for loving me through each and every step along the way.

 AUTHOR JENNIFER MILLER was born and raised in Chicago, Illinois but now calls Arizona home. Her love of reading began when she was a small child, and only continued to grow as she entered adulthood. Ever since winning a writing contest at the young age of nine, when she wrote a book about a girl with a pet unicorn, she's dreamed of writing a book of her own. The important lesson she learned about dreams is that they don't just fall into your lap – you have to chase them yourself. Most importantly, she is a wife and mother, and is very lucky to have a family that loves and supports her in all things. She also has an unhealthy addiction to handbags and chocolate covered strawberries, neither of which she cares to work on. For more information about Jennifer Miller, please visit www.jennifermillerwrites.com

Facebook – https://www.facebook.com/JenMillerWrites?ref=hl

Twitter – https://twitter.com/JenMillerWrites

Pinterest – http://www.pinterest.com/jenmillerwrites/

Sign up for my newsletter – http://goo.gl/JNRarR

Instagram - http://instagram.com/jenmillerwrites

Tsu - https://www.tsu.co/AuthorJenniferMiller

www.ingramcontent.com/pod-product-compliance
Lightning Source LLC
Chambersburg PA
CBHW060918250626
47159CB00008B/3062

*Some girls like to throw caution into the wind,
let fate take them where she wants them to be.*

But not Pyper Lexington. She's all about the plan. Graduate college and own a successful business have been marked off the list. All that's left of her perfect little plan is marrying a man equal to her father in success and wealth. And of course, adding to that the 2.5 children and picket fence, every girl wants that—right?

But fate has other ideas and like the old saying goes, 'the best-laid plans often go awry.' In walks Rixton Andrews, a cocky bartender with a sexy, southern drawl. He makes his intentions clear after a night they both can't forget. He wants Pyper – and he's determined to make her want him too.

But can a man of Rixton's status convince a princess like Pyper that he's the man she's been waiting for and that love can't be planned? Will the secret Rixton's keeping tear them apart? Or will Pyper's need to please others make her deny what her heart really wants?

ISBN 9780989407410

90000

9 780989 407410